WITH TIME OFF FOR BAD BEHAVIOR

By

Marc Sotkin

Happiness Always
Marc Sotkin

Merry Christmas Julie,
2011
Love Rhonda

For Adam, Michael, and Nina. You are my joy.

Table of Contents

ONE

The Beginning

The enormous buffet was so tempting even anorexic starlets couldn't keep from nibbling. Colossal mountains of jumbo shrimp, oysters on the half shell, an open bar for five hundred people — it was an elaborate spread even by show business standards. In addition to the fabulous food, to celebrate the end of the third and most successful season of the show, Paragon Studios had spent about a hundred and fifty grand to decorate the commissary to look like a bait shop. Worth every penny. It was kind of party only Hollywood can throw. More than giant spotlights crisscrossing the sky or long lines of limos, this shindig had real excess.

To keep the crowd of actors, writers, technicians, and network and studio execs musically amused, the Doobie Brothers had been brought in from a world tour, where most nights they played to stadiums filled with screaming fans. Evidently, for the right price, they were willing to come off the road to sit on a fake lifeguard tower entertaining the fortunate few who work on our show. It was incredibly cool. The Doobies were our party band. Only in show biz.

The highlight of the party, though, was the waitresses. Fifty gorgeous girls in bikinis serving champagne and caviar to the guests, who, in keeping with the nautical theme, had become a school of fish in the middle of a feeding frenzy. I assume the waitresses were gorgeous—it was hard to tell because their faces were hidden by papier-mâché helmets crafted to look like fish heads. If they weren't gorgeous, they definitely had great bodies. Pike and carp and walleyes with big bazangas and tight tushies.

Bazangas. God, I hate that word. But one of the occupational hazards of writing sitcoms in 1979 is having some network censor excise certain words from your vocabulary. We can't say "tits" on TV. We can't even call them breasts and that's what they are, for Christ's sake. So we call them bazangas or bazoobies or labambas. We have to call them something. After all, *In the Swim* is a show about two girls, Connie and Patti, who leave their homes in Chicago to become lifeguards in L.A. The network wants to see girls in bathing suits. Lots of girls. But none of them has breasts. Well, these fish waitresses, made to parade around in the skimpiest of bikinis, had some of the loveliest bazangas you've ever seen. It's the kind of thing I'm sure all the women in attendance found offensive and the men found . . . the men wanted to spawn.

"More caviar, Barry?"

I had eaten enough caviar to choke a sea horse. On toast points, on potato skins, by the spoonful. One more bite and I would forever smell like Eau d' Fish Egg was my cologne of choice.

"I'd love some." How could I say no to the loveliest of rainbow trout? You'd have to be crazy to throw this one back. "How did you know my name?" I asked, hoping against hope I didn't have a black bead of beluga stuck between my front teeth making me look like Alfalfa in an Armani suit.

"I'm a big fan of the show." She said the magic words. If she liked the show, she liked my sense of humor, and that's my main weapon. God, in His wisdom, has given all creatures the tools they need to get laid. Peacocks have their feathers. Pine Island chameleons have a face so ugly, other chameleons can't look at them. They also have these bright red appendages on their tongue, shaped like flowers to attract insects. Well, lady Pine Islanders like these flowers, too. One look at the tongue and it's your place or mine on Pine Island.

Barry Klein hasn't been given any extraordinary appendages, much to my dismay. But I do have the ability to make girls laugh and, as I've learned on my journey from boyhood to manhood, sometimes while they're laughing, I can get them to take off their panties. Not consistently. Or even very often. But the Pavlovian result of my limited success is that I always try to be funny to see what happens. If I can get a laugh, I've at least been accepted. Without it . . . without it, who am I? Like the salivating dog who's heard the dinner bell, I had to see if I could make this girl laugh.

Taking another cracker, I point to the caviar and ask the fish-woman, "Are these your kids? You must be very proud." I pop the cracker in my mouth and wait for results that are impossible to detect because of the damn fish head. Did she laugh? Did she smile? I need to know. Before I can figure it out, she swims away.

So, who are you, Barry, that you need this much acceptance? Oh, shit, don't start this again. Lately I've been often asking myself these "Who am I?" questions. I hate them. Introspection brings up all these feelings of inadequacy. I don't need to find out who I really am. Not tonight. Not at this great party.

"Barry, can I see you for a moment?"

I welcomed the interruption until I turned and saw Bobby Mitchell. Bobby's my boss, the executive producer and creator of *In the Swim*. He's also, at forty-four, the hottest guy in all of TV.

Bobby has five shows on the air, and four of them are in the top ten. Besides *In the Swim,* which is number one, he has the number two show, *Doing It Our Way,* the story of two girls who leave their homes in Phoenix to be models in New York. *Just Us,* the story of two girls from Milwaukee living together in Chicago and working at a meatpacking plant, is currently the number six show in the country. *All Aboard,* an innovative show about two girls from Miami who work for Amtrak, because they actually want to, comes in at number eight on the Nielsen ratings. And Bobby's latest creation, *We Want It All,* is mired at number sixty-six and is in danger of being canceled. *We Want It All* is the story of eight girls from all over the place who live together and want to be dancers in Vegas. The industry is wondering if Bobby has strayed too far from his creative roots, trying this eight-girls thing, but they're giving him a lot of credit for wanting to grow as an artist.

There's always somebody hot in TV. Norman Lear. Garry Marshall. But right now it's Bobby Mitchell who's on the cover of *Time, TV Guide and Guns and Ammo,* in an article on skeet shooting that proclaims him to be, "The hottest gun in the West." Bobby's gotten a lot from television: money, power, and a pinched colon that scares him to death. He's scared because he has no idea what will happen to him if his colon stays pinched. And he can only imagine what will happen if, during a meeting, it becomes unpinched, turning him into some kind of human balloon flying around the room as all his gas escapes. He tries, as hard as he can, to stay on the special bland diet that will keep the colon pinched just so, but can never remember exactly what's on it. The doctors have made it easy for him by allowing Bobby to eat anything white.

So here is Bobby with his cream cheese sandwich on white bread with a glass of milk, making sure everybody is having a good time at the party that's as much a celebration of his success as it is the climax of the *In the Swim* season. Dressed all in white, figuring anything that might help keep his colon stay put is worth a shot, Bobby, in a fit of fashion daring do, has added a bright red bow tie for a splash of color. At five foot three with a forty-seven-inch waist, Bobby looks more like a duckpin than a television mogul.

"Where's Tommy?" he asked.

"Gee, Bobby, I haven't seen him." I hadn't seen Tommy Cross, but I knew where I could probably find him. Either at the bar chugging a bottle of scotch or in his office doing a couple of lines of cocaine.

Tommy's my partner, sort of. We were discovered by Bobby Mitchell three and a half years ago when we were performing together in an improvisational comedy show. He hired us as writers. We had never written together, but Bobby made us a team so he could pay each of us half as much money. Sometimes we write together and sometimes we write alone, but usually people think of Tommy and me as a team. It's a union that doesn't appear to make much sense.

Tommy and I are very different people. My comedy is fueled by what I consider to be fairly normal Jewish neurosis. Tommy is driven by devils. Devils that cause the kind of pain that can only be quieted with massive amounts of alcohol and drugs. These devils also have a hell of a sense of humor. Tommy can write jokes. Biggies. He writes the kind of jokes that get an audience laughing hard. Too hard. Laughing so much, they miss the next three. Oh, some of them must hear the lines because they keep the laughing going. Rolling. Laughing women reaching into their purses for tissues to wipe away the tears of joy. Smokers, laughing so much, they start to cough that deep, raspy cough— wanting to get more air but the laughing won't let up. An entire audience laughing and coughing and spitting up phlegm. Is Tommy funny? Yeah, he's funny.

"Find him. I don't want him getting into it with Ben," Bobby says as he runs a finger around the inside of his mouth, unsuccessfully trying to get the sticky balls of white bread out from between his cheeks and gums.

Ben Fisher plays Connie's crusty Uncle Sal on *In the Swim*. Sal owns the bait shop on the show, above which Connie and Patti live, and right next door to Willy and Billy, two wacky morons who cut up chum for a living. Ben's one of those comics who's been around since they invented show business. To hear Ben tell it, *he* invented it—at Kutcher's Hotel in the Catskills. It was after an all-dairy dinner. Everyone at Ben's table was bored, so he stuck his cigar up his nose. Everybody doubled over with laughter. "Show business!" Benny cried.

It's true. He swears it. I'll never understand how Ben Fisher became a celebrity. His material was mediocre before he stole it from some other hack comic. He's the type of comedian who does "These kids today, with the hair and the beads" material. It's all stale and unimaginative. All except the burping routine. Yes, God has given Benjamin his gift, too. He can talk and burp at the same time. Not just a word or two. Sentences. Paragraphs. Ben can recite "The Charge of the Light Brigade" while burping. It's not exactly Noel Coward. It's not even Noel Coward burping. To my mind it's down-right disgusting. But enough people have found it amusing that Ben has built an entire career around this odd talent.

At first the burping routine was just like the rest of his act. Bad. He pretended he was a radio announcer doing a football game after eating too many hot dogs. Ben thought people would die laughing when he said "Bronko Nagurski" while he burped. A few did. Most wondered if they wouldn't have been happier sweltering in the New York City heat rather than driving upstate to have this man with bushy eyebrows burp in their face. Ben was not killing with the burping. Not until he met the only other person in the world who can talk and burp.

In 1956 he met a young comedy writer named Bobby Mitchell. Talk about meant to be. Ever since he was a child, Bobby would entertain friends at birthday parties by talking and burping. Bobby suggested that Ben drop the football bit and do the burping routine about a guy who's eaten too much stuffed cabbage and now he's trying to fuck his wife. Bingo. The material was so strong that even people who hated the burping had to laugh.

Bobby had his first paying job and Ben had five minutes that would get him from the Borscht Belt to the high-paying jobs in Vegas. For some reason, the same people who hated football and Nagurski loved cabbage and fucking. Suddenly Ben Fisher was bright and hip. Audiences would sit for fifty-five minutes listening and wonder what all the fuss was about. This guy was dull. Then he'd get to his last five minutes. The part about stuffing the cabbage and stuffing his wife, and all the time he's burping. Encore! Encore! And for a while he was smart. He wouldn't do an encore. He'd come out. Take a bow. One more burp. Screams.

"Good night, ladies and gentlemen, bbbwwwaaap." This was
the king of comedy. Then he made the mistake of believing the
audience. He would come back out and do five more minutes about
his mother-in-law's cooking. "And her mashed potatoes are like
rocks. The hard ones." Brilliant, Benny. Get off the stage.

Like a sky rocket. He came down like a sky rocket.
Suddenly his own agent wouldn't return his calls. Nobody cared
about Ben Fisher. And in 1975 when Bobby was casting *In the
Swim,* Ben was working at a hunting lodge in Minnesota as sort of
a combination entertainment director–night manager kind of guy.
Fortunately for Ben, he was still able to afford a subscription to
Variety. He read that Bobby was casting *In the Swim* and he called.
And he begged. The one thing you can say about Bobby Mitchell
is he's loyal. Do right by Bobby and he'll do right by you. So when
the man who gave him his first paying job called . . . what could he
do? Even though Jack Carter was practically set to play Uncle Sal,
Bobby went to the network and fought for Ben. Now, three years
later, Bobby's fighting for Ben again. Sending me as his emissary
to protect Ben from the rapier-like wit of my partner, Tommy
Cross.

"Hey, if Ben doesn't say anything about the writing staff,
Tommy won't say anything about Ben," I say, trying to reassure
Bobby who is now eating his sandwich and Rolaids at the same

time. At most wrap parties, this conversation wouldn't take place. Wrap parties are usually festive, marking the culmination of a long hard season of work and the beginning of the hiatus. The hiatus between seasons is one of the really great things about working on a sitcom. When a season is over, you're given about four months to heal. You're given time to grow new brain cells. Cells with new jokes and new ideas. It's a much needed break. I always feel that producing a season of situation comedy is like being in a championship fight with each episode being a round. A typical twenty-two-episode season is like a very long fight. The trick is not to get knocked out. Just be standing at the end of twenty-two. Some episodes will be good, some will be bad. Most will be just okay. If you have more goods than bads, you win. The wrap party is when everybody congratulates each other on not getting knocked out. That's on most shows. Not on *In the Swim,* which is probably the most emotionally taxing show being produced on network television. It's a show where you can easily get knocked out.

There is an underlying turmoil that drives this show. It starts with its stars, Lorraine LaBarbara and Mimi Simms. Like many of the other great comedy teams—Laurel and Hardy, Abbot and Costello, Mutt and Jeff—Lorraine and Mimi are physical opposites. Lorraine is a big, lusty blonde. Not technically pretty, but with an earthy beauty that suggests a joy of life not that different from everyone's favorite waitress at the local diner. Mimi is much smaller, petite really, with the manic energy of a frightened rodent. Besides the difference in appearances, they have one other similarity that too many of the great comedy teams throughout history had: they hate each other. It could be because Lorraine, who plays Connie on the show, is so close to Bobby Mitchell. She's known him all her life.

While growing up, Bobby used to put on shows for the neighborhood. During one production, he needed a little girl to play Hitler's daughter when Da Führer took her to nursery school. He found three-year-old Lorraine LaBarbara. She was a natural. She stole that show and every Bobby Mitchell show that followed. Lorraine's like a little sister to Bobby. That drives Mimi crazy. She's convinced that Bobby gives Lorraine preferential treatment. Now, why would anybody treat their little sister better than some whiny annoyance who is so paranoid she actually counts the words in the scripts to make sure that Lorraine doesn't get more words than she? I guess it's not fair to call her paranoid because Lorraine does get more jokes than Mimi and, to tell the truth, it's because Bobby tells the writers to do it. On some level he just likes to piss Mimi off.

"Barry, you've done it again. She has fifty-two more words than I do," Mimi will scream, after reading a particularly Lorraineladen script.

"Mimi, half those words are conjunctions. It's not like she has more jokes. In fact, this week you have more jokes than Lorraine," I say, hoping the truth will keep me from spending hours trying to squeeze fifty-two more words into Mimi's mouth.

"Fifty-two! And stop smiling!" It's hard not to smile when Mimi talks. Her voice sounds exactly like the queen of the Munchkins.

I remember when I was a kid, to entertain my friends, I would inhale helium from a balloon to make my voice sound like Chip 'n' Dale, the Disney chipmunks. The helium does something to your vocal chords, and my twelve-year-old buddies would roll on the ground howling as I would have Chip try to convince Dale to ask Daisy Duck for a blow job. It was great material for twelve-year-olds. My mother would warn me that if I inhaled the helium too often, my voice would remain in that ridiculously high register. I believed my mother and went on to Popeye and Bluto, trying to get hand jobs from Olive Oyl. Much better for the voice but, in reality, the Chip 'n' Dale material was stronger.

Maybe Mimi did too much helium. Her voice is right up there all the time. It's a mixed blessing. When she's doing comedy it makes her funny, but it has the same effect when she's trying to be dramatic. We can write a scene about Patti's dog getting hit by a truck and when Mimi says, "I'll miss you, Lucky," the audience will roar with glee. It's the voice.

So, Mimi hates Lorraine. Lorraine hates Mimi. For no apparent reason, they both hate the writers. Everybody hates Ben. And nobody particularly likes Willy and Billy, the actual names of the actors who play Willy and Billy. When we get to one of our wrap parties, the venom oozes out. Instead of publicly commending each other on a job well done, on this show the wrap party is a chance to humiliate each other in public. The insults thrown are always disguised as jokes. But, as with all humor, it only works if it has an element of truth.

"Just make sure Tommy goes easy on Ben," Bobby says, giving me one last warning.

"I'll do what I can," I say to Bobby as he waddles off to try some of the white rice pudding the network has sent over special for him.

Okay, time to find Tommy. I hope he's still lucid. Sometimes if I catch him before he goes into his walking coma, I can plant an idea in his head like, "Don't pick on Ben," and it will stick.

It's hard to make much progress through the crowd. Everyone seems to want to stop and wish me well. I hear, "Great season, Barry. I don't know how you guys keep coming up with those terrific scripts.

"Hey, how ya doin'?" I reply to someone whose name I haven't really forgotten. I'm not sure I've ever known it. I may have. About a hundred and fifty people work on the show, and although I've tried to learn all their names, I can't be sure I have. Last week, at the end of a rehearsal, a birthday cake was brought out for one of the stagehands. We all sang "Happy Birthday" to him. A good time was had by all . . . except me. When we got to the part where I loudly sang "Happy Birthday, dear Jack," everyone else sang, "Happy Birthday, dear Clyde." Clyde? For the past three years I'd been calling him Jack. I mean right to his face. "Hey, Jack, what's happening?" "Looking good, Jack." "My man, Jack." Why didn't he correct me? Could everyone else be wrong? Could all the "Clyde" people have all their heads up all their collective asses? Doubtful. Should I suddenly start calling him Clyde or could I make this Jack thing just a little joke between us with "Jack" being my special term of endearment for him? From that moment on he became the anonymous "Hey, how ya doin.'" It wasn't just him. Everyone became "Hey, how ya doin.'" It was safer than guessing. Safer, but not satisfying. Saying, "Hey, how ya doin'" feels just like asking myself, "Who am I?" It's unsettling. It's just another reminder that lately I've been off my game. Planet Barry Klein has been hit by an asteroid and knocked out of orbit.

Forget "Who am I?" How do you get your orbit back?

The Hey, how ya doin' in front of me is a carpenter who builds sets for a living. An older man, in his fifties, who, if he lived in Iowa, would build barns. Just an ordinary Joe. But this is Hollywood and he's in show business, so once a year he and the little wife get to dress up in their Sunday best and rub elbows with the stars of the show at the wrap party. And why not? He builds the sets on the number one show on television. He's part of the team.

"You remember my wife, Arlene?" Hey, how ya doin' asks.

"Of course. Great to see you." I can't remember his name from yesterday and he wants me to remember Arlene.

"Jerry just doesn't stop raving about the scripts you write," Arlene coos. I hear nothing after she says, "Jerry." I just pray that the Jerry she's talking about is the guy who's standing next to her because I'm about to call the man Jerry.

"Well, we did it, Jerry." I say with as much confidence as I can muster. He, too, has made it through the twenty-two-round fight, and now he wants to share the feeling of accomplishment. Let's raise our glasses together, we've made it old chum. "Everybody did a great job, Jerry." It's a gratuitous, extraneous "Jerry" but what the hell? If I don't get my life back together soon, I may never get to call him Jerry again. Now I get ready for the most important part of this conversation. I turn to Arlene, put my arm around Jerry's shoulder and in my most sincere of sinceres I say to Arlene, "This guy's the best."

Curtain. End of play. Arlene beams. She's proud of her man. He beams. The warrior victorious. Now they can drink plenty of free champagne, go home and have each other.

It's a conversation I'll have to repeat any number of times tonight. But right now, this one is over. As I move away I hear Mason Green shout, "Hey, Barry!" Mason Green is the network representative on the show. He's middle-management, sent to keep an eye on us. The network doesn't want surprises so Mason Green's mission is to know everything that's going on at *In The Swim*. What he doesn't know, right now, is that I don't have time to chat.

"Hey, how ya doin'?" I yell to Mason as I keep moving. Got to find Tommy. Got to keep going. Searching. Okay, maybe one more bite of caviar. No . . . keep looking.

Getting through the crowd is almost impossible. I stop after I feel someone grab my ass and hear, "You want to dance, Sweetie?"

I turn to find Marcia Heilger, my secretary. Actually, she's more than my secretary. For the past three months we've been seeing each other. Naked. We've been seeing each other naked at her place after work. We've all heard that lofty warning against diddling the help: "Don't shit where you eat." Well, I was shitting and eating and if Marcia had her way, now I'd be dancing.

"I've got to find Tommy," I told her. I don't care so much about finding him. I care about not dancing with Marcia. Not here. Not in front of everybody. I still like to believe that nobody knows I'm seeing her. Naked. I'm seeing her naked. Idiot. How did I let this happen?

"Well, then let's go outside and fool around," she purrs as she starts to move closer.

Leaving the party with Marcia would be too dangerous. Yet it still sounds tempting. Marcia looks great and there's a sexual energy about her that drives me crazy. That's how the seeing her naked thing got started.

Before I can decide, Marcia and I are interrupted by Harvey Lipshitz, the dialogue coach on the show. "Excuse me, Barry," Harvey says sheepishly.

I'm sure Harvey doesn't want to interrupt. But he's been sent on a mission, and Harvey's the kind of guy who, when given a job, does it and does it well. Don't believe me? Ask Harvey.

"What is it, Harvey?" I ask as I move ever so slightly away from Marcia.

"Your wife is looking for you."

It's not an asteroid or meteor that has me off course. It's the truth that's knocking me around. I have a wife, Linda, and she's here. A wife who I love or think I love or want to love. But instead I'm sleeping with this girl standing next me.

"Thanks, Harvey," I say almost absentmindedly, as a thousand thoughts race through my mind. I've never been with Linda and Marcia in the same room before. Earlier in the evening, while getting dressed, I pictured the scene; the three of us chatting gaily, bon vivants unflustered by Marcia and my improprieties. Instead, I fell slightly nauseous.

Harvey stands for a moment as if he's expecting a tip, then realizes he should disappear. As he slips into the crowd I explain to Marcia, "I gotta go."

"Barry, I hate this," Marcia says, under her breath. At least she's not making a scene.

"I hate it, too. Listen, I—" I give Marcia's arm a tender squeeze and throw her the tiniest kiss that can be thrown as I turn to leave. It could be a kiss or maybe my lips just twitched. It's hardly enough to make her happy, but it's going to have to do for now.

It feels like my life is just a series of encounters where I provide barely enough to keep someone happy. Bobby wants me to keep the show running smoothly. Mimi wants more words in the script. Marcia wants more time. Linda wants to know why I seem so distant. Hey, how ya doin' wants me to move to North Hollywood and play poker on Wednesdays with him and Arlene. Everybody wants something.

There used to be an act on *The Ed Sullivan Show* where some guy would spin plates on the end of a stick, then balance the stick on a table. He would wind up with about ten plates, each on its own stick, spinning like crazy. To keep them going, he'd have to run from one stick to the next, give each plate a little spin, then move on. By the end of the act, none of the plates were spinning as fast as they could. They were all going just fast enough to stay up. That's what my life has become. I keep hoping everybody's just happy enough to think they're getting what they want. But what do I want? What would make Barry happy? If I stop now to figure out what would make me happy, one of the other plates will fall. Forget it. Grab a glass of champagne and find Linda. What about Tommy? Forget Tommy. I've got to find Linda. I left her twenty minutes ago just to get a Perrier. Linda and I haven't been agreeing about much lately, but my being a louse is one we could get together on.

Toward the rear of the commissary, there are tables set up for people who want to sit while they eat. That's why Linda and I sat there before I went a wandering. She's still there. As I approach her I can't believe I sat her at a very large round table that could easily seat twelve people. She is alone and, of course being at the biggest table available, looks even more alone than if she were at one of the tiny tables for two. I've made her a wallflower. It's a rotten thing to do. If the plates are going to stay on the stick, you have to spin them once in a while and I haven't been spinning Linda at all.

"Sorry I took so long," I say, almost out of breath as if I rushed back as soon as I could. "Bobby wanted to talk. You having a good time?" Oh, man, what are you doing? You leave her for twenty minutes and then ask if she's having a good time?

Fortunately, the question is too dumb to answer verbally so Linda gets it done with a look. A look designed to kill, and if I was smart I would die or at least pretend to be dead.

"Can we go soon?" she asks, having served her penance at what amounts to no more than a very fancy office party.

"Right after the speeches. Bobby's worried that Tommy's going to do a job on Ben."

"Do you want to dance or something?" she asks. There is no malice or sarcasm couched in her question. Linda has the amazing ability of doing these great one hundred and eighty degree turns—and they're always to the positive. She's been left for twenty minutes and instead of being cranky, she's asking me to dance with a smile. And a pretty smile at that.

"Sounds great," I say, taking her hand and leading her to the dance floor. Dancing, holding each other as the Doobies sing "You Keep Me Running," seems like a chance to connect. A chance to be a couple. A chance to focus on Linda. Instead, I'm only aware of Marcia Heilger who, standing on the side of the dance floor, has her eyes riveted to me. I can't escape the intrusion. I'm the one who made the simple twosome a complicated threesome. What have I done? Where is my life going? What do I really want? I want to be with Tommy, consuming what ever he's consuming to shut this brain down so I don't have to hear these questions.

My introspection is interrupted by the realization that Linda has stopped dancing. She's just looking at me.

"What?" I ask, in an innocent tone, knowing I've been caught.

"You're a million miles away. It's like we're on a totally different wavelength. I don't know if it's you . . . or me?" Linda was searching for the truth.

"It's not you. I don't know what's wrong with me. It's like I've been nuts lately. I don't know what to do." I can't believe I'm going for pity. Poor Barry. He's been nuts lately. Can you forgive him?

Tears began to well in Linda's eyes, but they do not fall.

She's in control. "Barry, I've been thinking about this . . . a lot. I can't take it any more. I think we need some time alone."

"No, we don't," I say firmly, as if I have another solution. "I just need to . . ." I don't know what I need to do. Not fucking my secretary would help.

"It isn't working for me. Can we go?" Linda headed for the table to get her purse. Before she got there, the lights went out except for the spotlight that hit Bobby Mitchell who was standing in front of the fake lifeguard tower. I took Linda's hand, guided her back to her seat and settled in next to her.

"Hi, everybody. I hope you're all having a nice time," Bobby says loudly into the microphone in order to get everyone's attention. It's one sentence but it seems to take Bobby an hour to say it. Bobby's got a Northern drawl. He comes from Brooklyn where most people talk a mile a minute. Bobby talks slowly, in kind of a whine that makes a word like "nice" seem like it's got about fifty-seven syllables. "Nnnniiiiiicccce." He says "nice" a lot. Bobby believes in nice. He wants all his shows to be nice. "That's a good story, Barry, but make the end nice," he'll say to me after I tell him the storyline for each episode of *In the Swim*. His drawl is hypnotic. If you talk to Bobby for two minutes, you come away sounding exactly like him. You don't want to. It's not like it's a great sound. You just can't help it. I fight it as much as possible.

If Bobby makes too long a speech tonight the whole room will be saying, "That's nnnniiiiiiicccce." Fortunately, the wrap party is one of the times of the year Bobby doesn't worry about nice. He gets right to the jokes.

"We had a great year. Even though *The Enquirer* said we had a lot of emotional strife on the show, we had a lot of good times, too. We want to congratulate Mimi Simms. Besides having a great year on the show, Mimi got married."

This is not a joke. This is a setup. A surprise one at that. No one expects Bobby, or anyone else for that matter, to make fun of Mimi's marriage. Just before the season began, she had suddenly married Larry Brogan. Although only thirty-two years old, Larry is now on his fourth marriage. A drunk and a womanizer, Larry's a lousy catch. But Mimi's convinced she can keep him from straying. It's doubtful. The fact is, she's a plain girl, without much sex appeal, who is happy to have someone with Larry's sexual reputation show interest in her. Popular opinion is that he's probably more interested in the seventy-five-thousand dollars an episode she gets.

Bobby looks around the room, knowing that everybody is waiting for the kill. "Mimi's wedding was beautiful, though she did stop the ceremony twice to complain to the minister that Larry had more words to say."

Big laugh from the audience. Mimi's word counting is public knowledge.

"But I guess the worst part was after Larry promised to honor and cherish her and be faithful. Mimi will sometimes put up with more words, but now he had more jokes."

Screams. Even Mimi had to laugh at the idea of her keeping Larry's animal instincts under control. Maybe with a whip and a chair, but not with her body. Bobby had the party rolling but he knew we were getting to the dangerous part.

"We've decided that this year we'll have just one representative of the cast and one member of the writing staff say a few words. So, here is one of your favorites—the man who because of his acting ability was supposed to be on the series *My Mother the Car* as the car. Here's Uncle Sal . . . Ben Fisher."

As Ben makes his way to the microphone doing a little Chaplanesque walk, occasionally pretending to trip over his own feet, all I can think of is Linda's words, "We need some time alone." Time alone? How can she want time alone? I'm the producer of the number one show on television. God, that sounds shallow. Is this what I've become? Is this who I am? One of those schmucks who cares more about what he is than who he is?

Ben Fisher takes the microphone from Bobby as the partygoers give him a big hand. It's not that he's well liked. People in show business have this respect for longevity. Bobby hands Benny the mic and gives him a hug. For the life of me, I can't figure out why Bobby actually loves this man. It can't be just because of the three bucks a joke Ben gave him back in the old days.

Ben opens with his strength, a big wet burp that probably tastes more like caviar than he would have liked. The burp gets a laugh. Benny thinks he's got them. Like an old racehorse that's heard the bell, Ben is tempted to go right to the stuffed cabbage routine. He should have. Instead, after one more burp for good measure, he goes after the writers.

"Good evening, Ladies and Germs."

That Ben. Always keeping it fresh.

"We've had a great season, with some great acting."

Applause from the crowd.

"I just wish I knew what was going on with the writing. The writing sucks. I mean really sucks. These people don't know what funny is. I don't know why Bobby keeps these writers."

There are a few giggles from people too uncomfortable to sit quietly during this affront. Even Ben senses he might have gone too far. He tries another burp. Nothing. He puffs his cigar as he wonders if he should try the Bronko Nagurski material. I can tell by the angry look on his face that later, when he tells his friends

at Nate 'n' Al's delicatessen about the wrap party, he'll say that
the audience was bad. It would never dawn on him that it could
be his hateful performance. Bobby Mitchell rushes to take the
microphone to save his old friend from any more embarrassment.

"Thank you, Ben. How about a big hand for Ben Fisher?"
Bobby implores the crowd as he steers Ben toward his seat with
a slight push. As Ben walks, Bobby adds, "I'm sure he'd like
to say more but the U.N. wants him right away to try and settle
the problems in the Middle East." It's hardly a joke, but it gets
a big laugh as everyone is so relieved to get Ben off the stage.
Bobby wants to get this party over before it gets any uglier.
"Okay, moving right along, here's one of our great writers and
producers—Barry Klein."

How can I do this now? My wife is leaving me. That's what
"time alone" means. Every divorce starts with time alone. It's just
a stall. "I've got to do this," I say, turning to Linda.

"You want to do this." She knows me too well.

I can't let her leave me. I should fight for her. But what
could I do to make her stay? There's no time to figure it out.
There's a microphone in my hand.

"Thank you, Bobby," I say, walking into the bright
spotlight. "There are so many people to thank for doing a great job
this year. Our director, Michael Zylik," I say as I point out Zylik to

the crowd.

There is polite applause as Zylik, a truly handsome man with a slight English accent, stands to take a bow. It's hard to tell if the accent is real or not, but it, along with his good looks, is how Zylik has lasted a full season on the show. Lorraine and Mimi fawn all over him, following his every direction, good or bad. And he's smart enough to let "The Ladies"—our polite name for Lorraine and Mimi—do whatever they want.

After Zylik's bow, I add, "I guess the best thing you can say about Michael Zylik is that his name is worth forty points in Scrabble." It gets a decent laugh. Enough to let me forget that my life is falling apart and go on. I reach in my pocket and take out an envelope to go into my Johnny Carson "Carnack" routine. I hold the envelope to my forehead. "Cecil B. DeMille. David Merrick. Bobby Mitchell." I rip the end of the envelope off and open it with Carson's distinctive blow. I take out the card and read, "Name two great producers and a short man." Big laugh. I'm rolling. As soon as they settle down, I'll get to my jokes about Willy and Billy.

Unfortunately, before I get going again, I see a figure coming toward me through the glare of the spotlight. It's Tommy. Jesus, how can Linda leave me? Focus. As Tommy gets close enough for me to see his face, I'm relieved. He looks in control. All too often, when Tommy does coke, the right side of his face sort of collapses into a mini stroke. It's all he can do to keep the drool in his mouth when he speaks.

"Give me the mic," he says in a clear, firm voice.

"You've got it, Buddy." I give him the mic along with a pat on the back and head to my seat.

Tommy's words are slow and measured. "You know, there's a lot of talk about how the people on this show don't get along. How we don't respect each other. How sometimes we say things about each other, things that aren't appropriate. What people don't realize is that it's just our creative process. A process that sometimes is painful. But look at the work. This is the funniest show on television. The work is great. And sometimes we do get along. Just last week I was walking down the street with Ben Fisher, Uncle Sal, and . . . you know, part of the fun of being on a hit show is getting recognized. Well, some people saw us and they knew right away . . . they saw Ben with that big brown cigar in his mouth and those big bushy eye brows and they said, " 'Look, there's Lassie taking a shit.'"

Tommy gets a big laugh and a standing ovation from the writers scattered around the room. He puts down the microphone and heads for the bar.

I'm stunned. What happens now? Linda gets up and starts walking to the car. I have to leave. I have to deal with my marriage. On the way out I spy Tommy who is now surrounded by appreciative writers. He gives me a wave. I absentmindedly wave back as I follow Linda, wondering if I can keep us together. I also see Marcia. She blows me a kiss and gives the sexiest "Come hither" look I've ever seen in my life – her rebuttal to any sane thoughts I might have on the way home.

TWO

What's a Nice Boy Like You Doing in a Place Like This?

Linda and I both kept quiet on the drive home from the wrap party. I slipped in my *Allman Brothers Live at the Fillmore* tape. I wanted to escape into the sounds of "Whipping Post"—nineteen minutes and twenty seconds of the best blues-rock ever. It didn't help. The music couldn't keep me from thinking back to how much our lives had changed in the three and half years we'd been in California.

* * *

I met Linda in 1968 while attending the University of Kentucky. I'm not sure how I wound up matriculating to the Blue Grass State. But since ten of the 200 students in my high school graduating class wound up at U.K., my guess is that our guidance councilor, Mr. Schroeder, was getting kickbacks. It's the only explanation I can come up with for me ending up in Dixie or a gym teacher/guidance councilor being able to afford a Corvette.

Living in Lexington required certain adjustments from a nice Jewish boy from New Jersey. Corned beef or pastrami sandwiches, if you could find them, were served on white bread with mayonnaise, a sacrilege for anyone with carnal knowledge of rye bread and mustard. Also, an inordinate number of locals seemed to still be fighting the Civil War. They flew the Confederate flag with pride and hated anyone from north of the Mason Dixon line. But if you could get past the idea that this was 1968 and white people were still singing that "the darkies were gay," when obviously the darkies weren't even amused let alone gay, Kentucky wasn't such a bad place to be. It had some great things going for it: smooth bourbon, fast horses, and shiksas. Boy, did they have shiksas. Row after row of beautiful blonde gentile girls who had their nose jobs done by God centuries earlier in places like Sweden and, dare I say it, Germany. They were friendly, clean, and a few were even rebellious enough to date the descendants of Abraham and Isaac. Some of the girls, like Linda Harrington, were willing commit the ultimate act of treason and marry a Yankee Jew.

We were practically babies when we met. She had just turned eighteen and I was twenty. Blind dates were not something

I often went on, but a good friend swore that if I took this girl out I wouldn't be sorry. He wasn't wrong. When I picked up Linda, I got lucky. I mean really lucky. This was a great-looking girl. Shoulder-length blonde hair, gorgeous blue eyes, and a miniskirt that showed off a terrific pair of legs. She smelled good, too. Like lilies of the valley. Not like getting hit over the head by an entire basket of lilies. Just a hint. I wondered if she was going to mind having my nose near her neck all night.

The fraternity party we attended was a rush party where the brothers of ZBT tried to convince freshmen they could be happy being part of our group. For rush parties we were on good behavior. We wore jackets and ties and the rule was: if you got so drunk that you threw up on a prospective member, you'd have to clean him up. That kind of thing will get even a college kid to think twice about alcohol abuse.

Linda and I danced a little. Drank a little. And, to my surprise, talked a lot. I was supposed to be talking to the rushees, seventeen-year-old boys who thought twenty-year-olds were men, but I was having too good a time being with this freshest of flowers. We were relaxed. I didn't have to be "on" with this girl.

After the party, parked in my car in front of her dorm, Linda and I said good night and, for the first time, kissed. It was one of those terrific kisses where lips seem to know exactly where to go and how hard to press to achieve just the right temperature and humidity. A great kiss. Longer than either of us expected. So good we kept on kissing, knowing we were both in for some puffy lips. We kissed and kissed for about fifteen minutes. It was really nice. We were both practically purring. I'm a guy, however, and nice isn't good enough. It was time to make my move.

This was quite early in the sexual revolution and "Hey, you wanna do it?" was not yet in vogue. In its place, I had gotten into the habit of using the phrase "I love you" as a tool to convince girls that sex was a great idea. The theory was, you don't say no to someone who says I love you. It had been working pretty well on fourth and fifth dates. Lately, I had gotten sloppy and was using it on second and third dates with much less success. Now, on a first date, out of desperation, I whispered the magic words as I gently placed my hand over her breast.

Linda immediately sat up straight, opened her eyes, and said, "No, you don't." I was about to crash and burn. There was no graceful way out of this. Then she said, "You don't love me. Not yet, anyway."

She was wrong. Right at that moment she had me. She said those words so sweetly. So sincerely. She was right. All I could do was smile and say, "Yeah." We went back to kissing. Great kissing. We kissed and kissed and kissed. We kissed for two years, taking

time out only for food, water, and an occasional movie. After the
two years of kissing, I graduated from college. There was only one
way to keep the kissing going; we got married.

　　The first few years of married life were uneventful. We
moved to New Jersey, loved each other, and had dinner at my
parent's every Sunday. I wasn't the only Klein completely in
love with my new bride. Both my mother and father immediately
embraced Linda as the daughter they never had. My mother plied
her with her artery clogging Jewish cooking. In my mother's
house, chicken fat was considered a green vegetable. My father
jokingly chided Linda for her lack of good judgment in marring
a "nogoodnick" like me. He would then assure her, as he had me
while growing up, that the Klein Clan was very special and that I
would indeed succeed at whatever I put my mind to. It was a shpiel
I had heard and doubted many times as I looked around and saw
our anything but special, middle class, existence. I warned Linda
that this was coming from a man who also thought my mother's
collection of miniature ceramic dogs was special. Linda, however,
was touched by my father's sincerity and his belief in my abilities.
To insure his prediction for my success, my father offered me
the opportunity to become the boss's son; working for him in the
decorator mini blinds business. He enticed me by making the job
sound creative.

"You know, it's wonderful, you can make the slats of the blinds any color you want. You can be a Michael Angelo." That's the way he said it. Like it was two names. Like if Michelangelo had known about mini blinds, he wouldn't have given church ceilings a second look.

The pay was generous and from day one I would be the prince of mini blinds. How could I say no? Besides, my father was so excited about us working together. He couldn't wait to introduce me to our suppliers. And when we'd go to lunch, he'd proudly announce to the waitresses, "This is Mr. Klein, vice president of Windows by Klein." I was sure in their minds they heard, "Mr. Mushroom Barley Soup" as they tried to keep our order straight.

I learned all there was to know about mini blinds. How to install them and fix them and ship them. I learned that even though you could get the slats in any color, we only carried five of those colors. That's because ninety-five percent of the time you can convince people that they want one of those five colors. The other five percent, they really want drapes, anyway. I learned everything but how to sell mini blinds—actually, I knew how to sell them, I just hated doing it. I hated dealing with the people who didn't want their slats in white, black, navy, gray, or almond. I completely avoided the mauve people. I stopped calling on them. I'd leave the office to go call on customers and wind up just driving around.

Sometimes I'd take my briefcase and go to the movies. Then, I'd make up some lame excuse when I returned for why I hadn't sold just a whole bunch of mini blinds. It was a bad situation. Linda knew I was miserable, and it was hard on her. I had become very withdrawn and had taken to watching an inordinate amount of *Sesame Street* each morning before I left for work. Like most twenty-five-year-olds, I already knew how to count to ten. So, why was I spending up to two hours a day watching Burt and Ernie sing the rubber ducky song?

Linda tried to help me out of my funk. She'd ask how my day went, and I'd sing, "One, two, three, four, five, six, seven, eight, nine, ten." She'd nod with great understanding and ask if I thought a change of jobs might be wise. I'd answer, "Ten, nine, eight, seven, six, five, four, three, two, one." I could count forward and backward and she wasn't impressed. Did that mean the magic was gone? I was still crazy about her, wanting to kiss her every two seconds but didn't only because it made it impossible to drive.

Linda had every right to expect more of me. She had taken a job as a receptionist at a large textile company in New York City. Each day she'd spend three hours on a bus to go to a job she loathed just to help make ends meet. She didn't complain that she was too bright to be answering phones for unappreciative executives. She didn't complain about having to get coffee for the boss. And she didn't complain because she didn't get to stay home and sing "It Isn't Easy Being Green," like I did. Eventually, though, Linda had enough.

"Barry, when we were in college and we'd talk about what you wanted to be, you'd always say you were going to be a star. For some reason that didn't sound crazy—it made sense. You know you want to be in show business. Why don't you give it a shot? There are ads in the *New York Times* for employment agencies that specialize in jobs in television. Maybe you could check them out."

"It'll kill my father if I leave the business," I reasoned.

"It won't kill him. He just wants what I want. He wants you to be happy."

Linda was right. I couldn't spend the rest of my life doing something I hated. I would give my father the tragic news. The prince of mini blinds was abdicating.

The news of my departure from the mini blinds business didn't kill my father. His jumping up and down for joy gave him chest pains, but he did not die. I wasn't selling any mini blinds and had become the most expensive shipping clerk in the world. The prospect of having to support only one family thrilled my father. He even promised to help out financially if things got tough. Anything to get me out of the business.

Early the next morning I put on my best "Don't I look like

I'm in show business?" suit and headed for New York to get a jump on everybody else who wanted to get into show business that day. I took the seven-thirty bus, the same bus Linda took to her job. It was nice having her next to me on such a momentous trip. As I excitedly anticipated our arrival in New York, Linda slept. She looked so sweet. We had spent the previous weekend in the sun and now her freckles were coming out. I adored them. I couldn't believe how much I loved her.

From the Port Authority, we walked together, holding hands, down Fortieth Street. When we got to Broadway it was time for me to head off on my own. I had to go four blocks uptown and Linda was headed to her job on Thirty-Eighth. She kissed me, wished me luck, straightened my tie, and headed off into the throng. As I watched her go, I felt great.

I walked along avoiding any eye contact. I had learned early in life that if you make eye contact in New York City, it means you're looking at a nut. You look somebody in the eye and immediately they start screaming how you killed their brother or you're the devil's accountant or, if you're lucky, they give you a simple, "What the fuck are you looking at?" No matter what they say, they're nuts. I walked looking at stores. New York has lots of stores conveniently placed right next to each other so you don't have to make eye contact with nuts.

While window-shopping, I stopped to look at a watch that could show you the time in three time zones simultaneously. I was sure I'd need one of these once I got my new job in show business. After all, I'd want to know the time in New York and Hollywood and . . . somewhere else where they have show business. Okay, maybe I didn't need the watch. I needed to get to the employment agency. Before I could move, though, I sensed that there was someone starring at me. Don't look up, Barry. Walk on casually. Don't make the dreaded eye contact. I wanted to go but my feet wouldn't move. I felt there was something special about this person I had to see. As I slowly looked up, or actually down, I made eye contact with a black midget transvestite hooker complete with a bad blonde wig and facial hair.

"Want to party with Denise, honey?" she asked.

Now, I don't have anything against black women. In fact, I find them quite exotic. Midgets, I don't have particular feelings about midgets one way or the other. I don't like midget Republicans, but that's more of a political thing. I don't even mind talking to a transvestite if they're well read. But you put all three of these things together and dress it in a metallic red mini skirt and you get a pretty scary little person.

Denise was waiting for an answer. I didn't want to reject her outright. Yet I didn't really want to say yes, either. Besides the obvious turn-offs, Denise also had too much hair on her chest and arms to be wearing an electric yellow tube top.

"Sorry. I'm late for a job interview," I said, figuring the truth would be better than some lame excuse like, "I'm sorry, but I don't really want my family to be shamed for eternity because I was found dead in some Times Square hotel after being robbed and beaten by a black midget transvestite hooker."

"Then what the fuck are you looking at?" Denise shouted.

I should have known. On top of it all, Denise was a nut. As she waddled off, I felt sorry for her. I think it was more than the fact that even though her purple platform shoes gave her an extra few inches, they did nothing for her tiny bowed legs.

Walking the final block to the employment agency, I was plagued by thoughts of Denise. Why had she chosen me out of all the guys on Broadway that morning? Was it because I looked good? Or was it because I looked like a guy who would say yes to a black midget transvestite hooker? I was guessing the latter and doubting whether they'd let that sort of guy into show biz at all. Damn you, nutty Denise. I don't need this grief this morning.

I finally reached 19 West Forty-Fourth. It looked much too dingy to be the home of Top Talent Employment Agency. Yet there on the door, in worn letters, was a sign indicating that this was indeed the place and all I'd have to do was climb up three flights

of stairs to get there. Three flights and I'd be in the posh world of
show biz.

Four walls, one desk, two chairs. That's what the Top
Talent agency was. No receptionist. No water cooler. Nothing.
Seated behind the desk and a cheap nameplate was Sylvia Berman.
Sylvia was in her mid-fifties with the same bleached-blonde
bouffant hairdo she'd had since Jackie O had been in the White
House. She wore much too much make-up with lipstick straying
way past her already large lips. Her tons of cheap jewelry jangled
as she talked on the phone. She indicated I should sit down in the
chair conveniently located next to the desk. I sat down and began
to wonder not what I was doing here, but rather if I would be able
to get enough oxygen to stay alive. Sylvia was wearing a lot of
perfume. Bad perfume. I believe it's called Pavlovia. It's got a
heavy syrupy smell that won't go away. It's got a half-life of about
a hundred and fifty years.

I sat there waiting for Sylvia, wanting to breathe and
keeping my mind off the smell by concentrating on the cigarette
dangling from her lip. She had no trouble talking without
disturbing the ash that had to beat least an inch and a half long.

Sylvia had a live one the phone. A job to be filled! "And the
starting salary?" she asked. "Beautiful. Very generous. You know,
I think I have just the young man for this job. I mean it. It's just a

coincidence but he's right here." As she said it, she smiled at me and winked. I'm not sure which but either the smile or the wink knocked the ash from the cigarette and on to her desk. She ignored it.

"I'll send him over in fifteen minutes. Great. I'm sure you'll love him as much as I do. Okay. Thank you, Doll. Bye." She hung up without taking her eyes off me.

"And what can I do for you today, Doll?" Sylvia asked while batting her mascara-laden lashes. Sylvia evidently called everybody, Doll. It was an affectation that actually worked with her thick New York accent.

"Hi. Barry Klein. I'm looking for a job in show business."

Sylvia took a moment. She was either thinking or had slipped into a Pavlovia-induced coma. "Doll, I can get you a job in show business but it would be in sales. You'd sell TV or radio time. The truth is, you can make a lot more money selling something else."

"No, not sales . . . " I said, or actually whined. "I want to be in show business."

"Who doesn't, Doll. I, myself, thought about a career as an actress at one time. I was quite a beauty, you know." Sylvia was waiting for me to react to this beauty thing, so I went with the very diplomatic "And you still are."

Sylvia asked me what I'd been doing and I told her of my experience as vice president of Windows by Klein.

"You know, Barry, you've made quite an impression on me. You're a very special young man." Sylvia said this while she gave herself an extra little squirt of Pavlovia behind her right ear. Somehow I kept conscious as she continued.

"You could make great money in sales, Barry. I just got a call from a top-notch company. They're looking for somebody just like you. Why not go over and meet them?"

"What's the company?" I asked, figuring an interview wouldn't hurt and at least it would get me into some fresh air.

"BVD underwear," she said, with a smirk on her face. I waited for some indication that she was joking, but she just kept looking at me.

"You want me to sell men's underwear? An underwear salesman? Excuse me — I don't think I can do that."

"Just meet them, Barry. Look, you've got to have a job while you're waiting for your break in show business. These are nice people," she assured me.

If I said no, Sylvia would just keep looking through her files until she found me a job. I had to get out and breathe. As Sylvia gave herself a spritz of Pavlovia behind her left ear, and then one in the mouth, I said I would go meet the folks at BVD.

Sylvia was right. They were nice people. Mel Curtis, the vice president of marketing, couldn't tell me enough how much he liked me and how much he wanted me on the BVD team. Mel was one of these very positive, up people who at forty-five was doing his best to relate to the younger generation by wearing a Beatle wig to cover his bald head instead of a toupee. Mel was also a great salesman because somehow he convinced me to say yes when he offered me a job as the BVD salesman in Texas. They would train me, move me to Houston, and have me selling those BVDs starting the very next Monday.

As I left the BVD office, Mel said to me, "Barry, you're going to be a great underwear salesman. If you work hard, you can figure on pulling down five big ones a week." Mel and his three assistants fell to the floor laughing. Each of them saying over and over, "Pull down five big ones a week." Underwear humor. I should have just run away right then.

On the way home, I felt somewhat like Jack of beanstalk fame. Linda had sent me out to find a job in show business and I was returning, not with magic beans, but with a job as an underwear salesman. What in the world was wrong with me?

To my surprise, Linda thought moving to Texas was a great idea. Although she loved my parents, the idea of not eating with them *every* Sunday was quite appealing. Houston would give us a chance to be on our own. She made it sound like a great adventure. She was happy and excited, and after I told her we made love on the living room floor. We spent the rest of the night tending to each other's rug burns and wondering what Texas would be like.

Texas was actually fine. Selling men's underwear was the problem. I hated it. It was worse than mini blinds. At least when I was selling mini blinds I was the boss's son making more money than I deserved. There were good reasons for me doing something I didn't respect. But, when you sell men's underwear, respect is hard to come by.

There's something about selling men's underwear that most people find funny. As soon as you tell them what you do for a living, they give you the smirk. It's the same smirk Sylvia Berman gave me when she first told me about the job. I think these people are under the impression that if you sell men's underwear, you must be some kind of pervert. It's like they figure if you sell them, you must be putting them over your head and sniffing them. Once. I did it once. It's no big deal.

For two years I drove around Texas convincing every Billy Joe Bob owner of a men's clothing store that BVD was the way to go underwear-wise. I was actually pretty good at it. The early seventies were a boom time in Texas, and storeowners were willing to take my advice and put in a ten-foot rack of BVDs and watch the money roll in. After two years, Linda and I had saved enough to buy a small townhouse on the outskirts of Houston.

As we drove to the realtor's office for the closing, Linda snuggled up to me and giggled. She said she couldn't wait to make love in every room of the new house. I said I was sorry we couldn't afford a house with more rooms.

"Just put your John Hancock right here, Barry, and she's all yours." Big Jim Barnett, the realtor, handed me a pen with a picture of a cowgirl that, when turned upside down, made the young woman's dress go over her head and the words "Yah-hoo" appear across her panties. I was ready to sign but couldn't. As I stared at the pen, I'm sure the realtor thought I was trying to see what was behind the "Yah-hoo." I wasn't.

"Is something wrong, Bar?" Big Jim drawled.

"What is it, Barry?" Linda asked.

"I can't do this, Honey. If we buy this house, it means I really am a men's underwear salesman. Up until now I've been doing this because I didn't know what else to do. But I've never thought of myself as a men's underwear salesman."

Out of the corner of my eye I could see Big Jim smirking each time I said "underwear salesman."

"If I sign these papers, that's it. I'm stuck," I said, continuing my tale of woe.

"What are you talking about?" Linda asked, totally confused.

"Look, I can always get a job I hate as much as this one. I blew one chance to get into show business when I took this job. I don't want to blow another. I want to go to Hollywood," I said, feeling more centered than I had ever felt before.

"Are you serious?" Linda asked with a touch of excitement in her voice.

"I know if we go to Hollywood and I put my mind to it, I'll be successful," I said, suddenly quoting my father's cockamamie pep talk as if it were gospel. I'm not really an underwear salesman and you shouldn't be married to one."

"Thank God." Linda breathed a huge sigh of relief. Evidently the wife of a men's underwear salesman gets to see more than her fair share of the smirk herself.

After a quick kiss for me and an "Adios, Partner," for Big Jim Barnett, Linda practically ran to the car. As soon as we got home, I called Mel Curtis to give my two-weeks' notice and a strange thing happened. I expected him to tell me I was crazy to leave the security of the underwear business for the uncertainties of show business. Instead, he wished me luck and told me he respected my decision. Respect. It was something I hadn't really felt for two years. For the next few weeks almost everybody I told about my plans reacted just like Mel Curtis. People like the idea of somebody actually trying to make their dreams come true. When I told my parents, my father sounded happier than the day I said I would go to work for him. Even happier than the day I said I would stop working for him. He was genuinely proud that I had the courage to give it a shot. Either way, the Klein Clan was special. The next two weeks flew by. Everyday I'd bring home apple boxes from Safeway so Linda could pack more stuff for our trip to Hollywood. We only had about two thousand dollars in the bank and a couple of Visa cards but we weren't worried. We were finally on our way to meet our destiny. When the big day arrived, I forced everything we owned into a U-Haul trailer. Then realized I should have hooked it up to the trusty Ford *before* I loaded it. Unloaded it. Hooked it up to the trusty Ford. Re-loaded it and headed off to tinsel town.

THREE

Getting Into Those Pearly Gates
of Show Business

There were so many questions to answer when we first got
to Hollywood. Questions you wouldn't have to ask yourself in
other cities. Is the weather going to be this good every day? What
do you do first to get into show business? Do you really get to
wrestle a nude woman at the Wrestle a Nude Woman place? That's
right, Toto, we were no longer in Kansas or Texas or any place else
that resembled America. We were in Hollywood.

Linda and I spent the first couple of days driving around
the L.A. basin, deciding where to live. A tiny apartment in Santa
Monica about ten blocks from the beach seemed perfect. It was
small, but it had good cross ventilation, a nice group of palm trees
right outside our door, and it had Dave Larson.

Dave Larson was a twenty-five-year-old aspiring comedy writer. He had arrived in Los Angeles from Minneapolis with his Midwestern good looks and innocence about six months before us. To make ends meet, while he waited for his big break, he sold a little pot to friends and acquaintances. Nothing sinister. Nothing to call the cops over. In fact, in the mid-seventies, it was convenient having a pot dealer right next door.

Dave was a sweet guy who knew, ever since he was in high school, that he wanted to be a comedy writer. In his teens, he would write jokes for Johnny Carson and Dick Cavett. He didn't actually sell any of these jokes to Carson or Cavett, but he would send the jokes and be encouraged by the friendly rejection letters. Now, he had the rejection letters hung in the hall leading from his living room to his bedroom and used them as a lure for the girls who were so far down the Hollywood food chain of fame, they would go to bed with someone who even had a piece of Mr. Carson's stationery. Instead of jokes, Dave should have sent Carson and Cavett a couple of the joints he sold. His grass was really good. His jokes were not. They weren't really bad—just ironic, clever little jokes that didn't make you laugh. They made you say, "Oh, yeah."

"Hey, Barry, why did Agnew cross the road?" Dave would ask. To annoy him, I would sit there trying to figure out the punch line. Then, fearing the timing of his comedy gem was being completely put off, he would blurt out, "To steal something from the moron."

Even after Dave had gotten me completely blotto with his wacky tobaccy, it was tough laughing at that caliber of joke. After listening to Dave's jokes for about two weeks, I decided, with Linda's encouragement, to try writing. I was funnier than Dave. If he could be a writer, I could be a writer.

Dave loved the idea of having another writer next door. He was six months ahead of me in his career, so that made him feel like an old pro. He already had knowledge and was willing to share it. To get started in television, he explained, I first needed to pick a show I liked and write a script for it. This was called a spec script, and I would need one to show people my work. He also told me that we should smoke a number and go see a new improvisational comedy show that was opening that night in a small theater on Fairfax Avenue. It would be good fun and maybe we could steal a couple of funny ideas. Dave was so far ahead of me, he already knew about stealing ideas. Unfortunately, he just wasn't funny enough to know who to steal from. As it turned out, both pieces of advice were important.

The next day I would start writing my spec *Rhoda*. It was a show I liked, and I thought I could hear the characters in my head. In addition, Dave sold dope to somebody who worked on the show and thought he could get the script read by one of the producers. The second piece of advice, the one about going to the improvisational comedy show, turned out to be the stroke of genius.

Funny Bones was the name of the show—as well as the name of the troop of actors who would get up and perform any scene an audience wanted to see. If the audience wanted to see a woman having a baby in an elevator or ex-lovers sharing a cab on a rainy day, whatever, the six members of the *Funny Bones* cast would bound up on stage and improvise the scene. Most times they were very funny, and the audience loved them. It was a revelation to me. Here were people talking to each other in jokes as if it were another language. The cast had no time to prepare—they just got up and did it. Even if a scene wasn't that funny because someone in the audience had given a bad idea, you still had to love Dem Bones for having the courage to wing it and hope for the best. One member of the cast, however, particularly stood out. Six feet tall with jet black hair, piercing indigo eyes, and a pirate's swagger as he moved around the stage, you couldn't help but be impressed by the lighting-fast lines delivered by twenty-two-year-old Tommy Cross.

The show was one of the most exciting things I'd ever seen,

and when I found out that Wendy Marks, the show's director, had an improv class every Sunday where anybody could try to do what the troop did so well, I jumped at the chance. Although terrified at first, I found I could easily make the other people in the class laugh. When the regular cast of *Funny Bones* hung around class, I made them laugh, too. So, after just six weeks, when one of the guys in the cast decided to give up show business and become a priest (he wasn't really giving up show business, he was going into a branch of show business that paid better), I was asked to join the show. For the next ten months, every Friday and Saturday night, I would perform with the *Funny Bones* actors. I loved it.

Being on stage with *Funny Bones* was a time to forge my comedic metal. You can't learn to be funny. It's a gift. I don't know where the jokes come from. I'm just privy to them first. But you can learn to be funnier. You can get better at what you do. Playing in an atmosphere where you have to be funny in an instant is great exercise for whatever muscle it is that pushes the jokes out. Setting up the other actors - leading a scene down a road that you know will allow all of you to soar turns comedy into a team sport. You learn what works and what doesn't. You trust one another and so you take chances, knowing that if you bomb, your partners will do their best to save you.

From our earliest moments on stage together, Tommy

and I were smooth in our comic dance. During my first show, an audience member asked to see a TV cooking show being scrutinized by an uptight censor. Tommy immediately headed for the stage, stopping only to grab a wig, a wine glass and an apron from the nearby prop table. In an instant he was a hilarious half bombed Julia Child. I followed him, taking the role of the anal retentive censor. Tommy, in a drunken slur, told the imaginary TV audience that he was going to prepare a fabulous stuffed chicken breast. I immediately interrupted explaining that he wasn't allowed to say "breast" on television. Not unless he was reciting Joyce Kilmer's famous poem, *Trees*. "You can say, 'Pressed against the Earth's sweet flowing breast,' on TV," I explained. "But that's because the Earth has no nipples." It was a complex notion that seemed to form in slow motion. While I was saying it, I was both aware and surprised that Kilmer's poem, something I had not heard or referred to since elementary school had popped into my mind? And once there, where would I go with it? Yes, it was a clever reference, but where was the joke? Then "nipple", a word that for some reason almost always amuses people, thankfully showed up. The process and the awareness of it only took a millisecond. More importantly, it got a big laugh from our audience.

Tommy almost cracked up too. But he quickly regained his composure and shot back with a challenging, "A chicken has no nipples." Another big laugh.

In character, completely confused, I asked, "Then how do they nurse?" Joke. Joke. Joke. Tommy and I were off and running.

Linda didn't seem to mind coming to the show week after week either. Because they were made up on the spot, each show was different. So she knew she'd be in for a few laughs. She also helped out by selling coffee and cake to the audience during the intermission. There was a sense that we were both doing what we had to do to make my career happen.

It was a wonderful time for us. I'd work on my spec script in the mornings. Afternoons were spent with Linda, going to the beach or exploring the city. We spent lots of happy time together buoyed by the faith that something good would happen before the money ran out.

After a few months, *Funny Bones* really started to click. Word was getting around that the show was good. The *L.A. Times* gave us a great review. Comics showed up to steal material. Bobby Mitchell showed up to see if there were funny people he could use. There were. That's when Bobby asked Tommy Cross and me if we wanted to come write on his new show, *In the Swim*. He didn't even ask to read my spec script. What he saw on stage sold him.

When I joined *Funny Bones* it was just something to do until my writing career took off. But now, enjoying some success, I thought being a performer might be the way to go. But Bobby said we'd be making an incredible five hundred dollars a week. From nothing to five hundred a week. Easy decision. I was a writer.

The first day at work was like the first day of school. I got beat up. Not physically. Emotionally. In kindergarten it had been Roy Van Horn who had my number from day one. On my first day of real paying show business, it was Scotty O'Rourke who was giving me a hard time. Scotty was the guard at the main gate of Paragon Studios. It was a job he'd had since he was nineteen years old. Now, at age one hundred and thirty-five, Scotty was coming to the end of a career that should have ended during the last ice age. He was a permanent fixture and a studio legend, making any suggestion of removing him from his post a show business sacrilege.

As he checked his list for the fourth time to see if he could find my name and let me pass through the pearly gates of show business, I felt these incredible pangs of fear and loathing. This old man with a badge but no gun was going to keep me out of show business because of some clerical error. Even if my name had been on the list, there was no way he could see it looking through glasses that were too thick to be real. I was sure they had been given to him by Jerry Lewis after filming *The Nutty Professor*. He was wearing them only to honor Jerry.

"Nope, I don't see it," he said as he put his hand where the gun would be if they had let him have one. Was he expecting trouble from me?

"Maybe I could take a look," I suggested in a helpful tone.

"I said, I don't see it," he said a little firmer.

"I'm sure it's there. Just give me a peek. I've got strong eyes. I eat a lot of carrots," I said using a little laugh, hoping he'd think we were both in on this little joke.

He didn't laugh. He didn't smile. He just said, "You'll have to turn around. I don't see your name."

"You couldn't see the top row on an eye chart, you old fart!" I said a bit louder than intended. I was losing it.

Now Scotty really started reaching for the gun. It was becoming obvious why they wouldn't let him have one. Paragon Studios didn't want a pile of dead, snotty kids whose names weren't on the guest list messing up their studio gate. Just then, as Scotty was about to pee in his pants in anticipation of what he'd have to do to stop this intruder, he took one more look at his list and said, "I've got a *Larry* Klein . . ."

"Yes. That's me. Larry Klein," I of coursed.

"I thought you said Barry?" he asked cautiously. He was still unsure whether I would pull a tire iron from under the seat and smash his skull.

"Well, I'm nervous—this is my first day of show lisness . .
. oops, there I go again. Sometimes when I'm nervous I mix up my
b's and my l's." All Scotty needed was a little logic.

"Okay, Larry. You park in spot 53. If you're over the line
I'll have you towed," Scotty said in a cocky tone meant to indicate
that the cantankerous old man was back in control. It was a tone
I'm sure he learned in gate guard school along with the credo:
Minimus Populus Es Fortus—Let Minimum Wage Rule.

"Thank you, sir," I said, having no idea I'd have to repeat
the same scene every morning for the next two weeks until the
name Larry on the list was changed to Barry. I also had no idea I
would spend my entire morning shower, for the rest of my life,
plotting the murder of Scotty O'Rourke.

I quickly found "K" building, an old barracks of a thing
that housed all of Bobby Mitchell's shows. Each show had a group
of offices for the writers, producers, and secretaries. A handwritten
sign claiming that *In the Swim* would be on the second floor was
taped to the door. I wasn't sure if the sign was for real because
beside the announcement, there was a cartoon drawing of Bobby
Mitchell with blood spurting out of his butt and a pained Bobby
proclaiming, "Comedy is a pain in the ass." Here it was, first day
of school for all the kids, and already some wise guys were looking
for trouble.

The second floor could only be reached by a long climb up
an incredibly steep flight of stairs. When anybody reached the top
of the K building steps, they sounded old. No matter what kind of
shape you were in, the last few steps leading to the second floor
were punctuated with an out-of-breath "God . . . who designed
these damned things?" When I finally reached the top, I wanted to
plant a flag or something. Instead, I gave a wheezy "Hey, how ya
doin'?" to the pudgy boy waiting for me.

Howie Clark, the fellow writer who greeted me at the top
of the stairs, looked exactly like the Pillsbury doughboy. Or at least
how he'd look on his day off when he'd be wearing slacks and a
golf shirt instead of his usual doughboy nakedness. Looking like
the Pillsbury doughboy might be cute if you were a little kid, but
for a guy in his twenties it was kind of odd. I didn't know whether
I should shake Howie's hand or poke him gently in the side and see
if he'd giggle. I decided to go for the handshake. At least I thought
I did . . . I don't know . . . maybe I did give him a little poke. I'm
not sure, because as soon as I made contact with Howie, either
through shaking or poking, he slipped and began falling down the
long flight of stairs leading to the base of K building.

It was worse than horrible. He didn't just fall down those
steps—he bounced in slow motion so you could feel each bounce
as he hit step after step after step. His screams of pain stopped

about two-thirds of the way down. The rest of the way was just silent bouncing. Finally, he came to rest at the bottom. Lifeless.

What had I done? I stood at the top of the stairs frozen with fear. Poor Howie! And poor Barry. I was so close to show business and now I'd be out. Well, not out completely. I'd probably be writing the annual prison talent show, but that was little consolation.

"Oh, my God—somebody call an ambulance!" I wailed.

As I turned to go find a phone, there along with Tommy Cross was the rest of the *In the Swim* writing staff. All of them grinning from ear to ear. I'd been had. At the bottom of the stairs, Howie Clark was getting up. He wore a grin of his own as he waved to me before checking for broken bones. There were none, of course. Besides being a fine writer, this was Howie's talent. He could throw himself down a flight of stairs and land unharmed. He would repeat this process ten times today as he greeted each new writer with a long fall. Those who had worked with Howie before weren't scared, but they still enjoyed the show. Some, fearing Howie might give up his suicidal stair dives, offered cash contributions to start a "Howie Clark Chiropractic Care Fund."

* * *

Because Bobby Mitchell couldn't spend all day at each of his shows, a producer was hired to steer the ship. Phil Miller was

Bobby's guy for *In the Swim*. He would be the one telling us to make the stories "nnnniiiiiiiiccccce." He would be the one deciding what stories we'd be telling. Which jokes were funny enough. Which jokes weren't. For Tommy Cross's and my taste, Phil was not nearly funny enough to be making judgments about anybody else's jokes. It didn't matter much, though. Phil would be the first in a long line of people to produce the show. It seemed like every six weeks or so, whomever was producing at the time would decide to do something that either Lorraine LaBarbara or Mimi Simms would protest. Tempers would flare, and at some point somebody would say, "Either they go or I go."

When a show is a hit, it's pretty easy for the studio or network to decide who stays and who goes. America doesn't give a damn about Phil Miller. They love Lorraine and Mimi. Let's see, who do we back? So long, Phil. So long, Mitch, Jimmy, Jamie, Morty, Harry, and Erica. Each of these people got to the point where they wanted the show to be their vision. Each, in their own way, made a stand for creative integrity. And each got a nice buyout when the studio had to pay off their contracts because Lorraine or Mimi absolutely couldn't work with them any longer. It was the only time The Ladies could agree on anything. They loved firing producers. Fortunately, the writing staff was usually left in tact so that production of the show could continue. We would keep cranking out scripts while The Ladies would make their management changes. Over the first two seasons, we learned how to write for television as the parade of producers continued. Some of the producers were good. Some were bad. Some, like Erica, were as crazy as The Ladies.

Erica Rodgers had never produced a sitcom before she got the job on *In the Swim,* but she had attended a lot of Hollywood parties. It was there she met and befriended Lorraine LaBarbara. Lorraine had an active Hollywood social life that she loved except when her friends would tell her how they felt about her show: "I mean . . . it's funny, but it's so *silly*." The show just wasn't very hip. Lorraine desperately wanted to be hip, so at the beginning of the third season she had the studio hire Erica to bring the show to a degree of cool that would make party-going more enjoyable. Bad move. Erica turned out to be a major nut case.

Erica would come to work each day in a flannel nightgown and bunny slippers. On her third day in charge, we found out that she had never actually watched *In the Swim*. This became evident when, at a meeting with the cast, she wasn't sure who played Connie and who played Patti and in an exquisite blunder thought Ben Fisher was the prop man and asked him to run out and get her a pack of cigarettes. Everyone was furious with Lorraine for bringing in someone so unqualified. I made Ben's blood boil when

I asked him if he wouldn't mind picking up our lunch while he was getting Erica's cigarettes.

Mimi threatened to walk off the show if Erica wasn't fired immediately. To save face, Lorraine maintained that it would be good for the show to have someone with a fresh outlook produce it. That normally wouldn't have been enough to convince anyone. To cement the deal, she also promised Mimi that the next four episodes would be "Patti shows." In an attempt to keep some sanity on the show, we had always tried to do an even number of stories that featured Lorraine or Mimi. Now Lorraine was offering four Mimis in a row. Mimi took it. No one asked the writing staff if we had four Mimi stories. It was assumed that whatever The Ladies wanted, the writers would find a way to oblige.

The next four weeks were a disaster. Besides being totally inept, Erica was in the middle of a boyfriend breakup, so she spent most of her time in her office crying and drinking Singapore slings. She loved her slings, wanting them prepared following her strict instructions: garnished with an orange slice, a wedge of ripe pineapple, and one of those little paper umbrellas. Toward the end of week four, we had run out of umbrellas, and when it was suggested that she might reuse an old one she went crazy. How dare anyone entertain the thought? No, she'd quit before she'd drink a Singapore sling without a fresh umbrella. The studio wasn't about to miss out on this opportunity. If Erica quit, the studio wouldn't have to pay off her contract. When the proper garnish for her drinks failed to arrive, Erica, true to her word, drove off the lot. She was gone and another attempt to find a producer began.

By this time, Tommy and I were thinking we should get our shot at this thankless job. After all, we were the ones really running the show during the parade of producers. We were the ones working an average of eighteen, man eating hours a day to keep it funny enough to stay on top of the ratings.

The working hours had been a big adjustment for Linda and me. We no longer had our afternoons together. We had almost no time together. We each had our own worlds, which we weren't sharing with each other. There were lots of weeks when I'd see Linda only as she was getting up to go to her morning workout. I would still be zonked from working until 3:00 A.M. when she would slide out of bed. We'd throw each other very perfunctory kisses. She'd ask how the show was going. I'd mumble something about how Lorraine and Mimi were the Sacco and Vinzetti of comedy and then go back to sleep.

After a little more than two seasons, Tommy and I felt we deserved a promotion. We no longer wanted to unofficially produce the show. We wanted the title and all the benefits that came along with it. We assumed there were benefits. There had to be. People kept taking the job. Why should we have to keep teaching outsiders how to keep Lorraine and Mimi happy when we knew what to do? It was time for a meeting with Bobby Mitchell. If we didn't speak up, we had no one but ourselves to blame.

I called Bobby and asked for a meeting. Surprisingly, he said he'd meet with us right away. We didn't know if he was doing this because he was desperate or if he didn't want to give us the chance to really plan our strategy. Either way, we had no choice. After Tommy took a quick toot from one of the "caine" family of drugs, we headed for Bobby's office.

On the walk to Bobby's, I suggested to Tommy that if we got the promotion it might be time for him to take another stab at sobriety. He had, at other times, checked himself in to the appropriate version of Celebrity Detox in an attempt to clean up his act. Unfortunately, he needed more than resolve to resist the Siren's call of his chemical dependency, and would always wind up falling off the wagon.

As we approached Bobby's office, Tommy half-heartedly promised he'd give another trip to rehab some thought. "I just got a brochure in the mail from some fancy private hospital up in Santa Barbara. Maybe I'll go there. They actually made the week of sweating, puking and shaking sound fun," Tommy said with a self-deprecating grin. Then, shaking his head at a sobering realization, he added, "Jesus, the brochure came in the mail. Can you imagine the fucked up mailing lists *I'm* on?"

Bobby wasn't headquartered in K building with the writers. He had a plush suite in Paragon Studios' administration building. Traditionally, creative people wanted to be as far away from the men and women who ran the studio as possible. Bobby wanted to be right next to them. His theory was, if they thought of him as one of their own, they'd be less likely to screw him out of the huge profits he hoped to share in when all his hit shows went into syndication. That was the television jackpot. Once a television series had filmed a hundred episodes and had finished its network run, the studio could then sell the show to individual stations in each market. The shows could be re-run forever making each episode worth millions of dollars. The studios were notorious for not sharing those millions with the creative folks who had contracts promising them a piece of the profits.

Arriving at the oversized mahogany door marked BOBBY MITCHELL PRODUCTIONS, I took one last look to make sure the drugs hadn't made Tommy's face fall into his shirt pocket. He looked okay. We went into the reception area, which was occupied by Alice Martin, Bobby's secretary. A well kept, attractive woman in her mid-forties, Alice had been with Bobby for over fifteen years, moving with him from show to show. She was totally dedicated

to him and was intensely protective. When you worked for Bobby
Mitchell, you learned early on to get in Alice's good graces. I
always liked her, so that didn't take much effort. I gave her a warm
hello before she sent us in to see Bobby.

"Soooooooo, how are things on the show this weeeeeek?"
Bobby asked us as we tried our damnedest to ignore the lump of
white fish stuck on his front tooth. I guess he felt obliged to ask
about the show since he made a small fortune from it. In truth,
Bobby had little to do with the everyday running of *In the Swim*.
He hated the bickering that went on so he avoided the show as
much as possible.

"Well, Mimi's a little upset because we have her getting
wet again this week and she thinks we're doing it because
somebody pointed out she looks like a stork when her hair is wet,"
I explained.

"Are you?" Bobby wanted to know.

"Yeah," said Tommy. "But it's funny."

"Fine. As long as it's funny," Bobby said. The bottom line
was simple. If it's funny, it stays. "Now, what can I do for you
boys?" We were only penciled in for ten minutes. Bobby was
getting right to the point.

"Well . . . we think that rather than bring in another
producer who really doesn't know the show, we should get a shot

at it." There. I got it out.

"Do you guys think you're really ready?" he asked without making eye contact but instead going through the bowl of antacids he kept on the coffee table. He was looking for a specific flavor to take care of this specific pain in the gut that Cross and Klein were causing.

"We're ready," Tommy said firmly and directly.

"Absolutely," I stuttered. I wanted to start yelling, "Bad idea, bad idea! Sorry—it won't happen again!" But I knew Tommy would kill me if I did. There was, of course, the chance that Tommy wouldn't hear me. The cocaine had stimulated his postnasal drip problem so that he was now making an expectorant sound with his nose and throat that Yiddish medical books describe as *gehechting*. It was either the bad idea or the horrible noise, but Bobby wanted us out of his office as soon as possible.

"I'm going to have to think about this, guys," he said. "Give me a couple of days."

"Sure. No problem," I said as I guided Tommy out of the office. Bobby's request seemed reasonable. Even though he was Mr. Television, he'd still have to get Lorraine and Mimi's approval of whomever was to become the next producer.

As Tommy and I made our assent of the K Building steps, we saw a few members of the writing staff waiting for us.

"So, come on . . . what haaaappened?" Rhonda Silverman, one of the staff writers, called down to us. Rhonda had grown up in the same neighborhood, on the same block, as Bobby Mitchell and Lorraine LaBarbara, and so suffered the same whine. They had all played together as kids and when Bobby and Lorraine started making it in show business, Rhonda asked if she could come play again. The answer was yes. And why not? Rhonda was pretty funny and could really write for Lorraine. She had the sound. The voice. If you closed your eyes, you didn't know if you were talking to Lorraine or Rhonda.

Rhonda had given up her job as a data analyst in the button down world of Wall Street and came to seek her fortune in free wheeling Hollywood. She was a bright Jewish girl with an IQ of a million who had read everything ever written because she never had a date in high school, claimed she didn't care, but tried everything she could think of to attract a man. She had one of those tight New York, Jewish faces. The ones with the fairly big nose, the kinky black hair, the pasty white skin, and enough beauty marks that if you played connect the dots with them you'd probably have a pretty detailed picture of an American eagle. The more money she made in show business, the more she had done to improve her looks. She had her big nose done and wound up with a big fixed nose. She had her hair straightened, but even the slightest bit of humidity would make her look like Bozo the Clown. She spent every spare minute on a tanning table she kept in her office but, alas, she was from one of the tribes of Israel that didn't tan. She burned. As a result, she always looked like one of those girls who goes to the beach once a year and falls asleep in the sun and gets that horrible lobster red. Even though Rhonda was quite likable, she wasn't helping herself.

"Bobby said he'll think about it," I reported as I headed for my office.

Fred Maxwell stood next to Rhonda, listening intently to the details of the meeting. "Did he say anything about me?" he asked in the scared tone in which he customarily spoke.

"Yeah. He said you're the new president of show business," Tommy snarled as he headed for his office. "It'll be official just as soon as you write a fucking joke."

We all laughed and then caught ourselves. Fred Maxwell had not written a joke in quite some time. For years, Fred had been a successful writer and was supposed to be the main man on our staff. Instead, he'd been intimidated by Tommy and me. Our experience in improv made us fast. We could come up with the biggies when we needed them. Fred needed time. Too much time. So he just stopped writing jokes and started telling stories about his years on *Mister Ed*. It drove Tommy crazy. We'd be at the rewrite table at two in the morning, trying to figure out some new way for Willy and Billy to hit on Patti and Connie, and Fred would start telling us, yet again, about the time Ed took a crap on Wilbur's shoes. Fred had even produced a couple of shows himself over the years and probably hoped that Bobby would remember that. Then, in a sudden epiphany, Bobby would name Fred the new producer of *In the Swim*. Fred already knew his first order of business: get rid of Barry Klein and Tommy Cross, the two wiseassess who broke his joker.

"Bobby didn't mention you, Fred," I said. "He didn't say much about anything. We just told him that we thought we deserved a shot at running the show, and he said he'd think about it."

Heading for my office, I suddenly felt depressed from our meeting with Bobby. I really wanted the promotion. To walk into Bobby's office and have him welcome us as the new princes of show business would have been perfect. Then I could pick up the phone, call Linda, and tell her we got it. Well, I couldn't call and realized that even if I did, Linda wouldn't be home.

It was Tuesday, and Tuesdays had become group meditation day for Linda. She had joined a group of other show business wives, women who didn't get to see their husbands very much, either, because of the horrendous hours show business demands.

They met every Tuesday in Malibu Canyon where they'd burn sage, chant, and perform other rituals in an attempt to find inner peace or kill another afternoon. For most it was an honest attempt to create a life of their own. Linda said she found it fulfilling. It didn't seem like much fun to me.

Getting this promotion would be fun. More than fun, it would be a huge step. Comedy writers want to become producers for a variety of reasons. One of the biggest is artistic control. Producers decide whose jokes stay and whose jokes go. They decide what stories you tell. They go to meetings at the network. And although the network people would know that Bobby Mitchell was "the man," they would start looking at me as one of "the men" of the future.

There's a large group of good writers who will never become show runners. They may get a credit at the beginning of the show that says "Producer." But they don't really produce the show. The credit is just something they demand when negotiating their contracts. They never get the creative control or the really big bucks. I wanted it all – the money, the power, and most importantly, to be the one who decided which Chinese restaurant we'd order take out from when we'd work late.

I passed through my outer office and Marcia Heilger was there putting lotion on her legs. Marcia had been working for me for about a month. My previous secretary, Beth—the one who could do not only the typing and dictation and other secretarial tasks but also took care of my life—decided to take a job at a small production company. Actually, she wasn't that terrific on the clerical stuff; she made a lot of mistakes. But she was a wiz at the taking care of life stuff.

Whenever I traveled, I let Beth make all the arrangements. When I'd land at some strange airport, there'd always be someone from the airline, someone in a blazer, to meet me at the plane and make sure I was a happy camper. I didn't even know the airlines had these people in blazers. Beth did, and she made sure they were there to meet me. Beth also made my restaurant reservations. In Hollywood that's a big deal. It's not easy getting good tables at good restaurants. It was easy for Beth. She wasn't afraid to say "show business" to get what she wanted. Those were the magic words. She'd say "show business" and somehow there'd be people in blazers and good tables, and flowers in hotel rooms, and life was good.

I was devastated when she said she was leaving. I wanted to find some way to get her to stay. After all, she'd be doing the same work at her new job but they would call her "assistant to Mr. Kimmel." At Paragon Studios the secretaries were unionized so I couldn't call her "assistant to Mr. Klein." She'd never be my assistant. She'd always be just my secretary. So even though she'd

be doing the same damn thing, probably for less money, she left.

In Hollywood, credits mean everything. They define who you are.

When Tommy and I were first made partners, it took us a week to

decide if we were "Klein and Cross" or "Cross and Klein." After

I lost an odds defying thirteen coin flips in a row, I gave in to the

"Cross and Klein" billing. Beth was no different. She didn't want

to be someone's secretary. She wanted to be someone's assistant.

Now Mr. Kimmel's life was being taken care of instead of mine.

Although Marcia worked for both Tommy and me, she sat

right outside my office door in a small outer office that served as a

waiting area for anyone wanting to get in to see us. After about the

first three days on the job, I noticed that at least four times a day,

Marcia would apply skin cream to her legs. She wasn't bashful

about it, either. She'd hike up her dress, exposing her shapely

legs to about mid-thigh and then slather on the Jergens. It was

during these first weeks that I found out that Marcia had been a

ballet dancer before coming to Paragon and, thus, the attention to

leg care. In the world of ballet, if you don't make it by the age of

twenty-three, you're not going to make it. So even though she had

performed in the corps d' ballet of a number of major companies,

Marcia realized she was never going to be the big swan on the

lake. She'd always be twirling around the prima ballerina for meager money.

Marcia was ambitious and although she loved to dance, she hated the lousy pay. One night after a performance of *Giselle*, she was told she wouldn't be dancing for a few nights. The company wanted to try out a new seventeen-year-old wunderkind they had discovered at a dance school in Minneapolis. Marcia knew what this meant. Six years earlier she had been the wunderkind from Riverside, California. She saw the handwriting on the wall. Actually, the handwriting was on her contract and it said the company could replace her whenever they wanted. So she left the world of dance and went to work in the secretarial pool at Paragon Studios. That was not her true ambition—she wanted to direct feature films. Not that she was doing anything to prepare for such a career. But she did look good in a baseball cap. And in her mind, she was preparing. She was working for the two guys who might become the producers of the number one show on television. She knew her star was hitched to ours, so when I walked into the office after my meeting with Bobby, she quickly put down the leg cream and the legs and asked me how it went.

"Great . . . I think it went great," I said as I tried to keep up a front of confidence. I hadn't known her long enough to show my real emotions. I could have told Beth anything. She was my biggest fan, and if anything went wrong, she'd start figuring out right away what would make me feel better. Beth would somehow get me this promotion. Come back, Beth. Forget Kimmel.

"Well, if there's anything I can do . . ." Marcia wanted to help but she didn't know how. Beth would know.

"Thanks. Would you close the door and tell Donna to come in here?" If I was going to sulk, I wanted Donna Morris with me.

I was in love with Donna Morris. It was no secret. Everybody knew. Even Linda knew. Donna and Barry were in love, and that was that. But it's not what you think. There was no sexual vibe between us whatsoever. We were simply best friends. Luckily, there was no threat to Linda, either. She knew that Donna and I weren't each other's type. At five-foot-nine and medium build, I was too short for Donna. Physically, we just didn't match up. Besides that, Linda and Donna liked each other. They both looked forward to the times when Donna would join Linda and me for an occasional dinner together.

When Donna first came to work on the show, Rhonda Silverman immediately started snooping around wanting to know what was going on between us. Everybody was wondering, but Rhonda spoke the unspeakable.

"So, are you doooooing iiit?"

"No, we weren't doing it. We hadn't even thought of doing it," we both explained.

"They're dooooooing iiit," Rhonda insisted. The teasing didn't bother us and so became a senseless game in which everybody lost interest.

I knew Donna was special from the moment I saw her on the stage at the Comedy Store, a nightclub in Los Angeles that features stand-up comics. Normally, I didn't have the time to go to nightclubs. Most weeknights I worked to at least eleven o'clock and then headed home. On weekends, when Linda and I finally got some time alone, she preferred a quiet night of dinner and a movie. She didn't like the hype of Hollywood parties where everyone, including me, was "on" all the time. She wanted a little peaceful time together. Going to a place like the Comedy Store usually meant we'd wind up standing in the back alley schmoozing with the comics and other writers. Well, I'd schmooze. She'd watch. It wasn't a particularly enjoyable evening for her. So I didn't get to the Store very often. However, shortly after going to work on *In the Swim*, we had an unusual Monday night.

Monday was the first day of our production week. We would start at ten o'clock in the morning, sitting around a big table on Paragon Studio's famous Stage 7. It was not a stage in the traditional, theatrical, proscenium sense. It was a sound stage. The entire huge building, big enough to hold dressing rooms, bleachers for an audience, the four permanent sets plus one weekly additional set, cameras, and everything else you need to do a show was referred to as "the stage." Over the years, some of Paragon's biggest movies had been shot on Stage 7. People like Clark Gable, Spencer Tracy, and Marilyn Monroe had done their best work on Stage 7. Oscar-winning performances had happened in this building. But, like everything else, show business changes and now television was the big money maker, not movies. Paragon had transformed this building — which should have been designated some kind of artistic shrine — into the home of *In the Swim*. I'm sure all sorts of spinning was going on in any number of graves when a marquee with Lorraine LaBarbara and Mimi Simms's names was put over the door. Anyway, Monday mornings the cast and writing staff would sit around the big table and hear that week's script read aloud. It was an exciting and scary time for the writers. This was the first time you'd hear whether your jokes worked or not. It was a simple system. If people laughed the jokes were funny. If they didn't . . . well, if they didn't it meant you had to rewrite them. Come up with new jokes. Some writers would argue, "Hey come on, that's funny. An audience will love that joke." It didn't matter. No laughs meant it wasn't funny enough.

There were other pitfalls at the table. The script could be funny but the story might not make sense. That meant more rewriting. Then there was the biggest danger. Either Lorraine or

Mimi could simply announce, "I don't like it." Those were the worst rewrites. Those were the ones where you'd have to throw the script out and start all over. When Lorraine or Mimi didn't like a script on Monday morning, it meant an all-nighter. It meant we wouldn't be going home. It happened often enough that Linda had begun making plans on Monday nights. She'd get together with her meditation friends and go hear some yogi talk. She knew, even if I was available, I wouldn't want to tag along. I cared only about yogis who stole picnic baskets, not the ones who could tie their feet behind their necks.

So on this strange Monday night, when the script was funny and the story worked, and Lorraine and Mimi liked it, I was finished with work around six-thirty. Linda had already left to go hear some Mahatma Mahesh Mashugi, so I had the night to myself. Instead of going home and getting some much-needed rest, I headed for the Comedy Store with Tommy.

Seated at a small table in the back of the Comedy Store's main room, Tommy and I were hardly paying attention when we heard, "Okay, right now, we've got a terrific new comic. She's from Long Island, New York. Let's hear it for Donna Morris!" Mark Baxter, the Comedy Store master of ceremonies was once again promising us a terrific new comic. He'd been making the same promise all night and now at ten-thirty I had no reason to believe him. Baxter himself was a very average comic. The only reason he had become master of ceremonies at the Store was that he was dating Mitzi Shore, the woman who owned the place. As stand-up comedy grew in importance, Mitzi had become one of the most powerful women in Hollywood. She was the one who decided who got the "good spots" on the evening's schedule and who didn't. She could determine who got to audition for the producers of the *Tonight Show* and who didn't. All sorts of talented people, people like Richard Pryor and Jay Leno and Robin Williams, had to be nice to Mitzi in the late seventies so they could get the good spots. Some, like Mark Baxter, had to date her. Even then, he didn't get the really good spots. He got to be the emcee every night and do his act in drips and drabs in between the other acts.

Monday night was open mic night at the Store. That meant anybody could sign up to do five minutes. It was the night all the new comics got to work. But even on Monday nights there was a pecking order. Somehow, Mitzi had to convince the customers that she wasn't cheating them on the five-dollar cover and two-drink minimum, so she saved the good spots for the funniest of the new comics. So far, none had really been funny and I wasn't expecting much more from the terrific new comic from Long Island. I couldn't have been more wrong.

Unlike most of the comics who bound onto the stage, Donna walked cautiously. It may have been because she was a big girl, about six foot one, not fat, but big. It's tough for a girl that size to bound and have it look anything but scary. Donna knew that, so she walked. It was a good first sign. She started right into her act without asking the audience, "How ya' doin' tonight?" Since eight o'clock, every comic, one every five minutes, had asked the audience "How ya' doin' tonight?" Weren't they listening? We said we were fine five minutes ago. Yes, we're having a good time. No, none of us are from out of town except for the Korean couple who have no idea of what's going on.

Donna talked about her life back on Long Island. How she worked in a falsie factory. The audience loved her. I had found a soul mate. Just as people had laughed at me for selling underpants, they were laughing at her for making falsies. Only now she was laughing with them. She couldn't help herself. She was having a wonderful time. She was hot.

The five minutes flew by. When the little spotlight on the side of the stage lit up the large poster of Eddie Cantor's face, the sign for the comics to know their time was up, the audience was disappointed. All night long that light had been our savior, a reprieve from some other class clown telling us how weird stewardesses are. Now the light was taking Donna away from us. I wanted more. I wanted to talk to her.

Talking to a comic at the Comedy Store isn't the toughest thing in the world to do. You go behind the building, into the alley, and there they are. Big names, little names, they're all back there, smoking cigarettes, shooting the breeze with their friends. Going over the set they just finished. Deciding which jokes should stay in their act and which should go. Deciding if the audience was bad or if they had an off night. Griping about the spot Mitzi had given them. If only she'd give them better spots, they know they could kill, too.

This was a time when the comedy boom was just beginning. Soon, every town would have its version of the Store. The Comedy Barrel, the Laugh Stop, Hoo Ha's ad nauseam bringing mediocre comedy to a shopping center near you. As the industry grew, and so the demand for comics, the talent pool got badly watered down. People who were just remotely funny were coming to the Store to start their careers. It was here, in the back alley, they would lick their wounds from a bad set and maybe steal a joke or two from another struggling flop. The alley was where I'd find Donna.

Tommy decided not to come with me. He would go to the bar, have another Scotch and water, and try to find a woman who found his slurred speech and droopy face attractive. Because he was more interested in the Scotch than the women, he didn't really care whether he succeeded.

I walked into the alley and found Donna. She was looking around for somebody who obviously hadn't shown up yet. Smiling at a few folks, she made no effort to talk to anybody. She was standing there alone. Alone and uncomfortable. Just a few minutes before, she had total control of hundreds of people. They all loved her. Now, you could tell she wanted to run.

"Hi, Donna. I'm Barry Klein, executive story editor on *In the Swim*. I made sure I got my credits in the first sentence. If she knew I was in the biz she might not call a cop, or worse yet, ignore me.

"Wow, *In the Swim*. I love the show," she said quite sincerely.

"Yeah, well, I loved your set. You're very funny." To someone who's funny, I had just said the equivalent of "You're incredible looking and I love your body."

She looked down, embarrassed, and said, "Yeah, yeah, yeah. Do you want to get some coffee?"

The "yeah, yeah, yeah" was perfect. It said we both knew she was funny, I was funny, and that we could get past that and go talk. But the request for coffee was confusing. She asked me out. I was married. Was this a date? Was this allowed? Was this just coffee? It didn't matter. There was a connection here.

I suggested we walk down Sunset Boulevard to the Source, a health-food restaurant that had about the best organic, brown rice pudding in the world. I had begun to eat health food on Linda's advice. At first the idea of writing jokes without a constant stream of crème filled Ho-Ho's and Ring Dings seemed like the same kind of advice that Samson got from Delilah when she said he'd look good with short hair. But the world of tofu and whole grains did make me feel better and didn't seem to change my twisted view of the world.

Donna and I headed for The Source. The talk was easy. We had so much in common. East Coast. East Coast. Funny in school. Funny in school. Married. Married! Donna was married to Andy Edmundson, a very normal guy who worked as a CPA. Andy was only semi-supportive of Donna's career, which was why she used her maiden name on stage. She had just had a baby three months before and Andy didn't like having to be Mr. Mom when he got home from work so that Donna could go work the comedy clubs. She didn't know what was going to happen once her career took off and she'd have to go on the road.

We talked about the business and life and made each other laugh. A lot. We ate rice pudding and drank mu tea until way past our bedtimes and then promised we'd get together again soon. As we exchanged phone numbers, I wondered if this would be a show business bullshit "get together real soon" or a genuine one.

The next day at work, I told Bobby Mitchell that he absolutely had to hire this girl from the Comedy Store to write on *In the Swim*. I had never met a funnier woman. Bobby didn't take long to decide. He knew the value of funny and how hard it was to find. If we could make a deal with Donna, he'd be happy to give her a try.

Donna wasn't sure she wanted the job. All her life she had wanted to be a performer. She had never considered writing. I explained that the idea of a steady job would probably be more attractive to her husband, Andy, than having his wife traipsing all over the country trying to establish herself in the world of stand-up. Plus, we'd get to laugh together every day. It worked. She took the job.

Why wasn't Donna Morris in my office yet? I was growing impatient. I picked up the phone and buzzed Marcia. "Did you tell Donna I want to see her?" I asked in a less-than-friendly tone. My meeting with Bobby had made me testy.

"She said she'll be right there. Do you want some coffee or something?" Marcia was trying her best. Her best was annoying. She had been here a month and hadn't figured out that I don't drink coffee. Coffee plays havoc with your adrenal glands. It's poison.

Kimmel is going to live forever from drinking spring water with fresh lemon and I'm getting poisoned by a girl with greasy legs. I was about to make myself completely crazy when Donna walked in.

"What's doin', M'Love?" Donna asked as she sat down on the small couch across from my desk.

"Bobby's going to make Tommy and me sweat," I told her. "He said he needs a couple of days. A couple of days for what?" I wanted Donna to have the answers I didn't have.

"Do you want to smoke a number?" Donna asked as she pulled a neatly rolled joint from her shirt pocket. "Dave had some Pungent Purple Buddha Buds."

I had made the mistake of giving my neighbor Dave Larson an assignment to write an episode of *In the Swim*. It was an awful attempt at comedy, which Dave considered a political tour de force. He had Connie and Patti going to the White House and hiding under the president's bed. It made no sense. We had to rewrite the whole thing. Dave had become the show's visiting pharmacist, hoping it would get him another assignment. It got him on the lot to make deliveries, but that was as close to show business as Dave would ever get. Lately, to keep his customers happy, Dave started getting gourmet pot. Pungent Purple Buddha Buds, Triple Sticky Thai Stick, Mendicino Hot Tub Express, all powerful, all making

Dave indispensable.

I wasn't sure I wanted to take Donna up on her offer, having always prided myself for not smoking dope on the job. Recreational smoking was fine. After work was not unusual. Never on the job. I didn't want to be like Tommy. But now with all the stress of waiting to hear from Bobby and still having to get a show out this week and not having fun and all . . .

"Sure, why not?" I said, not even bothering to rationalize my sudden slip in form.

"Come on, we'll head up to Tower Records, grab some rice pudding at the Source, and be back in plenty of time for the run-through." Donna laid out the itinerary for the afternoon. It was the perfect prescription for fun. Each afternoon, at the end of their workday, the cast would perform that week's show for the writers so that we could see what was working and what wasn't. These end-of-the day performances were called run-throughs. Afterward, the actors would go home and the writers would head for the rewrite table. The rewrite table can be the most fun in the world or it can be Hell. Basically, you're sitting in a room full of funny people who are trying to make each other laugh. When something funny is said, a secretary writes it down. Most of the time is spent amusing each other on things other than the script. Somehow, though, the work gets done and you have a great time. On those rare occasions, however, when no one feels funny, and there are lots of jokes to write, the rewrite table is Hell. Those are the times when you understand why comedy writers get paid handsomely. It's when you find out who are the real pros. Donna and I could enjoy our little field trip and easily be back for the run through.

We jumped into her Mercedes 450 SL and headed out the studio gate. Scotty gave us a half-hearted wave and a disapproving shake of the head. He could have been shaking his head at so many things. I know he didn't approve of the expensive cars we all drove. There aren't that many people who are professionally funny, so those of us who are get paid a lot of money. Usually one of the first things somebody in Hollywood does when they start making the big bucks is get a nice set of wheels. Donna had chosen a fire engine red Mercedes convertible with a top that never went up. If it rained, she would drive her old beat-up Honda. On the three hundred and sixty sunny days a year in southern California, she'd drive the Merc with the top down.

Scotty drove his old, beat-up Honda every day. He also didn't like the idea of people driving off the lot in the middle of the afternoon to have fun. He could hardly grasp the concept of fun, let alone taking off if the mood suddenly struck. Why should these spoiled brats be allowed to leave? I think what bothered him the most was that when we returned he'd have to once again figure out who we were.

I lit the joint and took a long hit of the Buddha Bud. Boy, it was too bad Dave wasn't as funny as his dope was good. It was wonderful, happy dope. The kind of stuff that makes you giggly. Donna cranked up the stereo and we blasted through the city, grooving to Gino Vinelli. That's how good the dope was—we were grooving to Gino Vinelli.

It was nice shutting down my brain. I told Donna that I was getting tired of dealing with so many problems. What would Bobby decide about the show? When would Linda get over this guru phase she was going through? At first I didn't mind it. It seemed to make her happy and not notice how much I was gone. But over the past few months it had become an issue. Linda had found one guru to follow and had started down the path of enlightenment. It seemed like she smelled of incense all the time. I hadn't told any of the people at work because I knew they would have a comedy field day with it, but Linda had started to follow Vishna, a thirteen-year-old kid from India who God had allegedly sent to save the world or at least straighten it up a bit.

I couldn't see the attraction. In fact, I resented it. Linda had pictures of this kid all over the house. I'd go to the kitchen and there'd be His Holiness on the fridge. In the bathroom, there he'd be, pasted right behind the toilet, staring at me at the most inopportune times. I'd freeze up and have to sit down with my back to the picture and pee like a woman. Was this the road less traveled? Once she took me to meet him. Well, not really meet him but see him.

Every Sunday, Vishna's followers would meet for something called satsang. They'd get together and testify how joyous he'd made their lives. On this particular Sunday, the Wiz himself was going to be there. The Raiders were playing Pittsburgh and I was going to have to see Vishna. My hope was that he'd have the game on or at least know the score. Of course, he'd know the score; he was omnipotent. The score of the Raider game would be easy. So there I was, in a room full of people expecting the messiah and I was hoping for a New Age version of the Amazing Kreskin. "Now, before I save the world, the score of the Raider game is . . ."

The meeting took place in the Terrace Room of the AmFac Hotel, out by the airport. It was a typical hotel meeting room except that it was loaded with fresh flowers. Especially at the far end of the room where, sitting on a folding chair on top of a riser, was His Holy Smokes himself.

Linda and I got at the end of the line which headed toward Vishna. I didn't want to wait in line. The last thing I heard on the radio when Linda dragged me from the car was that the Raiders were about to score. They were on the Pittsburgh fifteen-yard line.

I figured there was time to get in the hotel, sit down with Vishna, and get a little play-by-play from the Grand Poobah. But there was no way I'd get to the front of the long line before the Raiders got into the end zone. I told Linda I was going to cut in front of the line. I could tell that this was the kind of crowd that wouldn't make a stink about a line cutter. They were all trying to be such holy goody-two-shoes, perfectly in tune with the universe. Nobody was going to give me a "Hey, buddy, no cutting in line." But Linda wouldn't hear of it.

"Is it worth all that bad karma just to find out the score of the Raider game? Do you want to come back in your next life as some kind of reptile because you need to know if the Raiders are covering the spread? Is that what you want, Barry?" Linda asked these questions, figuring she had me on philosophical grounds.

I had not yet stepped on the path of enlightenment nor did I care to. I headed to the front of the line with Linda right behind me whispering, "You'd better stop this instant."

As we got near Vishna I could see people bowing down in front of him and kissing his feet. I wondered, had Linda kissed this guy's feet before? I couldn't remember her ever kissing my feet. Maybe once, early in our marriage, when we had read in a dirty book about sucking on toes. But that was different.

"Do you kiss this guy's feet?" I asked in the tone of a

husband scorned.

"I haven't yet. But I'm thinking about it." She seemed embarrassed, as if the question was too personal. Then she added, "Barry, don't do this, please."

Before I could decide what to do, a guy in a white robe had grabbed my arm and was steering me toward Vishna. It was my turn to meet the Master.

"Share in the joy and then leave a donation," he said in an ethereal version of "Step right up and see what's inside the big top."

There was no way that I was going to give Vichna's little piggies a smoocheroo. Instead, to get his attention, I asked, "Score of the Raider game?" The guy in the white robe was not amused.

"No talking to His Holiness. Just share in the joy and leave a donation" he said quietly yet firmly, giving my arm a little squeeze.

"I just want to get a score on the Raider's game." Again I spoke to Yahweh's boy. "What do you say, kid—do you like football?"

The whole Terrace Room gave an enlightened gasp. Suddenly the guy in the white robe went from dove of peace to rock concert bouncer.

"All right, pal, you don't want to kiss his feet? You're out of here." He grabbed my arm more forcefully this time and, without making a scene, steered me toward the door. With my free hand, I blew a kiss at Vishna's feet. He smiled. He thought it was funny. Nobody else did. Especially Linda. Over the years of our marriage I had seen her upset. Never like this. It really affected our relationship. We stopped having sex.

I finished my story about Linda and Vishna as Donna Morris and I drove toward Tower Records. It had been two weeks since I had known my wife in the biblical sense. That, on top of the stress from work, had me completely out of sync. I needed help. I was hoping for a little sane advice from Donna, like, "Don't worry, she'll get over it." A little insane advice like "Go back and see Vishna again, and this time give his tootsies a little peck," would have been fine, too. But the advice she gave me was a total shocker.

"If you're so unhappy, why don't you just have an affair?" she said just as we pulled into the parking lot.

"Have an affair? What's that supposed to mean?" I couldn't believe she'd said it. I'd known Donna for three years. We were as close as two people can be without seeing each other naked. Was she suggesting that *we* have an affair or *me* have an affair or what?

"I've been having an affair for, I don't know, the last four months. It's made me a lot happier."

"What do you mean you've been having an affair?" I

asked, completely confounded.

"I've been having an affair. No big deal. Are we going in the store or not?"

"No, we're not going in the store. Who are you having an affair with? How come I don't know? I thought we told each other everything?" I hated the way I sounded. Donna and I had always been the fun in each other's life. We were always nonjudgmental. Now I was jealous.

"Brian Fox. I'm sleeping with Brian Fox, okay?"

Brian Fox was the producer of *All Aboard*. Their offices were down the hall from ours. We saw the writing staff of *All Aboard* all the time.

I was totally confused. First, one woman I loved, Linda, wasn't sleeping with me because she was in love with some flying carpet jockey. Then the other woman I loved, Donna, who I wasn't sleeping with because it never entered my mind to sleep with her, was sleeping with somebody besides her husband. I could take her sleeping with her husband—that's what she was supposed to do. If she was sleeping with somebody else . . . well that was cheating. On me!

"Brian Fox? He's not even that funny," I said, suddenly the scorned lover.

"I'm not seeing him for funny," she said. "I've got you for

funny."

Well that helped...a little.

"Come on, Barry, you mean you haven't even thought about fooling around?"

"Of course, I've thought about it. Who hasn't? But I'd never do anything, though." At least that had always been my intent. I had been faithfully married to Linda for eight years. Yes, there were times when it was difficult. But what about commitment? What about trust?

"Look, Barry, I'm not telling you to have an affair. I'm just saying that if you do, it's not going to make you fall off the earth. Do I seem any different to you over the past few months?"

"Do you mean other than the fact that you've lost thirty pounds, got a great haircut, and you look fabulous?"

"I didn't think you noticed."

"Of course, I noticed. It just seemed like the kind of thing we don't say to each other."

Donna blushed. We had never even acknowledged that we were aware of what the other person looked like. This was new territory. It was too uncomfortable. We had to get out of the car and into the record store.

Donna and I finished our record shopping, our rice pudding at the Source, then headed back to the studio. I was so confused by Donna's revelation about her affair and from the Buddha Bud that I didn't even notice when Scotty O'Rourke made me get out of the car so he could frisk me. Normally, I wouldn't let him scream, "Up against the wall and spread 'em," without finding out what he intended to do after "they" were spread.

The run-through was uneventful, though I was sure that everyone in the cast knew I was stoned. They all seemed to ask me very complicated questions to which I could only respond, "Huh?"

Afterward, when I went to back to my office to check my messages before heading to the rewrite table, Marcia Heilger was creaming her legs. She had swung around with her back to the door and had both legs straight up in the air. I stood there for a minute watching and for the first time wondered where those legs led. I asked her if there were any calls and she swung around with the legs still in the air. She gave me a big smile before putting them down.

"Nothing's going on here. It's been dead. I wish I could have gone with you for fun this afternoon."

I didn't know how to respond. It was a remark that seemed out of character. I mean, I was the boss. This seemed awfully familiar. Maybe I was just being an old fuddy-duddy. Maybe she was just being friendly. Maybe I was standing by her desk too long without giving any response at all. Move it, Barry.

I got to my office to regroup. It was quiet. Now was the time for control. For regaining my center, valuing the important things in life. That's how you deal with the stress, my boy. As, I sat there, composing myself to go back to the rewrite room, one important thought stuck in my mind. Man, those were some legs.

FOUR

Take My Drum Roll...Please

It had been a week with no decision from Bobby Mitchell as to who the new producer would be, and Bobby was no longer returning my calls. I paced outside Stage 7 waiting to talk to him. Bobby would always come there on Friday nights so that he could introduce the cast to the studio audience before we filmed the show. He loved the opening night thrill we'd get on Fridays. These were the nights we'd find out whether all our rewrites paid off, whether we'd fixed the story and made the jokes as funny as they could be. Our weekly play was debuting in front of a live audience. And since *In The Swim* was a hit, our audience was not made up of people who simply wanted to see how a television show was made. No, these were our fans. These people were the reason we stayed up late every night trying to make the show as good as it could be. Sure it's fun watching television, but it's more fun making television. Fridays were the most fun. They were always exciting, and a good show would make for a good weekend.

As The Ladies and the rest of the cast would have the finishing touches applied to their make-up, Bobby would go from dressing room to dressing room giving well wishes and some last-minute assurances that the script didn't stink and that the show would be fine. Then, at exactly five minutes to eight, Howie Clark would play a tympani roll (none of us could play the drum, but Howie consistently came the closest to doing an actual drum roll) as I would introduce "The number one producer in television today . . . Bobby Mitchell!"

The audience always welcomed Bobby as if they knew him, which was a fine testimonial to his two thousand-dollar-a-month publicist. Bobby wanted to be famous, and so he paid to get his name mentioned, in any way, in the most obscure publications. When the audience came to see *In the Swim,* they either knew Bobby as the show's creator or, if they had read the "Paw Prints" section of *American Cat Owner,* they knew him as the owner of Plato, "a cat who loves to sun himself in the living room window." Talk about money well spent. Talk about a unique cat.

On a typical Friday night, I'd introduce Bobby and he'd come out and talk with the audience for about ten minutes.

He'd do a few jokes, ask if anybody was from out of town, and, invariably, there'd be somebody there from Brooklyn. They'd talk about the neighborhood, and Bobby would do his strongest material about growing up in Flatbush. It was all very charming until one night when I caught Bobby giving some kid from the audience twenty bucks before the kid took his seat. The money was for the kid to say he was from Brooklyn. Bobby was planting a shill, making sure he got to do his "A" material. Then, after the less-than-authentic chit-chat between Brooklynites, Bobby would introduce Ben Fisher. Benny would come out and burp for the folks, which was a walk down memory lane for our older fans but a confusing gross-out for the young set who had no idea what this old fool was doing. Ben, of course, would win them over with an extremely endearing, "You kids don't know nothin' about funny." Another generation brought into the fold.

After Ben had turned off half the audience, Bobby would grab the microphone, make a joke about Ben, and then introduce the Ladies' moronic neighbors, Willy and Billy, America's favorite perverts. Forced to become masters of the double entendre by the constant surveillance of the network censor, the boys' sophomoric, off-color, humor was constant, although more bawdy than raunchy. They were greasy, low-class ragamuffins any normal woman would never give a second look at. Because of that, we often

had a large contingency of abnormal women in our audience.
Women who would scream with delight when Willy and Billy
were introduced. Women who would wriggle with joy when Willy
would say, "Hey, lady, I can see your underpants." Willy and Billy
would then sing a song from their Willy and Billy album, and the
women who came to see them would throw pieces of paper with
their phone numbers written on them. Willy and Billy would finish
their song, pick up the papers with the phone numbers, and head
to their dressing room to look over their booty and smoke a joint.
They never liked to go before the cameras straight. They might say
the words right.

After Willy and Billy had left the scene of the crime, Bobby
would introduce The Ladies. Once again, Howie Clark would have
to make the tympani sound like it was excited as Bobby would fire
up the audience. "Ladies and Gentlemen, the stars of the number
one show on television, Connie and Patti . . . Lorraine LaBarbara
and Mimi Simms!"

Spotlights would crisscross the audience as the P.A. system
played the show's theme song. The audience would always go wild
and give The Ladies a standing ovation as they came out and took
a bow. Everyone was psyched and ready.

That was on a normal Friday night. On this particular
Friday night, Bobby decided not to come to the show. He didn't

want to deal with Tommy and me. He didn't want to see us staring
at him with puppy dog eyes, wondering what was taking so long
for him to decide our future. He would simply avoid the scene
all together. Fifteen minutes before the show was to begin, I was
relaxing on the couch in the set of Connie's and Patti's living
room, chatting with Nick Martini, one of our cameramen, when
I saw Alice Martin approaching. Seeing her dour look, I wasn't
expecting good news. Alice politely asked Nick to excuse us, then
took me aside

"Bobby's colon isn't right," she whispered to me.

"What does that mean, Alice? He's never missed a Friday
night and his colon has never been right." I didn't want tonight
to be the night that Bobby let me steer the boat. Not without any
warning. Not without telling The Ladies he wouldn't be there.

"I'm very sorry, Barry. He had to leave. His colon just
wasn't right." Alice said it firmly to let me know I should just
accept my fate.

"Not right how? Has he lost control of his bodily
functions?"

"I didn't ask. Shall I tell Bobby that you need to know?"
Alice asked, quickly losing patience.

I was treading on thin ice. Like most executive secretaries,
Alice had more power than her job description indicated. Bobby

trusted her completely and, in his absence, she was his eyes and ears. If I had any chance of getting to Bobby for a decision, I had better be nice to Alice. She was the one who controlled access to his busy schedule. She was the one who always had his ear. She was also the one who doled out Bobby's Laker tickets if he couldn't get to the games. Producer or not, that was a perk I didn't want to give up. I needed to stay on Alice's right side. Still, I took one more shot.

"Intros start in fifteen minutes. This is a raw deal, Alice." I had made my position pretty clear.

"Fine, I'll let Bobby know you feel that way," Alice threatened as she walked away.

Okay, Barry, it's time to take control. It's time for you and Tommy to show you can be producers. I walked up to Tommy's office and found him chopping a sizable pile of cocaine with a razor blade as he kept his phone cradled between his shoulder and ear.

"Well why don't you just leave and move in with me?" he said sweetly to the person on the other end of the conversation. "Why? Because I love you, that's why. Will you at least think about it?" After a pause he added, "I'll talk to you tomorrow. But there's a key under the back door mat if you want to come over tonight." He punctuated the offer with a kiss, then hung up.

"That sounded serious. New girl in your life?" I asked. Tommy and I knew surprising little about each other's personal lives considering how much time we spent together. When not working, we tended to talk sports or politics or show business news. He never seemed comfortable talking about personal relationships. For the most part, he was a mystery to me.

"It's not a girl. It's my mother," he answered, not giving me any details in typical Tommy fashion.

"So, Oedipus, aren't you afraid that having Mom move in is going to put a crimp in your social life?"

"When I was six my mother and I left my father because he was always beating her up. Over the next seventeen years she . . . actually we, until I was sixteen and split, lived with five different men. They all eventually beat her up. Then last year she tells me she knows why she can't live with men. She tells me she's gay and she's moving in with Rita, the head of the paint department at the Sears in El Segundo. Last night Rita beat her up."

"Is she okay? What are you going to do?" I asked with genuine concern.

"She's fine. And I figure the best thing I can do is snort some of my buddy, here," he said as he arranged his cocaine into neat little lines. Tommy wanted to retreat into his private little world.

"You can't do that now," I said, more worried about the problems awaiting us on stage than about Tommy's personal problems. "We have to go see Lorraine and Mimi. Bobby can't make it to the show.

"Colon?" Tommy asked as began herding his white powder back into its jar. Not its vile — its jar. Maybe we were making too much money.

"Possibly. I think he just didn't want to deal with us. Come on. We've got to get the show on the road." I watched as Tommy carefully coaxed the last few specks in and then licked his finger as he headed out the door in front of me.

On the way down to the stage, we decided to start with Lorraine. Chances were she'd talk to Bobby after the show. We wanted her to tell Bobby what a good job we did. We felt that Mimi was more likely to go berserk over Bobby's absence so we decided to start off with the easy one.

I gently knocked on Lorraine's dressing room door.

"Who is it?" she yelled in a tone I imagine Cinderella got all the time from her cruel stepsisters.

"It's Barry and Tommy," I answered with all the good nature I could muster. I didn't want any fear in my voice. They'll turn on you if they smell fear. Fear or cheap cologne. As a rule, you don't want to smell of either.

There was a long pause with no response. After a moment Tommy and I both silently mouthed, "Barry and Tommy who?" Because the Ladies both seemed so self-centered and because of the constant staff changes, Tommy and I had questioned, from time to time, whether Lorraine and Mimi had any idea of who we were or which was which. Now, Tommy and I had the same thought at exactly the same time. It wasn't a surprise. It happened often. We'd both race to the same punch line while writing a joke. In life we were very different, but comedically our minds were on the same track. We were about to break up laughing when the wicked stepsister screamed, "Well, get in here!"

We entered to find Lorraine sitting in a director's chair, in front of her make-up mirror, reading about her latest battles with Mimi in *The Enquirer*. She was wearing the *In the Swim* bathrobe the writing staff had given her the previous Christmas. It was nice to see she had kept it. What wasn't nice to see was her lovely left breast. The front of the robe was positioned so that Lefty was pretty much out in the open. Surely she must have noticed it. Was that what took her so long? Was she positioning her robe so that we'd have to see her breast? Was this part of the producer's test? If so, this was a trick question. What do you do? Tell her? Not tell her?

"You're tit's hanging out. Cover it up, would ya?" Tommy said with a little laugh in his voice. I couldn't believe it. Duck and cover. That's what they taught us in grade school when we waited for the Ruskies to attack. Maybe I should do that now? This explosion wasn't going to be any less devastating.

"Oh, sorry." Lorraine covered up and gave Tommy a coquettish grin. They were relating on a level I didn't get. A he-man level. Maybe that's all she was looking for. Tommy had acted from strength and it worked. Now, as they both were staring at each other with ridiculous grins on their faces, it was time for me to produce.

"Listen, Lorraine . . . Bobby isn't going to be here tonight. We just wanted to stop by and say have a good show." I gave her a little pat on the shoulder as I wished her luck. She touched my hand as she thanked me. It looked like we were getting lucky. Someone had slipped some human being drops into Lorraine's iced tea and she was treating us, not only to a peek of her breast, but to some pretty civil behavior.

"Colon?" she asked matter-of-factly.

"Colon," Tommy and I answered in unison.

"Are you going to do the introductions, Barry?" She asked a question I hadn't yet answered myself. Someone was going to have to entertain the audience during the pre-show warm-up. I had seen Bobby do it enough times to know what to do.

"Of course I'm going to do it," I said, as if there were no

other option.

"Well, then, you have a good show, too." Lorraine was wishing me well. As we left her dressing room, I immediately started trying to figure out what she was up to.

We proceeded to tell Mimi the news of Bobby's absence, hoping for the same reaction we got from Lorraine: "You have a good show, too." It was the perfect thing to say. If Mimi could say the same thing, for now, life would be perfect.

Mimi threw things. She literally started picking up jars of make-up and throwing them at Tommy and me. We didn't run. We didn't duck. She wasn't throwing very hard, so we started catching the jars. Then, at some point, after perhaps five or six jars had been launched, I caught a missile of moisturizer and instead of putting it down, I tossed it to Tommy. Mimi was throwing at me and I was tossing to Tommy. It had become a game. It was fun for Tommy and me, infuriating for Mimi.

"Stop that! Stop having fun!" She was in the middle of a tantrum. But instead of obeying her, Tommy tossed her a jar of make-up. It drove her crazy. She caught it and immediately threw it at me again.

"Hey, I didn't throw it at you," I protested, as I tossed it to Tommy who kept it flying by sending it Mimi's way. She caught it and again aimed it at my head. I caught it and threw to Tommy who threw to Mimi. The jar was now moving pretty fast in the circle. I began to sing.

"The wonder ball goes round and round . . ."

Tommy joined in. "To catch it quickly you are bound . . . "

Then Mimi joined in. "If you're the one to catch it last, then you are out, O-U-T, and that is that."

The three of us ended the song with a big finish. We began to laugh. Mimi's rage was spent. She wasn't sure what to do. Neither did we.

"Have a great show, Mimi," I said as I indicated to Tommy we should get out of there while there was peace.

"Thanks, guys. You, too." She said it! She said we should have a good show, too. This was going to be all right. Now we just had to tell Ben and Willy and Billy. Willy and Billy would be easy. They wouldn't care. But Ben would be a big pain. We knew he'd start complaining immediately.

So, when our knock on his door was met with a less-than-loving "What the hell do you want?" I stuck my head in the door and blurted, "Bobby's not here tonight, Ben—have a good show." I then closed the door and Tommy and I walked away. As we walked to Willy and Billy's dressing room, all we could hear was Ben's rage. He was a wild man.

We passed Larry Brogan, Mimi's husband, and Donna

Morris. Larry was holding Donna's hand as he spoke to her. He was probably hitting on her judging from the uncomfortable look on her face. As we passed, Donna tugged on her ear with her free hand. That was our "save me from this" signal.

"Donna, Lorraine needs to see you right away. She has a script question," I said as Tommy and I kept walking. It was enough to rescue Donna from Brogan.

After Tommy knocked on Willy and Billy's door, we learned a lesson about dealing with them. Don't knock on their door. As soon as Tommy knocked, we heard Willy call out, "Just a minute . . . ," then the frantic sounds of them cleaning up their drug paraphernalia. With Willy and Billy, instead of knocking, you had to call out, "Hey, guys, are you in there? It's okay. It's us." Once they knew it wasn't the studio security, they wouldn't have to bother cleaning up their act. This time we didn't know, and so we had to wait for them to clear all evidence of drug abuse from sight. Eventually, the door cracked and Billy's head came out along with a large cloud of grass-laden smoke.

"Hey, guys," Billy said, recognizing us through eyes that had closed down to barely slits. He wasn't inviting us in.

"We need to talk to you," Tommy said as he pushed by Billy and entered the dressing room. I assumed Tommy knew what he was doing so I followed. Billy looked out the door to see if anybody was tailing us and then closed it. Willy was on the couch trying to look casual. He looked stoned. Tommy told them about Bobby not being there. They were thrilled. Willy and Billy, as it turned out, hated Bobby. Their show business futures had been on the rise when Bobby Mitchell cast them on *In the Swim* or, more accurately, talked them into doing the show. He told them they would be co-stars of the show, Lorraine's and Mimi's equals. They weren't. They were made second bananas right from the beginning. Very funny second bananas. But bananas, nonetheless. Not seeing Bobby Mitchell was just fine with them.

We wished them well and then headed back out toward the set. It was show time.

Drum roll (kind of).

"Ladies and Gentlemen, the number one producer in television today . . . Barry Klein!" Howie Clark had to play the drum and make my introduction at the same time. He couldn't do it. His brain automatically went to the introduction he had heard every week for three years. It was all he could do to substitute my name for Bobby's. The audience didn't seem to care or know the difference. They gave me the same resounding welcome they gave Bobby. They had come for a good time and weren't about to let the fact that Barry Klein was standing in for Bobby Mitchell ruin their night. And I wasn't about to ruin it for them either. I went right into

Bobby's "A" material. I did all his jokes. I even claimed to be from Brooklyn when somebody in the audience yelled out they were from the old neighborhood. I did great. Even when Ben Fisher tried to turn the audience against me, I stayed cool.

"Why are you laughing at this guy? He's nothing." Ben snorted with fire and hate coming from the nostrils of the dragon.

"Who is this man? All right, which one of you brought this nut with you?" I scolded the audience and they loved it. "I love this guy," I screamed in my best Jackie Gleason impression as I gave Ben a big hug. He was defeated. He had to laugh and pretend he was in on the joke.

Ben took a bow, blew a kiss to the audience, one to me, then headed to the bottle of schnapps in his dressing room. He didn't really have a drinking problem. But ever since his stand-up days in the Catskills, he wouldn't go on without a shot of schnapps to bolster his courage. Tonight he would take two: one for tradition, one to keep the bile of hate bubbling.

Willy and Billy were hilarious. Instead of singing one of their off-color songs, they recited the poem "Baby Land," by Emma Fosdick. It's a very sweet poem with the feeling of a lullaby. Having these two delinquents recite it was a brilliant comic twist. Of course, they did things like accentuate the "dick" in "Fosdick" and giggled moronically after they did. It was really very funny.

It was time for me to give the audience what they really
wanted. "You know them as their characters, Patti and Connie. We
know them as the stars of the number one show on television. Say
hello to Lorraine La Barbara and Mimi Simms." The audience
went wild — standing ovation. The Ladies were their usual dull
selves. The audience loved them anyway. The introductions were
over and it was time to film the show. Time for some serious
producing with much attention paid to a million details. During the
shooting, Tommy and I had to make sure that we had "the show
in the can," before we left the stage. That meant we had to make
sure that all the lines were delivered to our satisfaction. That all
the cameras had gotten all the shots we would need to assemble
the show in editing. Everything had to be right when we finally
called out, "That's a wrap." There was no going back if we missed
something.

The filming went without a hitch. Everybody seemed
to know their lines and we were done by ten o'clock. I quickly
stopped by everybody's dressing room and gave them a sincere,
"Great show." Only Mimi went through the "Do you really mean
it?" song and dance as she fished for compliments. I felt great so I
obliged.

"Absolutely. Mimi, I peed. When you guys got on the roof
and did that thing like you were skiing . . . I peed."

"Stop it, Barry," she protested, as she hoped for more. I told her to have a wonderful weekend and I was on my way.

I was flying on my way back to my office. We had won a round of the twenty-two-round fight. In addition, tonight I had filled in for Bobby and nothing went wrong. If this was some kind of a test to see how Tommy and I would handle show night, we passed it with flying colors. I headed toward K building to pick up my briefcase.

"Great show tonight, Barry." As I passed the commissary, there in the doorway was Marcia Heilger. It was a strange place to hang out this time of night.

"Thanks, Marcia. Are you okay?" I couldn't imagine why anybody would be standing in this particular doorway.

"Actually, I was waiting for you." She began moving toward me, not stopping until she was very close. Closer than people normally stand when they just want to say, "Great show tonight, Barry." Marcia was extremely close—she was practically rubbing up against me. It was obviously my turn to talk but all I could do was be aware of my increase in blood pressure. "You really were amazing tonight. The audience loved you," she said as she finally got tired of waiting for me to respond to her initial volley.

"Gee . . ." Oh, good Barry. *Gee*. Aren't you the wordsmith?

She was now looking right into my eyes.

"Listen, I just want you to know that I really admire the way you're handling yourself . . . having to wait for this producer thing to get worked out. And . . . well . . . you know, if you just want to talk some time . . . you know . . . get a bottle of wine and come over to my place . . . well, I'd like that."

Mommy! Help! Go to her place? Why the hell would I go to her place? Why do you think, bird brain? You go to her place and do the dirty thing. Oh, my God. There's no breathing going on. I've stopped breathing completely. Oh, come on, Barry—it's not like you've never entertained the thought of being with another woman in the eight years of marriage to Linda. I had, what I considered to be, a pretty normal fantasy life. But nothing so far out there. Even wanting to go to the Wrestle a Nude Woman place every time I passed it wasn't that odd.

But what should I say to Marcia? I would have to say something, that is, assuming my mouth would work. I knew there was a real possibility that I would open my mouth and nothing but a very dull "Aaaahhh" would come out. I sure wasn't being the suave playboy. I didn't hear "Sure, baby. You get the wine and then it's party time." I didn't hear anything until I heard Donna saying, "Barry, are you okay?"

Suddenly Donna was next to me and Marcia was sashaying

away. She had left me speechless on the street. Now Donna was checking up.

"Yeah, I'm fine." I managed to say as we headed toward K building.

"You hit a homerun tonight, Baby," Donna said, putting an arm around my shoulder as we walked.

"Uh . . . yeah. Thanks." I was trying to focus on Donna but my thoughts were still on the Marcia encounter.

"Just hang in there, Barry," Donna advised, adding a friendly kiss on the cheek before she headed off toward Brian Fox's office.

Driving home, I couldn't stop thinking about Marcia. There was no doubt about it, I was attracted to her. It's amazing what happens when you work with people who are just average looking. After a while, if you spend enough hours with them, you start finding whatever little bits of attractiveness you can hang your hormones on. There were late rewrites when I would even notice the sparkle in Rhonda Silverman's eyes. Now, normally, I would never think of Rhonda in any way but professionally or as a friend. But if it's three o'clock in the morning, and you'd rather be doing anything than trying to find a joke to get Ben Fisher out the door, then all of a sudden you're noticing that Rhonda Silverman has sparkle in her eyes. And you're thinking, "Yeah, I could fuck sparkle."

Well, now it was Marcia I was focusing on. It wasn't as tough coming up with reasons to be in bed with her than it was with Rhonda. Marcia had those fantastic dancer's legs and that graceful swanlike neck. She may never have been the main swan when she was a dancer but it certainly wasn't because of her neck. It was a beauty. See, all of a sudden I'm a neck man. Guys simply work with what's there. Neck, sparkle, what's the difference? I was quite sure kissing that neck would be a pleasure. Kissing wasn't the only pleasure I considered. In my mind I was debating the virtues of sleeping with Marcia. Rationalization is a powerful thing when you can even find virtues in the idea of cheating on your wife.

The debate raged on as I got home and crawled into bed. I had been faithful for eight years. Eight years, that's quite a record. I was just thirty, and when I'd tell people I'd been married eight years they were always amazed, in a very approving way. Then some guy, always a guy, and usually a single one, would ask, "Do you screw around?"

"Nope. Never have," I'd say with the quiet cool of a gunfighter who had survived countless showdowns. That would always blow the single guys away.

"Really? Never?" they would ask in a "Gosh, Mister" tone of voice.

"That's right, Bub. Not never." Wow. A guy in Hollywood who could turn down the temptations of the flesh. Unbelievable. This boy's all right. The approval from nameless others was enough to send me off into a fitful night's sleep.

The next morning, a surprisingly chipper Linda woke me with her humming. She was just laying there, staring at the ceiling, humming. Not a tune. Just nondescript humming. Now, normally I'd get irritated, if on my day off, I was awakened by a random hum. This time, I was too surprised by Linda's good mood to say anything. As sweet as Linda could be, the first few minutes of each day she was a bear. You kept your distance.

When she saw I was making a monumental attempt to pry my eyes open, she gave me a big smile and an even bigger, "Guess what we're doing today?"

Who was this woman? And what is she doing in my bed? "Whaaa?" I drooled onto the pillow.

She was smiling and talking. "We're driving up to Tujunga and getting our crystals."

More drool and more "Whaaa?" from me. I really hoped she was kidding. I had no idea where Tujunga was, but it sounded like a long trip. And why on earth would I want a crystal? A crystal what?

"Does this have anything to do with . . . what's his name?"

I asked as I coughed myself awake. I'd been smoking enough pot, of late, to develop a morning smoker's hack. It was a cough that had left me four years earlier when I stopped smoking cigarettes.

"His name is Vishna, Barry." She hated when I called him "What's his name." It showed such a lack of respect. I was hoping for a fight that would get me out of this Saturday drive to Tujunga. It didn't work. She was in too good a mood.

"I didn't find out about this from Vishna. I found out about this from an Indian woman, Roberta Shapiro-Dakota. American Indians have used crystals forever. She spoke to my Malibu meditation group. They're quartz crystals and you get energy from them. You know, like crystal balls? You can see the future and feel things. I held Roberta's. It's like they're alive."

"Shapiro-Dakota? Is this woman from a tribe of Israel or Apache or what?" I thought a healthy splash of skepticism might put out this fire of enthusiasm.

"Well, okay, she's not a real Indian. But she lived on a reservation one summer. And her spirit guide is an Indian," she said matter-of-factly as if I could just let this spirit guide thing go by.

"Me no wanna go buyum crystal today. Me wannum watch football. Hey, I think I am channeling Chief Thunderthud . . ."

"I don't want you making fun of this, Barry. We're going to Tujunga." With that proclamation, Linda kissed my forehead and jumped out of bed. The kiss on the forehead made it impossible to get a good fight going. I had no choice. I was going crystal shopping.

FIVE

A Hunting We Will Go

Tujunga was about an hour out of L.A. in a remote canyon
of the Angeles National Forest. The twisting mountain roads
led high above the smog of the city. Linda kept the directions
to Jonathan Reilly's house on her lap along with a letter of
introduction from Roberta Shapiro-Dakota. Jonathan Reilly was
Mr. Crystal, and one wrong turn in the canyon meant you'd never
find him. The letter of introduction from one of the crystal people
was a necessity if you didn't want to buy just a run-of-the-mill
crystal but were to see Reilly's really powerful, top-of- the-line
aura busters.

I was really enjoying the drive, taking my BMW through its
paces on the mountain roads. Finally, after a particularly winding
section of pavement that had us right on the edge of a rather steep

drop-off, Linda said, "Turn here."

"Turn where?" I asked, as I looked from side to side. Going right meant falling a few thousand feet to a certain death. Even worse, going left meant traveling up a dirt road, full of huge potholes and gravel, which would certainly ding the paint job on my beloved Beemer.

"Just get up there, would you, Barry? It'll be fine," Linda assured me.

I knew turning around and heading back home was out of the question, so I put the car in first gear and started inching up the road to Jonathan Reilly's house. As we went over the top of a ridge, we saw the house in the little clearing below us. It was an old, dark cabin probably built in the twenties. It sat peacefully alongside a flowing stream.

"Where are we supposed to park?" I asked, as we headed down the bumpy hill.

"On the other side of the stream. Just drive across," Linda said, as if she was giving directions to a cab driver who should know where he's going but doesn't.

"Drive across? Are you kidding?" There was no way I was taking my alloy wheels through a stream.

"According to Roberta Shapiro-Dakota, it's very shallow. You just drive across," she reiterated.

"Hey, even Christ was smart enough to walk across the water, not drive."

"Barry, I can't believe you. It's six inches deep—" Linda was out the door before she finished the sentence. She kicked off her shoes and walked halfway across the stream to prove her point. The water was up to her ankles. "See, Honey? It's nothing."

For a second I thought about driving over. Then I remembered all the cartoons I had seen over the years where somebody walks halfway across a river to show how shallow it is and then some schnook drives in only to find the water where the car is leads to a depth where the fish drive cars and a fish cop directs traffic at a busy intersection. I had seen this a lot. It happened to Porky Pig. It happened to Farmer Gray. It wasn't going to happen to Barry Klein. I turned off the engine and got out. As I took off my shoes and rolled up my pants, I explained to Linda that I just couldn't do it.

"Please, Barry. Just come on, would you?" Linda said as she walked easily to the other side of the stream.

I put my first foot in cautiously to test the temperature. A little cold, but not too bad. I started slowly, looking for good-sized rocks to step on, which were few.

"Would you come on? What are you afraid of?" Linda's rising impatience was getting on my nerves. I wasn't about to tell her what I was afraid of. She wouldn't understand. She hadn't seen the humiliation on Porky's face. She hadn't heard the fish laughing at Farmer Gray with their bubbly ho-ho-ho's.

I took my second step and then my third. I felt a little foolish holding my arms out to keep my balance as if I was on some circus high wire. As I took my fourth step, I suddenly plunged deeper. Much deeper. Instantly, the water was above my head. Everything was dark. I couldn't see Linda. I couldn't see the surface. And, although I could not see fish driving cars through a busy fish intersection, I could see my life flashing before my eyes. I knew I had to get to the surface and fast. Besides the lack of oxygen, there was the sudden realization that something squishy was under my feet. I broke water like an attack sub. Gasping for air, I saw Linda on the shore. She was standing with a skinny guy with long straggly hair. It was Jonathan Reilly.

"You gotta watch that one sink hole," Reilly told me as he laughed a laugh a little too bubbly and a little too ho-ho-hoey for my taste. Fortunately, I kept my wits about me. As I sloshed onto the shore and he extended his hand with a "Hi. Jonathan Reilly," I was able to squirt out all the water I had held in my mouth. It was a good long squirt and got a big laugh from Linda and Jonathan. I was thankful knowing that even close to death I remembered to take a mouthful of water to do the squirt and get the laugh. It was good to be alive.

The inside of Reilly's house was just as old and dark as the outside, plus it had the added feature of smelling musty. It was cold, considering it wasn't air conditioned, and outside the sun had heated the canyon up to the low nineties. It was also filled with an incredible collection of quartz crystals. On every table, every shelf, all over the floor, there were clusters of quartz large and small. They weren't displayed with any regard to style or presentation. There was a sense of chaos that made it impossible to take it all in.

"Can I get you some dry clothes?" Reilly offered.

"No, I'm fine," I shivered. I knew whatever was in this house would share the musk.

"Well, just look around. I'm sure one of our little friends will talk to you," he said, disappearing into the kitchen.

"Okay, don't be shy," I addressed the room full of rocks. "Where are you boys from?"

"Don't start, Barry," Linda warned. "Can't you feel the energy in here?" Linda closed her eyes and with a big smile on her face began to sway.

"What are you doing?"

"Getting ready to Om," she whispered.

Oh, Jesus. I really wanted to leave. While Linda continued to bliss out, I looked for a place to sit. I found a spot on the couch next to a sheet of newspaper full of crystals. They were single pieces, about six inches long. There were about eight of them on the paper, each incredibly clear except for the dense matrix of rock at the bottom. I slid the paper over, making room to sit, not caring that Reilly's couch would get wet. I could tell from the decor, or lack of it, neither would he.

Looking around the room, I heard Linda quietly begin her chant. "Ommmm. Ommmm. Ommmm." It seemed to call for a wise crack but I let it go. She was at peace. Some of the quartz clusters in the room were incredible. There were large ones that had to weigh hundreds of pounds with lots of clear wands reaching upward. There were massive single crystals that were perhaps two feet around that had an amazing sense of strength. Tiny, delicate crystals, gemlike creatures, danced with the narrow stream of light that came through the windows and refracted it into rainbows on the walls. As I sat there quietly for a moment, the place did feel good to my surprise and consternation. It was so much easier to be skeptical of this rather than accepting.

Jonathan Reilly returned from the kitchen with three teacups on a tray and offered me one. Normally, I would have said, "No thanks," figuring his kitchen was probably as dirty as the rest of the house and that the teacups would take on the same patina of filth. But I was still freezing, and the warm cup in my hands would be a great relief.

"Sure. I'd love some," I said, quickly taking the cup. Holding it with both hands, I pressed it first against my face and then my chest. Reilly didn't bother Linda with the offer of tea. She was having too good a time in her own little world. He set down the tray on a spot between rocks on the low table in front of the couch and found a corner of the table to sit on.

"So, what do you think?" he asked, as he placed a sugar cube between his teeth and began to sip tea.

"You have some pretty amazing things here," I confessed. "I've never seen rocks like this." The rocks were special. Even if they didn't do any of the things Roberta Shapiro-Dakota claimed, they were beautiful. They were works of art created by nature. Even I could appreciate that.

Reilly began telling me all about the quartz. How it amplified electronic waves in a steady rhythm, which is why they use it in quartz watches. How that same amplification applied to the energy of the universe giving those people who had quartz kind of a hi-fi system to tune into. He talked about sign waves and amplitude and things from high school physics that I had long forgotten. He was like a mad scientist of crystals. Before long he had me moving around the room from specimen to specimen. Here was one that was too dense to let the light in, so he polished one face exposing an incredible world of other minerals growing inside the quartz. There was another with a water bubble trapped inside that had lived for the tens of millions of years since the crystals were formed. I was spending the afternoon with a New Age Mr. Wizard, and each new crystal was more fascinating than the one before.

"Have you held one, Barry?" he asked, as he handed me one of the crystals from the newspaper lying next to me. It was initially cool but quickly warmed to my touch. It was about seven inches long and maybe three inches around. It was heavier than I imagined, weighing perhaps a pound and a half. The top half was clear, not like a drinking glass but mostly clear with an occasional imperfection. The imperfections, however, were wondrous. They were like mirrored planes, more dense than their surroundings, suspended within the clear section. The planes reflected light and sparkled. The six sides, though all of different widths, met perfectly at the tip. The lower half of the crystal was made of milky, less opaque quartz mixed with a brown sandstone. It was much rougher than the smooth upper half but was the perfect size to grasp. It felt comfortable in my hand.

"Close your eyes and tell me if you feel anything," Reilly whispered.

I didn't want to feel anything. I didn't want the rock in

my hand to have any great importance other than the fact that it
had survived millions of years and still looked good, the goal of
everyone in Hollywood. But there was no question, I felt a slight
buzz in the hand with the rock. It was subtle. So subtle that it could
be explained away. It could be anything. It could be . . . it could be
. . . it could be . . . anything. Okay, there wasn't a clear explanation
for what I felt. I switched the crystal to my other hand. The buzz
moved with the stone. Was Linda onto something with these rocks?

"Yeah . . . there's like a buzz," I finally admitted.

"That's the energy." Reilly smiled, revealing what was left
of the sugar cube. "Just enjoy it," he instructed.

I sat there with the crystal in my hand, still aware of the
slight tingle, and began getting into the visual pleasures of the
rock. It was incredible. I was getting lost in it. Without seeing
specifics, there was a sense of past and future, of all time, living in
this clear stone. I was smiling. It made me feel complete.

I had no idea how long I'd been looking at the crystal when
I realized Linda was standing next to me. She was struggling with
a crystal cluster that was about two feet across and must have
weighed about forty pounds. She had it cradled in her arms as she
waited for me to acknowledge her.

"I'm sorry. I didn't know—" I was a bit dazed.

"It's okay." Linda smiled. "Pretty nice, aren't they?"

"Yeah," I agreed happily. It was nice to be on the same wavelength.

"This is the one I want," she said as she tried to hold out the cluster in her arms. "Actually, I think it's the one that wants us."

I put my free hand on the cluster. It was more powerful than the one I was holding. It had a majesty about it.

"I think you're right." I turned to Reilly, "How much is it?" I asked, as I warmed myself with a sip of tea.

"I'll take a thousand. And I'll throw in your little friend," he said nodding to the crystal I still held.

I had to decide quickly. Was a thousand dollars a fair price? Too much? Much too much? Maybe the dark cabin and the torn pants were all an act. Maybe at night Reilly slipped off to his fabulous mansion in Beverly Hills. A mansion he could afford because he charged suckers like me a thousand dollars for a rock. Then again, diamonds are just rocks and they cost a lot more. I had not seen a lot of diamonds that were any more beautiful than the quartz cluster Linda was holding.

"We'll take it," I said, "if you carry it across the stream."

"Probably a good idea," he agreed with a laugh.

Driving back to L.A. with our new treasure, I looked at the cluster on the floor between Linda's feet. I wanted so much from this rock. Supernatural powers, divine intervention, something to give me the strength to stay on the straight and narrow. I wanted it to relieve the pressure of waiting for Bobby Mitchell's decision and wipe the constant image of Marcia Heilger's legs from my mind. I wanted it to make me happy. Linda rested her hand on top of mine. She gave it a little squeeze. We were both smiling. The rock was already working.

SIX

Casting the Monkey

"Can I help you?" Scotty O'Rourke asked as I rolled down my window.

I pointed my new crystal at him, hoping to vaporize him. Scotty immediately began to fumble for his nonexistent revolver.

"Marlon Brando to see Barry Klein," I said, before my powerful stone could melt him.

Oblivious to the world around him, Scotty began to scour his daily list of expected visitors to see if Mr. Klein was expecting a Marlon Brando. He gave a heavy sigh as he searched. Scotty knew he had heard of Marlon Brando and didn't relish the idea of telling him that he wasn't on the list. I felt sorry for the old guy.

"Scotty, it's me. Barry Klein."

"I see. Are you here to see Mr. Brando?" he asked, as he

now started to look for my name on the list of visitors.

Killing Scotty would actually be a good thing. I would be helping the studio. It might be good for my career. Scotty was taking too long. It was Monday and I had to get ready for the table reading of the new script, so I simply drove on to the lot. As I checked my rear view mirror, I saw the car behind me pull up to Scotty. I was sure the poor driver would be spending the better part of his day explaining that he was neither Barry Klein nor Marlon Brando.

I ran to the stage as quickly as possible. I wanted to beat Bobby there. Since he had chickened out on Friday night, I knew he'd be there on Monday morning. He did so little on the show that his Friday night and Monday morning appearances were the only reassurance to the network that we were, indeed, a Bobby Mitchell show. I knew the cast would talk about how well Friday night went. It was something we did every Monday. We'd reminisce about how hot the audience was, or which of the actors had a particularly good show. I was hoping that my performance as Bobby's stand-in would work its way into the conversation. Bobby needed to know I could handle the job.

I also wanted him to hear this week's script read. Donna Morris had written a terrific script and so Tommy and I really looked forward to doing this episode. It had two great things going for it: a chimpanzee, which The Ladies would love; and it humiliated Ben Fisher, which the writing staff would love. Yes, it was going to be a fine week.

We had wanted to do a monkey show for quite some time but had trouble coming up with a story that was either funny enough or compelling enough. Even on *In the Swim,* which was a pretty silly show, we wanted good, solid stories. A good story made the slapstick work better. It gave it a basis of reality. A spine to the silliness. So, although working with a chimp seemed like a natural for our show, up until now we hadn't come up with a story to our liking. It was Donna who finally solved the simian puzzle while we were trying to find a solution to another problem.

Ben Fisher's character, Uncle Sal, was a widower. He had a special friend, a woman named Yvonne, to fulfill his manly needs. Yvonne was a flamboyant character with a big blonde hairdo who loved to party, dragging Uncle Sal around in spite of his grumbling. Yvonne was played by Dee Dee Moore, a lovely woman, quite refined, who was nothing like the character she played. The best example of the difference between character and actress was that Yvonne loved how gruff Uncle Sal was and Dee Dee hated it. It wasn't Uncle Sal she hated. She hated Ben Fisher, especially having to kiss him with his rotten cigar breath. It was the only thing she ever complained about. I should have listened.

When we started the season, we got a call from Dee Dee's agent. She wouldn't be back. She had an offer to star in a series of her own. Her new series was also produced by Paragon Studios, so they, too, wanted her off our show. Because Dee Dee refused to come back, even to do one last episode where Yvonne decides to run away and join the circus, we had to come up with an explanation for the audience that didn't include her.

"What if, when she runs away to join the circus, a chimp stays in her place?" Donna suggested with a sly smile at a story meeting to solve the Yvonne crisis. "Then Uncle Sal gets drunk and has to pour his heart out to a monkey."

We loved it. Connie and Patti would get to play with a monkey, and Ben would have to kiss one. Perfect.

When I got to the stage, everybody was milling around, drinking coffee, eating doughnuts. It was getting close to ten o'clock, the time we'd sit down to read. Normally, about five minutes to ten, Bobby would give the greeting, "It's Monday morning, let's see what we've got," and the cast and writing staff would sit down to read the script. I scanned the room looking for Bobby. Instead, I saw Alice Martin walking toward me. I could tell she wasn't looking forward to delivering whatever message she had. Alice and I had always gotten along well. I could easily make her laugh. But waiting for the producing decision was taking its toll on our relationship. I knew she didn't like the way I talked to her on Friday night, and I planned on apologizing. As she approached, the apology left my mind. I knew she was bringing news from Bobby.

"Barry, there's trouble over on *We Want It Al*, she whispered to me as if this was news too important for everyone to hear.

"Don't tell me, they all have colon trouble?" I asked feigning as much concern for the entire cast and crew as I could muster.

"Yes. They all have colon trouble, okay?" Alice immediately walked away. Telling lies for Bobby was not her favorite thing to do, even though it was a big part of her job.

There was nothing to do but get the show on the road. We couldn't afford to waste any more time. Even if the script reading went well, there'd still be rewriting to do. I had to get this herd of people to the table but didn't want to use Bobby's Monday morning line. I had used too many of his words on Friday night. It was time to develop a style of my own.

"Madames et Messieurs, your table is ready," I said in my corniest French maître d' accent. Thank God for Donna Morris. She laughed her wonderful laugh. It's a laugh more infectious than strep. Once she gets started, others have no choice but to join in. Donna laughed and so did everybody else as they headed to the table. I think they were all surprised that I was loose enough to do the French bit in front of all these people. Tommy gave me a little shake of the head in disbelief and put his arm around my shoulder as we headed for the table. It felt great.

As soon as we all sat down, Mimi Simms read the episode title out loud. " 'The Monkey Show.' Does it have a monkey in it?"

"I don't know how you guessed, but, yes, it does," I said, feeling perhaps too loose. I could sense that everybody at the table got a little tense at this bit of sarcasm. The cast knew we always titled the episodes with exactly what they were about. We hated cute titles. When a freelance writer handed in a script about Connie losing a tooth entitled: "All I Want for Christmas . . . ," we immediately changed it to "The Connie Loses a Tooth Show." There was only one thing "The Monkey Show" could have been about.

Michael Zylik, the director, began reading the stage directions with his lovely English accent. It gave even "The Monkey Show" dignity. The cast joined in the reading of the script. It started out well. The jokes were working, and everyone was laughing. Even Willy and Billy were reading what was on the page. Most weeks, they'd try to improvise when everybody else was reading. Sometimes they'd come up with truly funny stuff. Most of the time they would bomb and throw the timing off on what we'd

written. This morning we were sailing. Right up until Uncle Sal got
a bit drunk playing poker with JoJo, the monkey.

The premise was that Patti and Connie want to go on dates,
so they ask Uncle Sal if he'd baby-sit the monkey. He doesn't want
to because it's his poker night, but reluctantly he agrees and the
girls go out on the town. Now, alone with the chimp, he begins
to play the poker game he's missing and has a couple of beers.
We dissolve to a few hours later and the monkey is winning the
game. All of Uncle Sal's chips are in front of JoJo, and Uncle Sal
is getting a bit sloshed from all the beer. They are both enjoying
the fine Havana cigars Uncle Sal saves for only the most important
occasions.

Uncle Sal tells JoJo about the note he's found from Yvonne
that explains how she's always wanted to join the circus. After
all, it's so much fun. JoJo nods his head in agreement. Uncle Sal
begins to cry. JoJo puts his arm around Sal who gives the ape a
big kiss. The scene works. Everybody around the table is moved.
Everybody except Ben. I could tell we were in trouble when,
while reading the poker scene, Ben began to read in a whisper. I
knew from the vein that was bulging on the side of his neck that
the whisper was not an acting choice. He didn't like the material.
When Michael Zylik read the stage direction, "Uncle Sal kisses
JoJo, long, hard, and deep," Ben got up from the table and walked

to his dressing room.

"I'm not doing this shit," he grumbled as he headed off. In an act of defiance, he lit his cigar. The Ladies had forbidden the cigar on stage. They didn't care if he wanted to smell like a humidor, they didn't want the entire stage to reek.

What to do? We'd read only about two-thirds of the script. Should we continue without Ben? Did he really mean that he wouldn't do this shit? He had to. This was the only shit we had ready.

"Why don't you all keep reading? Howie, you be Uncle Sal. I'm going to talk to Ben." I gave the instructions firmly and with confidence. The reading continued. Hey, I was producing.

I knocked on Ben's door and opened it, not waiting for him to invite me in. He was sitting on his couch reading *The Daily Racing Form*.

"What do you want?" he asked, without looking up from the paper.

"I want to know what your problem is. That's a great script." I sat right next to him on the couch. He would have to deal with me.

"You kiss the fucking monkey," he said, still not looking away from the list of horses running at Hollywood Park. The same horses that would take most of the exorbitant amount of money he got for playing Uncle Sal.

"You don't want to kiss the chimp? Fine. Lorraine will do it," I said, knowing he would never want to give a piece of business away to another actor. Ben whined a lot, but deep down he trusted me. If I wasn't going to throw something away, it must be okay.

"She's going to kiss him? Why would she kiss him?" he asked, finally putting the paper aside.

"Because the kiss works. The audience is going to love you when you kiss that hairy face. They're going to feel so sorry for Uncle Sal. Poor bastard. His girlfriend left him and now he's kissing this monkey. Ben, it's a scene where we're going to play the music."

Toward the end of most episodes, we'd have a scene where the emotional crisis would be solved. Patti and Connie would tell each other how much they needed each other's friendship or how much one appreciated the other. We almost always played emotional, sappy music under these scenes just in case the audience was too dense to realize the importance of what was going on. To Ben Fisher, these became "the scenes where you play the music." Over the years, to Ben's delight, we had given him a number of these scenes: when Sal and Connie went back to her mother's grave, when Sal and his mother resolved a quarrel that had gone on for thirty years, when Sal almost lost the bait shop to unscrupulous land developers and contemplated his future without bait. Although Ben did a credible job with these scenes, the toll was too high. All week he'd be a bigger pain in the butt than usual. Laurence Olivier didn't go through as much preparation to play Hamlet as Ben did to tell Willy and Billy how much it meant to get up each morning to dig worms. If Sal's beloved girlfriend Yvonne was leaving him for the circus, certainly we'd have to do a scene where we played the music.

Ben sat there looking at his cigar, trying to process what I had just said. I had been right about this kind of thing before. I could tell he was close to coming around.

"Maybe it's not the kiss that's bothering you," I suggested. I had to save the kiss. The show didn't work without it.

"No, it's not the kiss. It's the part where I say he's my best friend. We've spent three years establishing Frank from the bowling alley as my best friend. Now you want it to be some fucking monkey!" he lectured.

Like a good student I listened. "I know. That was stupid. Hey, sometimes we try stuff that doesn't work. You know that." My confidence grew. This would be an easy fix. We wouldn't say that JoJo was Uncle Sal's best friend. We'd find something else. Like if the monkey was the new guy at the Motor Vehicle

Department and Sal had to renew his license, how would Ben feel if Sal had to explain to the monkey that since his girlfriend left, he was afraid to parallel park? I considered the comic possibilities of having a chimp for a driving instructor and then decided against it. Too silly. Even for us. "Don't worry. I'll come up with something. I'm going back out. You need a minute?" I knew Ben would want to save face.

"Yeah. I'll be out in a minute," he answered without looking at me. He was already figuring what he'd tell the other cast members. How he got me to crawl. How he got whatever he wanted. I didn't care. The monkey was still in the show.

By the time I got back on stage, everyone had left. They had finished reading the script and Tommy had led the writing staff back up to K building. He didn't want to waste time. It was going to be a fairly easy rewrite. We'd be done before the next day's dawn.

"Barry, your wife just called." Harvey Lipshitz, the dialogue coach, had trouble fitting the words and his third jelly doughnut into his mouth. Harvey had stayed behind to clean up the snack table.

I picked up the stage phone and dialed Linda as I watched Harvey move from the jelly doughnuts to the bear claws while carefully avoiding any contact with the fresh carrot sticks.

"Barry, Ram Das is speaking in Santa Barbara tonight. If

you're working late I thought I'd take a ride up." Linda sounded in a particularly good mood as she told me her plans.

"Sure, that's fine. I don't know when I'll be finished." That was true. There were so many nights I thought I'd be home early and then something would happen and I'd get stuck at the studio. I didn't want Linda changing plans on my account. She had done that too many times. Besides, if I got home early and she was at Ram Das's talk, I'd get some much-needed time alone. No studio, no Bobby, no Marcia's legs. Just a little break to get myself together.

I walked into my office, before heading to the rewrite table to check messages. There was Marcia, legs in the air, applying the lotion. She didn't even try to hide anymore. She didn't swing around so I'd only see her back and the tops of her fantastic legs. No, she left them right there in front of me.

"Do you want to see the monkey?" she asked as she caught me staring. I didn't know what to say. Was she being as forward as I thought she was? This was too much. No, Barry. She's talking about the monkey from the show. Get with the program.

"Uh, yeah. Call casting and tell them I want to see monkeys this afternoon." I blushed, which made her smile, as I headed for the rewrite. Our casting department had gotten used to last-minute orders to "Find a monkey" or "Get me a guy who can chug a beer in five seconds." We never booked these acts in advance because all too often the script would change so much on a Monday that monkeys or beer chugging guys would get cut and we'd still have to pay them. So casting would have everybody on hold. When the call came for monkeys, they'd be ready.

Donna, Tommy, and I hit a groove. The first ten pages of the rewrite flew by. We were hot. The jokes were coming fast. Most were at Ben Fisher's expense. Before we knew it, we were up to page fifteen. We were rolling. Right until Marcia appeared at the door.

"Barry, Bobby Mitchell's calling," Marcia announced.

I ran by her. I went so fast I almost didn't notice Marcia's little grab of my ass as I went by. Almost, but not quite. There was no doubt about it. Now she was publicly making physical contact with me. It gave me plenty to think about on the way to the phone.

"Yo, Bobby," I said as I swept the receiver up to my ear. I was slightly out of breath from running while not breathing.

"One second, I'll get him," Alice Martin replied. I should have known he wasn't on the line. He'd never sit on a line waiting for me to answer.

"Baaaarrrrryyyy?" It was him.

"Bobbbbyyyy?" God, I hated falling into it so quickly.

"Listen, I'm sorry I've been missing you, but you know,

I've been having trouble."

"It must be quite uncomfortable," I said, hoping he wouldn't mistake my comment for genuine interest and begin a detailed conversation that might contain the word polyp or something else that might be growing in his pooper.

"You don't want to know," he said. He was right. I wanted to hear whether I was the new producer of *In the Swim*. "Listen, Barry, I need a favor," he continued.

"Whatever you need," I kowtowed.

"There's this guy, Tony Figarito—he cuts my hair. He needs to work to pay for his S.A.G. insurance. Find him something on this week's show."

Unbelievable. Not only wasn't he calling to make me a producer, he wanted me to put his barber on TV to cheat Blue Cross out of five hundred bucks worth of health insurance premiums.

There comes a time when a man has to take a stand for what's right. He has to push aside his fears of what might happen to him as a result of right action.

"Sure. No problem," I said. This wasn't that time. Besides, it wasn't that tough to do. Half the people in southern California belonged either to the Screen Actors Guild or the other actors' union, AFTRA, and they got their health insurance by working once a year.

"Thhaaaannnk you, Baaaarrrryyy." He was gone.

Nothing. Not a hint. Not a clue. I wanted to call him back and read him the riot act. You don't treat another person like this! What was he waiting for? I had seen the litany of candidates for the job heading for Bobby's office. People with more experience. People who knew how to do the job. Most were only willing to take it for a ridiculous amount of money. Lorraine and Mimi's behavior was no secret in Hollywood. Anyone taking the job expected to be fired. It might be worth it if you could get enough money up front or be guaranteed a payoff when The Ladies decided to get rid of you. That kind of guarantee is called a "Pay or Play" deal. It happens so often in show business that they have a name for it. But Paragon Studios wasn't willing to pay the big bucks. Not anymore. They were already paying off too many ex-producers' contracts. So Bobby began to see people who were less qualified—producers who couldn't write as well as Tommy and I, and people The Ladies would eat for lunch. Bobby did everything but put an ad in the classifieds to find a new producer.

On my way back to the rewrite room, Marcia was still standing in the doorway. She wanted to hear the news. This time as I passed her I put my hand on her shoulder. It looked like I did it just to get around her. At least I hoped it looked like that. It

took all the courage I had. The last thing I wanted was for Rhonda
Silverman to notice me touching a woman other than my wife
and begin making an awful scene to embarrass me. It was a risk
I had to take. I wanted to touch Marcia. I had to touch her. The
invitation to her apartment. The grab of the ass. The constant
creaming of the legs. It all took its toll. I was on the hook. I wanted
to feel her. Instead, I felt her silky blouse and imagined it was her
skin. My heart was racing. What a jerk. I only touched her blouse.
People touched other people all the time. Howie Clark was always
hugging all the women in the office. It wasn't threatening or
offensive. It was Howie. Why couldn't this be Barry?

I got to my seat and looked back at her. She smiled. The
touch had not gone unnoticed.

"What's the deal?" Tommy asked.

"He wants us to put his barber in this week's show." As I
said it I gave a little shrug of the shoulders to Marcia as if I was
reporting the information to her, taking her into my confidence.

Donna Morris threw a pencil against the wall in disgust.
"Fine, we'll make his barber the goddamn monkey. How can he do
this?" she asked.

Finding a place for the barber would be easy. He only
needed one line to qualify for his insurance. He didn't have to
be good. Chances were we'd cut him out of the show in editing.

Bobby wouldn't care. He didn't want the guy to succeed as an actor. Figarito was too good a barber, having the ability to take Bobby's few remaining wisps and make them look like a lacquered ashtray. Yes. Bobby's hair had a funny little dip in it that would be a perfect place to park your Marlboro. But he loved his hair. This was the right thing to do. Figarito would have his health insurance and a good show business story.

We made the barber a delivery guy who brought a telegram for the monkey from his stockbroker. The chimp would be making a fortune in the stock market and Uncle Sal would try to get stock tips from him. It only took a few minutes to write and we all liked it. We were about to move on to the next problem when Marcia came back into the room.

"The monkeys are ready," she reported.

Tommy stood. "Barry and I are going to go look at monkeys. You guys keep working."

As Tommy went through the door I don't think he noticed that Marcia was still in the doorway. She was waiting for me to squeeze by her again. I didn't waste the opportunity to touch the blouse. And this time, when I put my hand on her shoulder, she put hers on my waist. I couldn't believe how exciting it was. I inhaled to catch a whiff of perfume. She wore a fragrance that was very subtle. I was close enough to be aware of every nuance. I wanted more.

As Tommy and I headed for the casting office, my mind started thinking about what I would really like to do if I got off work early this evening. I wanted to see Marcia. No, I didn't. I was the guy who'd been married for eight years without cheating. I was going for the world's record. There's no such thing as just a little fooling around—either you cheat on your wife or you don't. Marcia's fragrance was still with me. I was trying to hold on to it as long as I could. No, I wouldn't see her.

Randy Hammer, our casting director, was waiting for us in his office. Randy was about as gay as a man can be. He had it all, the lisp, the swish, the limp wrist, the whole nine yards. He also had a tremendous amount of power, and he was good. As casting director for the number one show on television, it was up to him who got to see the producers. To get on the show you had to pass through Randy, literally. As a result, we never had a straight actor guest star on the show. Not that we complained. He always brought in actors who were more than competent, and the network and studio liked that we were hiring gays. They were able to point to our show as an example of affirmative action. In reality, it was just a way to keep Randy and his huge sexual appetite satiated.

"Oh, look who's here!" he squealed as we entered his office, which looked more like a boudoir than a place to work.

Randy had a tremendous crush on Tommy, so he was especially happy to see both of us show up to choose a monkey.

"Do you have monkeys for us?" I asked, not wanting to get into Randy's usual routine. If allowed, Randy would spend most of our time showing us pictures of young, boy-actors for whom he wanted parts written.

"I have three monkeys and they're all fabulous!" he exclaimed.

"Fabulous!" Tommy and I responded immediately. We couldn't let Randy get away with a "Fabulous" without pointing it out to him.

"Now, don't tease," he said as he led us into the casting room, an old conference room that had a few theater seats set up for the producers and casting directors and a well-lit area for actors to stand as they auditioned. Next to Randy's seat was an intercom on a small table. He pushed the button. "Ricky, bring in the first monkey?"

Ricky, Randy's straight assistant, brought in the first monkey. Randy insisted on having a straight assistant so he wouldn't have competition for his acting prey. Ricky was, however, pretty good looking, as Randy liked having a little eye candy around the office.

"This is Mr. Campelli and Choo Choo," Ricky told us as

he indicated where Mr. Campelli and the monkey should stand.
As soon as Mr. Campelli and his spider monkey entered, I knew
I was in for one of those show business days where you have to
constantly remind yourself that *everything* about it is appealing.

Choo Choo was one of the ugliest monkeys I'd ever seen.
Not that I'd seen that many, but, still, you can tell when you're
looking at one of God's little whoopsies. Choo Choo had the
mange or something. His fur was missing in many areas, showing
skin that had some sort of red blotchy disease. Some of the blotch
was thankfully covered by a little tuxedo jacket as well as the
obligatory bellboy's cap and a pair of red satin pants. Mr. Campelli
was dressed as an organ grinder, hoping that his costume would
spark an idea in us that would land both him and the monkey some
work. The worst part, though, was not Choo Choo's lack of fur.
It was what Mr. Campelli had done to the monkey's face. He had
shaved it down to the skin and then applied rouge, lipstick, and
eye make-up. Choo Choo looked hideous. Actually, he looked
embarrassed. When you cast monkeys, or any animals for that
matter, you quickly figure out that these poor creatures have little
desire to be in show business. This indignation was not something
Choo Choo chose to endure to reach his lifelong goal of being
an actor. Choo Choo had not seen Cheetah in a Tarzan movie
and thought, "Gee, I could do that." No, this was Mr. Campelli's

brainstorm of how to get to easy street.

Looking at poor Choo Choo, I hoped I wouldn't be having bad dreams for the next few nights. This was a creepy monkey. But having not yet seen the other monkeys, we still had to find out if Choo Choo had the talent to carry the role.

"Does he play cards?" Tommy asked looking down at the floor, avoiding the monkey's wild, darting eyes.

"Oh, absolutely," Mr. Campelli said, as he pulled a deck of cards from his coat, which matched Choo Choo's stitch for stitch. He then took five cards from the top of the deck and forced them into the monkey's hand. Choo Choo didn't really want to play cards so he threw them on the floor. Mr. Campelli tried to coax the monkey into the game by joking about Choo Choo's obvious inability to hold the cards.

"What's the matter, Choo Choo, you don't want to play today? Is it because I won so much money from you last night?" Mr. Campelli was trying to keep it light as he picked up the cards and again gave them to Choo Choo. This time he also offered the monkey a small piece of banana. Choo Choo wanted neither. Now what kind of monkey refuses a piece of banana? He began to scratch his red blotchy skin. We couldn't have this pathetic creature on the set all week. The Ladies would spend too much time worrying about him. Besides, it was clear that Choo Choo wasn't going to be able to play cards with Uncle Sal. In fact, other than being able to sit still while Mr. Campelli shaved his face, I couldn't see that Choo Choo had any particular talent at all. It was hard to watch.

"Thank you, Mr. Campelli, that's great," I said trying to sound like Choo Choo was still in the running.

"I can get him to do it better. Can I just have a minute with him alone?" There was desperation in Mr. Campelli's voice. I didn't want to think about what was going to happen to Choo Choo in this "minute with him alone."

"No, that's okay. He's so cute, he doesn't really have to do the card thing. The audience will love him." I wanted this freak show out of the room.

"Well, thank you. Audiences do love him. I could make him do the card thing in a day or two."

"I'm sure you could. We'll be in touch." I looked down at my casting list to see the name of the next monkey and to avoid any further conversation with Mr. Campelli.

Ricky brought in the next candidate. Actually he brought in a man named Joe Peters who was dragging a box, the size you'd transport a big dog in if you were going on an airplane. I assumed he had a monkey in it. He opened the door and tried to get whatever was in the box to come out.

"We're waiting." Randy was getting impatient.

"Yeah, well, Max was a little worked up when I tried to put him in the box so I gave him a couple of Valiums. He seems to have passed out." Joe was trying to pull the limp monkey from the box as he explained the problem.

"Look, these are very important men. They have no time for drugged-out monkeys." Randy was embarrassed by the situation. He had only called in three monkeys and the first two were bombing. "I'm sorry, Tommy, I had no idea." Randy put his hand on Tommy's knee as he apologized.

"Next monkey, please!" Tommy said as he bolted out of the chair and began to pace. There were two things Tommy didn't like. He didn't like Randy touching him and he didn't like that I would bust his chops about it later when we got upstairs.

"What's the hurry? Sit down, Tommy. Relax." I gave him my biggest Cheshire Cat grin as I indicated he should sit down again next to Randy. To make things worse, or better depending on whether you were busting chops or having chops busted, Randy patted the cushion next to him, an invitation for Tommy to return.

As Joe Peters stuffed the half of a monkey he had out of the box back in, he explained that the animal was more than capable of doing the card bit. He had some uppers in his truck, which he would force-feed the monkey and be back once his furry little pal came to. We told him that was a great idea, knowing that once Peters was out of the room, we would not have to see him again.

Ricky brought in the last candidate, a chimp named Betsy. I was glad it was a chimp. They're cuter than other monkeys and it's what I had envisioned for the role. Betsy was a mature chimp, however, with abnormally large breasts. We'd definitely have to put her in clothes. I wished her trainer, an old cowboy named Gus, had dressed her before bringing her in. Gus didn't waste any time. He sat Betsy down and began to deal. Betsy picked up the cards one by one and arranged them in her hand. She could play cards. Gus then took a cigarette from a pack in his shirt pocket and lit it. He laid the pack on the card table. Betsy took a cigarette from the pack and put it in her mouth. Gus reached over and offered her a light. Betsy took a puff and exhaled. She then began to shake her head up and down to indicate what a great smoke it was.

"Isn't she wonderful?" Randy cooed. He knew he was off the hook. This monkey would be fine. Or so we thought. Just as we were about to tell Gus that Betsy had the job, he tried to take the cigarette away from her. The chimp went crazy. She began to scream that wild, unbearably loud jungle scream. Next she began to jump up and down on the table. A mature chimp is big and strong and Betsy was now lifting a chair over her head. She was willing to fight Gus for the cigarette. Before the fight had a chance to escalate, Gus pulled a handgun out of his pants. Tommy and I hit the floor. I didn't want to die in some gunfight between a man and a monkey. What if Betsy got the gun and decided to get back at all the people who had robbed her of her perfectly fine monkey life for this absurd existence in show business? Would she take hostages and demand a plane back to the jungle? Or would it just be another case of random monkey violence?

As soon as Betsy saw the gun she became totally passive. She immediately sat at the table with her hands folded in front of her, eyes straight, not moving a muscle. I wondered what had happened with that gun. Had Gus shot it at her? Had he beaten her with it? Whatever he did, she sure didn't want any more trouble from the gun. As Tommy and I got up from the floor and quickly headed for the door, we told Randy to book Betsy. I felt sorry for Betsy but we had our monkey. The show would go on.

We got back to the rewrite table and found the staff hadn't done a thing while we were gone.

"I can't believe this. We finally get a night when we can get out at a decent hour and you guys just sit here?" They didn't know how much I needed my night alone.

"Guys, right after you left, Bobby called for Fred," Donna said with the concern usually saved for reporting the unexpected death of a relative.

Tommy and I looked at each other, jumping to the same conclusion.

"Did he offer him the job?" Tommy was now straight enough to focus on the end of the world as we knew it.

"Not on the phone. But when he left, Fred took his script with him. If he were coming right back, he would have left his script." Donna had put all the ugly pieces together. Fred wasn't planning on coming back tonight. He was probably planning his celebration dinner with his wife. I was planning a call to my agent.

None of us got any work done. All we could do was speculate whether Bobby might make Fred producer and what life would be like if that happened. Donna, Tommy, and I all agreed that we'd leave the show. Rhonda would stay.

"How could you work for him?" Donna asked as she turned away from Rhonda in disgust.

"I liiiiike Fred," Rhonda replied in very unconvincing style.

"You like the money." Donna was now in Rhonda's face.

"Potato, po-tah-toe." Yup, Rhonda liked the money.

Hours went by. We slowly made progress through the script. Every fifteen minutes we'd take a "dump on Fred" break. But each hour made the wait worse. To take a week and a half and then give the job to Fred was too demoralizing. I was really depressed. I needed to talk to someone. I needed to talk to Linda.

It was only four in the afternoon. She might not have left for Santa Barbara yet. I excused myself and went to my office. Marcia was at her desk putting lotion on her arms. I assumed the pores on her legs just couldn't absorb any more.

Talking to Linda was the thing to do. She'd give me one of her reassuring "If it's meant to be, it's meant to be" talks. Even though I put down her interest in personal growth, most of what she passed on to me was helpful. It just didn't seem like fun. Linda was always prescribing things like eating right and meditating and crystals and getting in touch with spirit guides. They all lead to a healthier, more centered, easier way of life. But there's a catch. They're practices that require discipline. You have to do them regularly to recognize their subtle influence.

At our home in tranquil Topanga Canyon, having moved from the hustle and bustle of the city, I'd quietly think about these practices and realized that when I used them on a routine basis, they helped me. They made me focused. They made my writing easier and brought Linda and me closer. But at work there was no time for those things. They didn't seem to fit into the glitz and glamour of show business.

I felt like I was living in two different worlds, and I was a bit of a freak in both. My show business friends didn't understand the new rock on my desk. Linda's New Age friends didn't understand my attraction to the "maya," the illusions of show business. The best of both worlds was what I wanted. Right now, I was off center. I needed Linda.

I dialed the phone and as it began to ring I started thinking how Linda would probably say that Fred Mitchell was on his journey and I was on mine. The universe is benevolent. I wasn't being put through this as any kind of punishment. Be patient. Things happen when they should happen and not when I want them to. All these things made sense, but not as much sense as when they came from Linda, and she wasn't answering the phone. Where was she? Had she left early to hear this Ram Das guy? Goddamn her and her search for enlightenment. I needed her. I slammed the phone down and headed for the rewrite room.

As I went by Marcia, I asked if Bobby had called. The answer was no and it came with a sympathetic look and a vote of confidence.

"You're going to get it, Barry. You're the best."

"Thanks, Marcia. It's nice to know somebody thinks so." I was standing by her desk. We had said all we had to say yet I was still standing there. I needed to get back to the table, but I wanted to stay.

"Barry, let's go," Tommy yelled, and I had no choice. I gave her a shrug. She gave me a wink. I went back to work.

Tommy, Donna, Rhonda, Howie and I managed to finish the rewrite at about nine-thirty but our hearts weren't in it. After my visit to Marcia's desk, I wasn't much help. I wasn't thinking of ways to get Willy to dance with the monkey or ways to make Uncle Sal look more ridiculous. Instead, I was thinking of ways to get Marcia into bed. It was the perfect thing to keep me from thinking about Fred. Later, as I packed my briefcase, I made a decision. Why not drop by Marcia's? She had invited me. I wasn't getting my work done because of thinking about her. I'd be better off going to bed with her and getting it over with. She lived only a few minutes from the studio according to her address on the crew list. Because producers need to be able to get in touch with the people who work on the show at any time, day or night, they're given crew lists with everybody's home address and phone number. Although we weren't the producers, the studio made sure Tommy and I had everything we needed to keep the show running smoothly.

I headed down Melrose to her place. Was I really going to do this? Was Barry Klein going to give up his medal as Married Guy Who Doesn't Mess Around? There was a parking spot right in front of her building as I drove by. That scared the hell out of me. What if she had plans for tonight? What if there was somebody up there with her? I drove around the block as I thought of how I should handle the situation. What I would say? What she would say? I drove around the block again. And again. And again. It was enough times for somebody watching me to think I was casing the joint and call the cops. Yeah, I'm sure I'll be made producer after the studio has to bail me out of jail for loitering in front of my secretary's building.

I drove off to think. The waiting for Bobby's decision had been stressful. The possibility of Fred Maxwell getting the job was a catastrophe of a magnitude that knocked me off my axis. No longer in a regular orbit, I felt life spinning out of control. What was I doing? What do I want? I wanted answers. I didn't want to go home, back to the little house in the canyon, to hear about the wonderful day Linda had and how she learned to levitate. I wanted relief.

SEVEN

Five Minutes Later You're Hungry Again

Driving aimlessly, unaware of where I was or how long it
had been since I had stopped circling Marcia's building, I looked
around for bearings. Things looked familiar. It was my old Santa
Monica neighborhood, but where? Then I saw the large neon sign
of the gorgeous girl in front of the Wrestle a Nude Woman place.
My heart was beating fast. I was out of control. The constant
thoughts of being in bed with Marcia made feeling centered
impossible. I had to do something to relieve this preoccupation.
Perhaps wrestling a nude woman would quiet my sexual stirrings
without being as big a transgression as sleeping with Marcia.
Maybe I wasn't really attracted to Marcia at all and what I simply
needed was an outlet for my fantasies. In that case, wrestling a
nude woman would have to be considered therapeutic . . . a good

thing. Having been tempted by the neon girl's electric dance since the day I got to California, I could no longer resist.

I parked, got out of the car, and approached the door. Terrified. There were no other cars on the street. I was alone, about to get my first glimpse at the seedy side of life—the other side of the tracks—the kind of place nice boys just don't go. Suddenly it dawned on me, what if the Wrestle a Nude Woman sign was just a front for some other illegal activity? Would I be beaten over the head the moment I entered? If the bad guys were going to beat me over the head, and I had no reason to believe they wouldn't, why would they let me wrestle a nude woman first? No, they would go right to the head beating and get it over with. That didn't make sense, either. It had been three years since we moved to California and the Wrestle a Nude Woman place had been here all along. Surely, somebody would have mentioned it to the police if all they were doing was beating people over the head.

I couldn't take my cowardess any longer. I was afraid of wrestling a nude woman. My God, Barry, for once in your life, live! If I was going to consider myself a writer, I shouldn't be afraid of experiencing things. It's what writers do. How can you write about life if you don't taste its fruits? All its fruits.

The door was locked. I knocked softly. I doubted anybody could hear it, but in my mind it still qualified as a knock. I could live with myself knowing that I had done all I could to get into the Wrestle a Nude Woman place. I was an adventurer. I was a writer. I was Hemingway, for Christ's sake. Having made this great display of manhood, I still had time to run. Before I could get my feet moving, the door cracked open. A small, old, Asian woman stuck her head out from behind the door.

"Wha you wan?" she said in a suspicious tone. It was as if even the people who ran the place couldn't respect someone who actually knocked on their door.

"Wrestle a nude woman," I mumbled, as I almost burst into tears.

"You come in." She opened the door just a little more. It was dark inside. I couldn't see if anybody was hiding behind the door, waiting to beat me over the head. The old woman was waiting. I had to do something. I went in. The woman looked to be about sixty. She was wearing an outfit stolen from one of the cocktail waitresses at Caesar's Palace in Las Vegas. It was one of those short, toga-looking things that was showing off her anything-but-lovely sixty-year-old legs. If this was somebody's idea of a sexy start to my wrestling a nude woman experience, they were wrong.

"You sit down." She indicated I should plant myself on a dilapidated couch that sat against the far wall.

"I'll just wait, thank you." That's it, Barry. Be polite. If you're nice to her, she'll be nice to you. She'll go get a really beautiful woman for you to wrestle. Like the ones in the pictures on the wall. She won't take off the Caesar's Palace costume and wrestle you herself. It was a horrible thought, but a distinct possibility. What if she was, indeed, the woman I'd be wrestling? My feet were not going to fail me. They started pointing themselves toward the door.

"You be he befaw?" Uh-oh. She was getting personal. What should I say? Would I get a better girl if I was a regular? Or would I get special treatment if I was a first-timer? As long as it wasn't her. God, don't make me wrestle this old withered chopstick of a woman.

"First time," I said, as I walked over to a picture of a gorgeous girl hanging on the wall. I pointed to the picture in a way that might suggest to Madam Mao that this would be the perfect gal with whom I'd like to get into the ring.

"Sissy dollah."

I had no idea what she was saying. "I'm sorry—what?" I squinted as I said it so she would think I was listening really hard.

"Sissy dollah. You give sissy dollah. You wrestle."

"Oh! Sixty dollars." Yes, of course. Money. I would need money. I hadn't thought about that. I don't usually carry much cash. If I have cash I spend it. So I usually don't have more than fifty dollars with me at any one time. Why hadn't I thought about how much it would cost to wrestle a nude woman? This was embarrassing. Forty-seven dollars was all I found in my wallet. It had taken years to work up the courage to come here. I didn't want to have to leave because of thirteen dollars.

"I have forty-seven dollars, that's it," I said, holding my wallet out so she could see there was no more money hiding from the Wrestle a Nude Woman coffers. She quickly took all the cash, then handed me a pair of large, olive green boxer shorts, which she pulled off the bottom shelf of the wobbly end table next to the couch.

"You put on. Den go der." She nodded toward to a beaded curtain separating this fabulous waiting room from the actual Wrestle a Nude Woman room. Before I could say a word, she went into her office, leaving me alone with my empty wallet in one hand and my olive green boxer shorts in the other. I looked at the shorts. Where had they come from? Where had they been? Who had worn them before me? Had they ever been washed? I immediately dropped the shorts and again thought about running. I had gotten at least forty-seven dollars worth of excitement. How much better could it be even if I did wrestle a nude woman?

Suddenly, her office door flew open. It scared the crap

out of me, though I was relieved to see she still had her Caesar's Palace outfit on.

"Chop chop," she scolded.

I immediately undressed down to my briefs, folding my clothes neatly over the arm of the couch, carefully avoiding the cushions. I put my wallet in the front of my briefs, figuring it would give me added protection, and I wasn't about to leave it just sitting there in the waiting room. Parting the beaded curtain, I stepped inside.

The dimly lit wrestling room was small, maybe ten by twelve, with mattresses covering the floor. On the walls were posters of girls, mostly Asian, in varying degrees of undress, wrestling with similarly unclothed girls. Other than the mattresses and the posters, the room was empty. I walked around to get a better look at the posters. I was at the far wall, the one the farthest from the beaded curtain, which was my only route of escape, when I heard the beads rattle. Someone had entered the room. My heart was pounding. Fear had me paralyzed, unable to turn around and see the naked beauty waiting to wrestle. If I could muster the courage to face her, I wondered if I should wrestle with her as hard as I could, or if I should just submit and let her throw me around and then pin me to the mattresses with her lovely breasts on top of my naked chest. It was an exciting thought. Exciting enough to get me to turn around and see the lovely creature waiting for me.

Well, I was right about one thing, she was a creature. A three-hundred-and-fifty-pound, and definitely of Asian descent, creature. Because of its large belly hanging over the genital area, it was hard to tell if it was a woman or a man. Anything this rotund would have breasts, so that was no sure way to tell. Its face looked sort of feminine, but whatever it was, I really didn't want to wrestle it anyway. In my mind, I could hear my mother scolding me, "Don't eat hamburger meat outside of this house and don't *ever* wrestle a nude woman."

"Okay . . . I say this, in no way to offend you, but I've got to get out of here." I moved toward the door as I explained I was leaving. The blob blocked my path and started taking slow, deliberate steps in my direction. I figured I could out-run it, so I gave a head fake to the left and ran like hell to the right. I was wrong. It was big and fast. It dove for my leg. A big meaty hand grabbed my foot then gave a quick jerk, knocking me to the floor.

"Come here, Cookie, I'm going to show you something," it said, as it rolled over revealing what I believed to be a vagina, though I'd never seen anything that big or that hairy or that scary before. Why was this happening to me? I had spent so much time fantasizing about wrestling a beautiful nude woman. In my dreams it was all so clear. And it was all because of that damn neon sign in front of the Wrestle a Nude Woman place. What ever happened to truth in advertising? Why didn't they have a big fat neon girl above the door instead of a gorgeous one? I had to figure out some way to escape as I was pulled toward her. There was no getting away. The she-monster began to wrap her arms around me. I was engulfed in her flesh.

"What's your name?" she asked, making small talk as she got me in a scissor lock, her enormous legs around my waist.

"Uh . . . Mason Green," I groaned, as I struggled to get free. Mason Green, the network representative assigned to *In the Swim* was little more than a bureaucrat who, from time to time, would demand unnecessary changes in the scripts. An occasional thorn in my side, his was the name that popped into my mind.

Evidently, because of my hesitation, it wasn't a convincing answer. Before I could catch another breath of air, the massive legs squeezed my middle again.

"Come on, now. What's your name?" she grunted, sounding irritated that our relationship was not based on honesty and trust.

I felt terrible for Mason Green's family as I once again swore I was him. They would have to endure the shame once his name appeared in the obituaries with the details of his horrible death at the Wrestle a Nude Woman place.

Suddenly a big paw grabbed between my legs. My whole

sexual life flashed before my eyes. Fortunately, my wallet was there to protect me. Or so I thought. Sumo girl was pulling off my briefs. As they went below my knees and my wallet fell to the floor, I was totally exposed. There was nothing I could do to stop her. With her legs wrapped around my waist and my arms pinned to my sides by her one-handed bear hug, she completely controlled me. With her free hand, she grabbed my wallet and opened it.

"Barry Klein," she read from my driver's license. "You know, Aki doesn't like men to lie to her." Her name was Aki. I knew I should remember that when I tried to piece this nightmare together for the police.

"Are you the Barry Klein who writes for *In the Swim*? Aki asked.

How could she know that? There was nothing in my wallet that said where I worked. Oh, great. Here I was, having the shit beat of me by a telepathic whale. What should I do? Should I tell her the truth? She hurt me the last time I lied.

"Yeah, that's me," I said, making a pathetic attempt to reach my underwear. It was impossible the way she had me.

"Don't move." Suddenly, she let go and jumped to her feet. Just like that I was free, gasping heavily, trying to get air into my lungs. I started to get up.

"I said don't move!" Of course, she had. When will I learn

to listen? I froze, not moving a muscle. As she left the room, my mind was racing. What was she going to do to me when she came back? How did she know about the show? Did she like it? Did she hate it? Would that determine my fate? I began to think about all the fat jokes I had written over the years. I liked writing fat jokes. Now I was going to pay. Rhonda Silverman used to warn me that I was hurting the feelings of fat people, and I would just laugh at her. Well, now, she would get the last laugh. Killed by a fat girl. How perfect. Had I written any fat jokes specifically about fat Asians? If I had, surely the coroner would list that as the cause of death. A particularly offensive scene about some rotund "Number one son" who couldn't get enough mu shu pork came to mind. I was a dead man.

Before I could figure out my next move, Aki returned wearing a bathrobe. It made me feel self-conscious because all I had covering me was the wallet I had dared to retrieve in her absence. Aki had something in her hand. It looked like a script.

"Mr. Klein, I know you must get asked this about a thousand times a day, but I've got this spec script . . . it's an *All in the Family* . . . and well, is there any way I could get you to read it?"

Incredible. Even the Wrestle a Nude Woman woman had a spec script. Wasn't there anyone in California who was what they claimed to be? Were there any waiters who were actually waiters and not actors who happened to be waiting on tables? Were there any doctors who didn't drop the names of their show business patients in an attempt to align themselves with the lights, cameras, and action? Were there any nude women who were wrestling just for the love of the sport and not just doing it to earn a living while waiting for their big writing break? Well, Barry, you could ask these pertinent questions of this woman who is capable of snapping you in two like a rice noodle or you could take her script and get out with your life. I immediately took it to cover my backside.

"I'd love to read it. I'm always looking for new writers." It's amazing how, compared to being totally naked, you can feel completely clothed with just a wallet and a spec script.

"I hope you like it. It's about Archie going to a Wrestle a Nude Woman place."

"Well, at least you've done your research," I said, sweeping up my underwear and heading for the door.

"Should I call you in the office? You know . . . to see if you like it?" she asked. I guess for some reason she suspected I might not get back to her.

"No, no—I'll call you. Sometimes I'm hard to reach." That's all I needed. I could just hear the howls when Marcia came into the rewrite room to announce there was somebody from the

Wrestle a Nude Woman place on the phone for me. It was just too much ammunition for a room full of comedy writers.

"Okay. But you will call, won't you? My friends think it's really funny."

I could tell Aki wanted out of the wrestling biz. She suddenly seemed human as she walked me to the beaded curtain. I was glad that's where she stopped. She let me get dressed in private. Well, almost in private. The old woman took one more peek from her office to see if I was still alive.

Leaving, I was thrilled to see my car hadn't been stolen. I tossed Aki's script on the seat next to me and took off. After a few blocks, the fear began to fade. My trip to the Wrestle a Nude Woman Place had been exhilarating. Just the fact that I had gotten myself to do it. I guess there were sexual implications, too. For the first time in almost a decade, I had been naked in front of a woman other than Linda. It felt okay. I certainly could do it again. Perhaps with someone more attractive than Aki.

I had only driven a few minutes before realizing that my experience with Aki had not helped me to feel centered. On the contrary, I felt more out of control than ever. Had I left too soon? Is wrestling a nude woman a two-out-of three falls experience? I had to quiet this churning chaos. But I wasn't ready for the solitude of Topanga Canyon. I headed back to Hollywood.

* * *

When Marcia opened her apartment door and saw me
standing there, she was, to say the least, surprised.

"Hi," she said, as she looked me up and down, trying to
figure out what I was doing there.

"I was wondering if that invitation to drop by was still
good?"

The sudden appearance of two lovely nipples pressing
against her T-shirt was my answer as she swung the door open and
pointed me in. It was late, eleven-thirty, and Marcia was relaxing
in a pair of cut-off sweatpants. They showed off her legs, which
were buffed to a high polish.

The apartment was fairly new so it was clean and fresh.
There was a good-sized kitchen that opened to a dining room–
living room. The parquet wood tiles were a cheap imitation of
the real thing and Marcia had the sense to cover most of it with
cheap imitation Persian rugs. The place was sparsely furnished,
a reminder that it wasn't easy living alone in Los Angeles on a
secretary's salary. There was a dining room table and chairs, a set
that, judging from the amount of chrome and fake wood Formica,
was probably bought from someone who claimed to be the Dinette
King. A sectional couch with lots of throw pillows sat behind a
cocktail table. Because it looked so much like a squat version of

the dining room table, I assumed the King threw it into the deal. I sat on the couch thinking Marcia would join me.

"Would you like some wine or something?" She looked delicious as she asked.

"Sure."

We didn't talk at all as she got the wine. I wanted to, but couldn't think of anything to say. Finally, she came back with two wine glasses, gave me one, and lightly clinked hers against it. We both sipped.

"So, what are you doing here?" My God, she was being direct. She wanted to know the deal and she wanted to know right away. I tried desperately to come up with some witty answer. There was nothing.

"I don't know. I've been married for eight years. I've never cheated on my wife. But since you came to work, I can't keep my eyes off you. Or my mind. When you touched me in the rewrite room tonight, I thought I was going to go out of my mind."

"I know. Me, too."

Thank you, Lord. I was still expecting her to not have any idea what I was talking about.

"So, what do you want to do about it?" she asked.

"I want to do lots of things, but first I want to kiss you." She gave a little smile and waited. I would have to make a move.

I leaned in and kissed her, putting one arm around her while holding the wine glass in the other. It made a passionate embrace impossible. Unfortunately, I didn't realize that until after I had put the cold glass in the middle of her back. That ended the first kiss with a small scream from Marcia. I could have been devastated. I should have been devastated. But I had made it through the first kiss without falling off the couch. In my mind that made it a success. Besides, after the scream we both laughed.

"Can I take that before you hurt someone?" She took my wine glass and put it on the cocktail table. Then she laid across my lap so that we could be in each other's arms even though I was sitting up and her legs were on the couch. Now we were free to kiss and hug and explore. All I could think about was how much I wanted to touch her . . . and how amazing it is that you can put wine glasses on Formica and never have to worry about them leaving rings. The idea of putting a glass down without a coaster was heresy in my mother's house. Now, at one of the most critical moments of my life, a moment when I see my left hand, the hand that's still wearing my wedding band, about to play with this girl's body, all I can think about is the miracle of Formica. Marcia must have sensed I was drifting and that all I needed was more than one tongue in my mouth to bring my concentration around to the task at hand. All thoughts of my mother and the damage that wet stemware can cause quickly disappeared.

Serious fondling began. I wanted to feel her body next to mine, but it was impossible with her across my lap. I didn't want to stop kissing. I tried slowly shifting my weight but, as it turned out, I was sitting on the crack where the two sections of the sectional couch met. Each time I tried to move a little, they'd move a little farther apart. It wouldn't be long before I'd slip down to the floor. The impending disaster was impossible to ignore. We had to stop kissing.

"You know, whenever I've thought about this, I always saw us naked in bed. Do you think we could make that happen?" All right! Listen to you asking for what you want.

Marcia sat up, which sent the couch sections sliding apart. She wound up on the couch. I landed on the floor.

"I hope this looks cute and vulnerable instead of like I'm a total dork."

She reached down to help me up. "Come on." She led me by the hand toward the bedroom. I quietly followed.

All the bedroom had was a king-size bed and a TV perched atop a wooden milk crate. It seemed sparse. On the other hand, I couldn't think of anything else we'd need.

"Why don't you make yourself comfortable? I'll be right back." Before she left, she switched on the TV and turned up the sound. "The walls are kind of thin."

A noise maker! She must be a noise maker! Oh boy, oh boy. I began to get undressed as I watched the sports report. I was naked well before she got back and had to decide whether to get under the covers. I struck as casual a pose as one can strike when getting ready to be naked in front of somebody who's never seen your stuff before. I semi paid attention to a story of how Bob Macadoo was blending in with the Lakers as I waited for Marcia to come back. She was coming back, wasn't she? I mean, this really would be life doing its worst. What better way to teach me a lesson than to leave me here totally naked. Well, totally naked except for my wedding ring. I quickly removed it, jumped out of bed, and stuffed it deep into my pants pocket so it wouldn't fall out. When I'd get home, I didn't want to have to come up with a story of where my wedding ring was.

Jumping back onto the bed and reassuming the casual pose, I began to think about what kinds of retribution the universe might have in store for me if I went through with this. It was the universe's fault that I was here at all. I'd been a good boy and now Fred was going to be the new producer of *In the Swim*. Why be a good boy? The universe had taken too damn long. The debate ended when Marcia came back into the room. She was wearing exactly what I hoped she'd be wearing. Nothing. She looked great.

She stood next to the bed for a moment so I could admire her. She was, indeed, a redhead. Not only that, she had trimmed her pubic hair into kind of a close cropped crew cut that was shaped like a heart. I was guessing: not a virgin.

Marcia and I did the deed. It wasn't bad. It wasn't great. But it wasn't bad. There had been more exhilaration when I had finished wrestling Aki. As for going to bed with Marcia, I was just glad it was over.

EIGHT

Grace Seems Much Higher When You're Falling

Scotty O'Rourke lay dead in a pool of blood, his skull crushed by a blow from his own metal flashlight. As the police searched his shabby, one-room apartment, they were disheartened by the lack of clues. It looked like another Los Angeles murder would go unsolved.

"Barry, would you hurry up? I've got to get into the shower." Good wife Linda thankfully interrupted my morning's fantasy version of Scotty's demise. I had made up an ending that was too gory even for Scotty. Better, however, to think about doing Scotty in than continue thinking about the previous night. Although I had gone to sleep confident that *shtupping* Frau Heilger was in no way going to affect my marriage, I wasn't so certain when I woke up.

The first half of my morning shower was spent, not dreamily concocting the old Irishman's final curtain, but rather, giving myself a thorough once-over in search of any signs of VD. I had not heeded Mr. Pedlosky, my high school gym teacher's sage advice from health class; "Fellas, don't go into the wrong neighborhood without protection." I was never quite sure what Pedlosky meant until this moment when it became clear that a condom was the protection and the area between Marcia's legs was, without a doubt, the wrong neighborhood. I scrubbed my entire body hoping to wash away my feelings of guilt from breaking a major commandment. As I got dressed, kissed Linda good-bye, and headed for the office, I swore again and again on all that was holy—if all that was holy was still paying any attention to me—I would never, ever commit such a mortal sin again. I had to admit, though, I did have fun . . . and how about that fuzzy little valentine? Woof. Stop it! Don't you realize you're lucky you weren't struck by lightning while driving home? That's what you deserve.

I had to get myself to stop the mental flogging. I made a mistake. Anybody who had been under the pressure I'd been under might have slipped up once. Okay, so I won't get a medal. But they won't drum me out of the corps, will they? Surely, a just and forgiving God will understand one minor transgression.

Climbing the stairs of K building, I wasn't looking forward to spending the rest of the day in paradise lost. When I reached the top, there was a diversion. Tommy was playing hall golf. He was lining up a putt, trying to get his golf ball into a tipped-over coffee cup.

"Fred's gone. His office has been cleaned out. He took everything," Tommy said as he stroked the ball into the cup. I was glad I hadn't gotten there any sooner. It was a long putt, and I was sure we would have bet a few dollars as to whether he would make it.

"Has anybody tried to find out where he is?" I asked, doing about as much detective work as the police did for the bloodied Scotty in my early morning daydream.

"Nope." Tommy picked up the ball and cup and headed for my office. I followed while trying to imagine what had happened to Fred during his meeting with Bobby. Apparently, Fred had not become the new producer of the show. That would be good news. Maybe the new producer didn't even want Fred on the staff. That would be bad news. Because Tommy and I hadn't been consulted on the firing of Fred, that probably meant we weren't the new producers.

Tommy and I walked toward my office. Marcia was at her desk. "Hi, there," she said, obviously directing the greeting to me.

My God, does she have to be so cheery? Why doesn't she just stand on her desk and announce to the entire floor what we did last night? Would it be any less obvious? Settle down, Barry. Just say hello and everything will be fine.

"Hey, how ya doin'?" I said with no real feeling and no need for a response.

"Fine. How are *you* doin'?"

Did she have to ask? "Okay . . . I guess." I closed my office door just as I said it. In retrospect, I suppose sending flowers would have been a more appropriate way to say, "Thanks for last night." I didn't want to do that, though. I didn't even want to think about it. As soon as I shut the door, the phone rang. She wasn't going to leave me alone.

"You don't have to be such a grump. Nobody knows."

"Uh-huh." I tried to make it sound like I was talking about something else entirely. I didn't want Tommy to know what was going on.

Marcia continued, "And Bobby Mitchell called."

"Why didn't you say something?" I couldn't believe she had spent so much time on how are you's and don't be a grumps.

"I was going to. But the way you ran through here . . . " She wasn't going to let me get away with treating her badly. An apology was coming, but she had already hung up. I immediately called Alice Martin.

"Hi, Alice. It's Barry. Bobby called?"

"Yes, Barry. Can you and Tommy come down here?"

"Do you know what he wants?" I was hoping to get a little hint. I was sure Alice knew something.

"No, I don't. Just come on down." She said it in a singsong way that meant she knew exactly what he wanted.

Tommy and I took off for Bobby's office. On the way past Marcia's desk I stopped, looked her in the eye, and smiled. "We'll be back soon, okay?" That was my apology.

"Thank you." She accepted.

Tommy and I got down the K building stairs faster than the bouncing dough boy, Howie Clark, ever had. We arrived at Bobby's office out of breath and Alice took us into his office. We sat in the two wooden captain's chairs directly across the desk from Bobby who looked up from the script he was reading. He didn't waste any time.

"Guys, Fred Maxwell is gone. He didn't want to work on the show if you two were producing. Start looking for a replacement."

Tommy and I waited for more. After a minute of watching Bobby continue his reading, it became evident that was all he was going to say. Tommy and I glanced at each other, confused as

to what had happened. That was it? After another minute Bobby
looked up.

"Is there anything else, guys?"

"Are you saying that we're the producers?" Tommy asked
what I couldn't. I was afraid Bobby would laugh out loud and give
us a hearty "Of course you're not the producers."

"Yeah. You're the producers. Hire somebody to replace
Fred." He said it like we were bothering him with trivia.

"Sure, no problem," I said in an attempt to reassure Bobby
that he had made the right decision. And in case he missed the
point, I added, "Thanks, Bobby. You won't be sorry." Then,
standing to leave. I offered my hand to Bobby to shake. He seemed
surprised to see it but shook it anyway. He then shook Tommy's,
picked up the phone, and instructed Alice to get him Grant Tinker.
As Tommy and I were leaving the office, Bobby called to us.

"Don't screw this up, guys."

Well, I guess that's kind of like, "Congratulations, I know
you'll be great."

About halfway back to K building, it sunk in. We were,
indeed, the producers of *In the Swim,* even though I was a bit
ticked off by the way it was handled. I mean, there couldn't have
been less of a ceremony. It would have been nice if someone from
the studio or cast or Bobby's office had wished us well. And what

about a raise? Were we getting a raise or a bigger office? Did anybody bother to tell our agent, or did he just agree that whatever Paragon Studios wanted to do to us was fine with him? We'd been given the job because nobody else would take it. That was the truth. But we were the producers of a hit show. Now, even if the job killed us, at least we'd get a decent obituary in *Variety*.

When we got to the top of the stairs, the writing staff and secretaries from our show and a bunch of the people from *All Aboard,* the show that shared the floor with us, were waiting for Tommy and me. They were all holding paper cups filled with champagne. Alice Martin had called ahead to tell them of our promotion. Donna Morris had kept a couple of bottles of champagne hidden in *All Aboard's* refrigerator. She'd been confident all along that we'd eventually get the promotion.

We had a good little celebration. Tommy even pushed Howie down the stairs. We partied for about a half hour and then like usual it was time to get to work. We agreed to meet in the rewrite room in ten minutes. That would give everybody time to sober up some and take care of any personal business. In spite of all the fun and laughter that surrounded our work, there was always enough discipline to get re-focused. For me this discipline came not from any deep seeded work ethic, but from the fear of what the studio would do to me if I screwed them.

Heading to my office to call Linda with the good news, it
dawned on me that the universe had come through even though
I'd made a substantial moral slip-up. It was a time for thanks and
promises that I wouldn't slip up again. I got to my desk and began
to check my messages when I heard my door close. Marcia had
followed me in and now was moving toward me. Before I could do
or say anything, she planted a big wet one on my lips. I was scared
that Tommy or Donna or Rhonda or everybody at the party would
barge in while we were kissing. But I didn't stop. I wanted to be
cool enough to handle it.

"See that. I knew you'd get it," she said, as she stroked my
face. She was certainly more comfortable with the situation than I.

"Thanks." I slowly took a step backward before turning
toward my desk, trying to make the move look casual. The truth
was, I knew getting caught with Marcia would be incredibly
stupid. Two very powerful congressmen, Wilbur Mills of Arkansas
and Wayne Hays of Ohio had, in recent years, been shamed
out of office by sex scandals. Mills was sleeping with a foreign
woman, Fanne Foxe, a stripper who went by the stage name of
"The Argentine Firecracker." Hays, like me, was sleeping with
his secretary. Taxpayers were outraged when they learned that the
woman couldn't even type. If discovered, I doubted that Marcia's
all-American secretarial skills would make my job any more secure

or my shame any less than that of the ousted politicos.

"I want you to come over tonight to celebrate." She wasn't asking me. She was telling me. Had things moved along that quickly? We'd only been together one time. As I had explained to the universe, that was a slip-up. It didn't mean we'd automatically continue to get together. Just the opposite — we definitely weren't going to see each other again. How was I going to tell her?

"Sure, fine." I'd tell her that things were over between us at her place. Just in case there was crying or screaming or some other scene I didn't want happening at work. I'd just go to her place, tell her, split, and get on with my life.

Not knowing my intentions, Marcia smiled, bent down, and kissed me again.

"I'm going to be thinking about you all day. You and that glorious cock of yours."

Holy shit, Barry, did you hear what she said? She said "your cock." Right in front of you. What kind of woman actually calls it that? A hooker? A porno queen? Stopping this before it went too far would be a daunting task. Nonetheless, I was determined to get back on the straight and narrow. "Married for eight years with only one slip up," suddenly had a ring to it.

* * *

When I arrived at Marcia's she had already gotten out of

her work clothes and slipped into a black teddy with matching lace panties. As I entered the apartment she did a sexy little pirouette and said, "This is for you, Mr. Producer."

"Marcia, we have to talk," I replied in a very businesslike tone. I took her hand and led her to the couch. I let her sit down first so that I could position myself at least five feet away from her. I began to explain that seeing each other wasn't a good idea.

"I'm not comfortable with us kissing in the office. It makes me nuts," I said.

"Weren't you nuts the past few weeks just wanting to be with me?" she pointed out. "That was nuts."

"True, but I don't want to ruin my marriage. I've been with Linda for a long time."

"I don't want you to ruin your marriage, either. Look, I don't want you to leave your wife. You're a happily married man. I don't want you to be miserable."

Gee, I didn't realize she was so concerned about my marriage. Maybe this would be okay. At least on this plane. I would deal with the burning for eternity in Hell when I got there. No, Barry. Be strong.

"What happens if you fall in love with me? You're not going to care about my marriage if you fall in love." I was sure I had her there.

"Fall in love with you?" she asked incredulously. "Sweetie, I just want to have some fun." She was moving toward me.

Okay, here's the thing about having sex. It's a lot like baking cookies. When you bake cookies, you should always throw away the first batch. They're going to be okay, but they won't be great. There's something about getting the cookie sheet warmed up or something. It's the second batch that's a keeper. Same thing when you're in the sack. Everybody's too nervous the first time. "Am I big enough?" "Am I small enough?" "Am I hard enough?" "Am I soft enough?" The first time is tentative. The second time, you can get down to serious screwing. And, of course, that's what Marcia and I did.

It was wild and uninhibited. We started in the living room and moved to the bedroom only after a stop in the dining room for a candle and then the kitchen for some wine. I felt alive—electric—like I'd never felt before. It was great right up until I slipped with one "I love you." I couldn't believe I said it. I knew I didn't love her. What I meant to say was, "Man, you've got a wild pussy." But it just came out, "I love you."

Marcia said, "Shhhhh" and proceeded to perform at least three different acts that I assume can only be found in the *Supplemental Guide to the Karma Sutra*. Wow. It was perfect. Until we finished, lying in each other's arms, sweaty and spent, and I heard her whisper, "I love you, too."

I got home about twelve-thirty and found Linda already asleep. When I slid into bed, she awoke just enough to kiss me. I didn't know if I should tell her the news of my promotion. That would really wake her up. Then she might want to celebrate. Not good. Linda was like a bloodhound. She would certainly pick up Marcia's scent. Even though I had showered thoroughly at Marcia's, my upper lip still retained the slightest wisp of her perfume. The good news would have to wait until morning.

Lying in bed, waiting for sleep to shut my brain down for the day, Marcia's scent was an unrelenting reminder of what had happened on the night I planned to tell her we wouldn't be seeing each other again. I began to bargain. How many more times would I be able to be with Marcia, and how should I space those times out? The sex was too good to pretend that it wasn't going to happen again. I'd have to ration it while trying to find some way to end the affair. That would be the right thing to do. Wouldn't it? Unless there was some way to keep both Linda and Marcia happy. Could I do that? I fell asleep without a satisfactory answer.

I spent the next few months trying unsuccessfully to stop seeing Marcia. I hated lying to Linda. Even worse, I was beginning to have performance problems at home. One night, I became aware that even though Linda had her hand in my pants, a move that up until now had always gotten the desired results, I had a dead chicken between my legs. Being a good sport, and loving a challenge, Linda did all she could to revive Mr. Limpet. It just wasn't happening. All the thoughts I could muster, hoping to fall upon just the right fantasy to revive my libido, were in vane.

"What's wrong?" Linda asked, having never seen this problem before.

What could I say? I've been doing it with my secretary and I bet that's got me all messed up in the head? Right. Why not just start writing alimony checks and get it over with?

"I don't know," I sighed. "Maybe it's all the pressure at work. You know, sometimes I wonder if it's worth it." Nice touch, Barry. Like you'd give up show business for a minute even if it was the reason for your amorous slump.

The truth was, work was going well. Tommy and I had settled into a rhythm. Week after week, we were turning out good shows. We replaced Fred with Aki, the nude wrestler. After finally reading her spec script, "Archy Wrestles a Nude Woman," I had no choice. The way she described Archy Bunker's reaction to the huge, naked, Japanese woman was side-splitting. When Archy finally had to tell someone what had happened to him, he tells Meathead. It was a great scene in a great script. Once I got Aki to swear she'd never reveal how we met, I gave her script to Tommy and Donna. They loved it, too. We immediately hired her. As a result, the writing staff was stronger than ever. We were sailing along. The Ladies were happy. The studio was happy. Bobby was happy. Happy, happy, happy. Everybody but me. Having the show run with no apparent problems just wasn't enough.

If only my personal life could run as smoothly as my professional life. I needed advice but had nowhere to turn. I thought back to a lecture my father had given me when I was thirteen. It was his version of a sex talk although it was completely void of useful information like how or when "Tab A" was inserted into "Slot B."

"Barry, don't go to bed with a woman unless you're completely in love with her. Otherwise, you'll suffer the curse of the Klein Clan," he warned, in an ominous tone.

"Curse of the Klein Clan?" I nervously queried. "How can we be cursed? I thought the Klein Clan was special."

"We are special. That's why once a woman has been to bed with a Klein, she'll never want to let him go," Dad cautioned.

"Sounds like more of curse on the woman," I said, suspecting, even at thirteen, that going to bed with one of the Klein men couldn't be that big of a deal.

"I'm only telling you what my father told me," he explained. "I never wanted to test it, so I've only been to bed with your mother."

My parents "doing it" was, of course, too disgusting a thought for my teenaged mind, so the conversation quickly came to an end. Over the ensuing years, I would fondly think back on the ludicrous story as woman after woman had absolutely no trouble, whatsoever, being done with me surprisingly soon after bedding down.

Now, I began to wonder. What if my father was right? What if this was some kind of random curse that took a while to warm up? What if, because of the Klein Curse, I would never be rid of Marcia? How could it be the curse? Marcia wasn't the problem. I was. Each time I'd have performance problems with Linda, I'd swear to myself I'd stop going to bed with Marcia. Yet that's what I always ended up doing. Sex with her was like heroin. Being without it wasn't an option. But the trouble it was causing was getting worse and worse. I hated myself for becoming a liar and a cheat. Linda kept asking what was wrong and assured me she sincerely wanted to help. She eventually suggested we get professional help.

"Barry, I think we should see a marriage counselor," she announced one night in bed after another unsuccessful attempt at conjugal bliss.

"How come?" I asked. I would have had to be catatonic

not to know why we needed help. I wanted help. But I suspected the marriage counselor would dig around until the truth came out about Marcia. Like any addict, I kept my stash hidden.

"How come?" Her frustration began to boil. "Let's see . . . we have no sex life, we hardly see each other, and we never talk anymore!"

"Oh, come on. It's not that bad. We talk. Besides, when would we go see this counselor? I get up. I go to the office. I come home."

"I can't believe you won't go," she said, stung by my unwillingness to help find a solution to our problems.

"Maybe after the season," I said, rolling over with my back to her in order to end the conversation. What was the matter with me? Why was I willing to risk everything I had with Linda to be with Marcia, a woman I didn't really like? Not that she was so unlikable. Other than sexually, though, there just wasn't any connection. I didn't respect her, either, because she was a woman who would go to bed with a married man. What a hypocrite! So what? Hypocrites have needs too.

Time went on and the lies grew bolder. I started claiming to have to work on Saturdays and Sundays and that the studio switchboard was closed on weekends so that Linda couldn't reach me. Then I'd spend the day in bed with Marcia. Always in bed.

She'd want to do other things—go to a movie, go shopping. No thanks. Occasionally, she'd even threaten to stop seeing me if we didn't go out. Yet she couldn't stop, either. We were suffering from the hopeless condition that exists when two people are totally wrong for each other but their genitals work so perfectly together that there's no way they can control themselves. Marcia and I had it bad.

After seeing Marcia for only about two months, I was forced to concoct the ultimate lie—an excuse for why I'd be away from home for an entire weekend. Marcia wanted us to go away together and had been working on me continuously. I gave in one night, in a moment of weakness, when it was obvious she wouldn't undress until I agreed. I never really assumed we'd end up going, and if I stonewalled and pretended that I forgot, maybe Marcia would forget it, too. Well, not forget it, but she'd get so tired of repeating how I broke my promise that she'd drop it. Wrong. Not only wouldn't she forget it, but she went about her business planning our weekend out of town.

"Why do we have to go away? Why can't we just spend the weekend at your place?" I pleaded.

"Because I don't want to spend an entire weekend in my apartment. I know you. You won't want to go anywhere because you'll be afraid someone will see us. You'll just want to stay in bed and order in pizza." It sounded to me like she had a pretty good plan there. "Barry, I don't know why you think people care what you do." she said smugly. "Everybody knows we're seeing each other. Why don't you just relax and have a good time?"

"What do you mean everybody knows? How do they know?" I thought I'd been so careful to cover my tracks.

"You leave the rewrite room ten times a night to come make-out by my desk. Don't you think they suspect something?"

"Bladder trouble. They suspect bladder trouble." The idea that anybody knew was too much for me to handle. I still wanted to be that nice Jewish boy from New Jersey who made good in Hollywood. Married for eight years, you know. And in Hollywood. Who stays married for eight years in Hollywood?

"Fine. They don't know. Let me show you where I made reservations." She was holding a brochure and telling me about the place we were going to but I wasn't listening. All I could think about was that she had already made reservations. In whose name? What if they called my house to confirm the reservation? What if they called just to tell my wife what her cheating husband was up to? Marcia was going on and on about how each room had its own private hot tub and I was figuring what to tell Linda when she'd ask me why I had removed all the phones in the house. It was the only solution I could come up with to avoid unwanted calls.

I hoped I'd do better if a call actually came from La Mancha, the Palm Springs resort I'd be going to the very next weekend.

Marcia laid out the whole plan. We'd leave right after the show Friday night and still get to Palm Springs early enough to soak in the hot tub. Marcia would not be sidetracked. She was going away with her fella for the weekend even if he did have a hangdog look on his face.

"What's wrong now?" she asked in a tone that suggested I better not have any problems with her plans.

"I just wish I knew what I was going to tell Linda."

"Tell her the truth, Barry," she said, as more of a dare than as a bona fide suggestion.

"I can't do that!" I didn't like talking to her about Linda. To me, Linda wasn't any of her business. It's hard enough spinning all those plates. It's a lot tougher if the plates talk about each other.

"You know you're going to leave her, don't you?"

How dare she sit there so calmly, so sure of her prediction? No, harlot. I'd be married to Linda forever. I was going for the record. Life might be in a bit of a mess at the moment, but I'll always be with Linda. Linda and I make sense together. Marcia and I, on the other hand . . . Marcia and I . . . Marcia was at the other end of the couch playing with herself. She threw her tiny silk panties at my face and winked. I was at her mercy.

The ultimate lie I ended up telling Linda was that Bobby
Mitchell was taking the producers of all his shows to the desert
for a weekend of story meetings. Bobby was known for taking
producers to exotic spots to think up new episodes. It was tax
deductible, and it was a good excuse to spend a weekend with a
bunch of funny guys. Because I had recently been promoted to
producer, this would be my first weekend away with Bobby, I
told her. It seemed like a believable story. I don't know if Linda
believed it, but she accepted it as another in a long list of reasons
why we wouldn't be spending time together.

That Friday night, after the show, Marcia and I left for Palm
Springs. We pulled up to La Mancha at about one o'clock in the
morning. A uniformed guard came out of his little house that stood
by the large wrought-iron gate. The entire resort was surrounded
by an eight-foot-high wall. Privacy was obviously an important
thing here at La Mancha. I liked that.

"Barry Klein," I announced to the guard as if I was alone.

"Good evening, Mr. Klein," he said, without even looking
in the car to check out Marcia. "Did you have a good trip?"

"Fine. Thank you . . . Vinnie," I replied, reading the name
tag on his shirt.

"Here's your key, sir. Casida number seventeen. You can
take care of the paperwork in the morning. Enjoy your stay." With

that he handed me a key and opened the gate. What a relief. For the last half hour I'd been dreading our arrival and dealing with Vinnie or some version of Vinnie. I didn't want to go through the "Mr. Klein and . . . Mrs. Klein?" routine. I didn't want the judgmental looks. Vinnie made it easy. I loved Vinnie and made a mental note to try and find out his last name. He'd be the perfect replacement for Scotty O'Rourke after I killed him.

    "There's seventeen," Marcia announced, pointing to a sign barely visible in the moonlight. We pulled in and headed for the casida which, evidently, is Spanish for "just a condo." The place was reasonably comfortable. It had a small living room with a kitchenette and a separate bedroom. At the end of the living room was a sliding glass door that led to a small hot tub surrounded by a high wall, ensuring complete privacy. On the table in the breakfast area was a flower arrangement and a basket of fresh fruit. The fruit was from the management. The flowers were from me. I had enough sense to know I needed to do something nice for Marcia. It had been such a struggle getting me here, and there was still the question of whether I would whine and be miserable all weekend. That certainly wasn't my intent, but with me, who knew? I had called the front desk at La Mancha earlier in the day and asked them to arrange the flower delivery. It should have been a simple thing, but they had to complicate it by asking me what I wanted to put on the card. I didn't want to put anything on it—once I expressed something on the card, there would be proof of my feelings for Marcia. At first, I told the girl at the desk to just put "Barry" on the card, but she wouldn't do it.

"You have to put more, Mr. Klein. Whomever you're bringing is going to want more than just 'Barry.'" She had been through this before, knowing not to say "your wife" or "your friend" or some other variation of "the woman you're going to be shacking up with all weekend." Instead, going with the very safe and grammatically correct "whomever." You have to listen to someone like that. Together we came up with "Love, Barry." Surprisingly, it worked. Marcia was thrilled with the show of affection, no matter how minute.

The first night at La Mancha was great. We had fun. We had lust. Everything was terrific until, as we slipped off to sleep, I wondered if Linda was waiting up for me to call with the phone number as I had promised. It was three-thirty. Marcia was asleep. I could sneak off to the living room and call. Surely Linda would have gone to sleep by now. I didn't know what to do. It was the fuel for a fitful night's sleep.

Marcia woke up about nine-thirty the next morning and found me in the kitchen. I had been up since six, racked with guilt, and snuck off to the local Safeway to buy groceries for the weekend. I was hoping to convince Marcia that we would stay in the condo for all our meals. My plan worked through breakfast. We had bagels, juice, and coffee in bed. We had a little of each other for dessert and then I turned on the TV, hoping to find some early morning sporting event other than professional bass fishing. Marcia immediately turned the set off.

"Let's go play some tennis," she said as she rolled on top of me, punctuating her request with a kiss.

"Maybe later." Her body felt good. I didn't want to move.

"Come on. Let's go." With that she jumped up and pulled her tennis outfit from her bag. There was no getting around this. I was going to have to go outside.

When we walked onto the tennis court, my heart went to my throat. There, playing in the early morning desert sun, was Bobby Mitchell across the net from his wife. For a split second the optimist in me kicked in and I thought, "Well, at least I didn't lie to Linda. I'm spending the weekend in Palm Springs with Bobby Mitchell." Then an overwhelming sense of embarrassment took over. I was a liar and a cheat and now other people would know that, too. I wanted to run away, hoping Bobby hadn't seen me. Bobby and his wife had finished their set and were heading for the courtside bench. The same bench where Marcia was putting her racket cover.

"Hi, Bobby," Marcia said, pleasantly as pie, as if she and Bobby had been buds forever.

"Great to see you," Bobby replied, having absolutely no idea who this person was. It didn't matter. It was probably someone from the studio or a fan or somebody who deserved a genuine Bobby Mitchell greeting.

"Marcia Heilger from *In the Swim*. I work with Barry," she said, pointing to me.

The moment I heard my name I did an about face, hoping they hadn't seen me. Before I could start running, Marcia called out, "Barry, it's Bobby."

I froze. How silly would it look if I zipped my racket cover over my head? Bobby's wife might not know which Barry I was if my face was hidden. The giant "Prince" across the cover might lead her to believe I was eccentric royalty. Bobby, of course, would know and might be offended that I chose to say hello to his wife while wearing a vinyl bag instead of a normal tennis hat. I slowly turned to greet them. I wanted to vanish into the desert but stood there silently as introductions were made all around. Bobby's wife had met me a couple of times at studio functions. She knew I wasn't married to this girl who was now shaking her hand. We were all very polite, acting as if nothing was wrong. I sat on the bench and watched them leave the court.

"I'm sorry, Barry, I didn't know." Marcia was trying to make it better. She knew she couldn't. The damage had been done. We played a half-hearted set of tennis. She would have allowed me to go right back to the room if I had wanted, but what was the point? The wound had been inflicted. The rest of the weekend was spent with me wanting to go home. Needing to go home. But I couldn't do that to Marcia. I had to spend this weekend with her if she was going to be waiting for me in bed after work. Or whenever else I needed to be there with her. She, in turn, made our stay as bearable as possible. We stayed in the room most of the time. Instead of going to the pool, we played in our private hot tub. We watched TV and played backgammon. We cooked our meals in the room and made it through the weekend.

I never recovered from the chance meeting with Bobby and his wife. Over the next few weeks I felt increasingly worse about cheating on Linda. But it didn't stop me from doing so. In fact, I was increasing my time with Marcia. I kept finding reasons not to be home and became very moody. Linda asked me repeatedly what was wrong. "Nothing" was my answer. "Everything" was more like it. Each day I prayed for the courage to tell the truth. I couldn't. I waited weeks. I waited months. The TV season moved on. The show moved on. More and more time spent with Marcia. Constantly telling Linda I needed time alone. Time alone wasn't just a lie to tell Linda. It was also an option no longer really available to me. Because as the season ended, I could no longer stand myself.

NINE

The Bumpy Ride Home

The Allman Brothers were seventeen minutes and forty-two seconds into "Whipping Post" when Linda hit the eject button. We hadn't said a word to each other since we left the wrap party.

"You'll have to let my lawyer know who she should contact about the settlement," Linda began.

"Lawyer? You already have a lawyer?"

"Yes. And you should have one, too."

"When did you get a lawyer? You just told me we needed time alone about an hour ago. Aren't there a few steps before the lawyer? Shouldn't we go to a marriage counselor or something?"

"I've been to a marriage counselor," she said calmly. "And I've asked you several times to come with me. But you either think that our problems aren't bad enough or you're too busy."

"Well, can't we go now?" I asked, sincerely – beginning to comprehend the serious consequences of my foolishness. "I'm sure the therapist can help us find a way to work this out."

"The therapist was the one who suggested I leave. If I stay, you'll just make me crazier, because that's the way I feel, Barry. Like I'm crazy."

You're not crazy," I said, dismissively.

"Either I'm crazy or you've been lying to me," she said, a touch of accusation in her voice.

"Lying?" I asked, with as much innocence as I could muster.

"Oh, come on. If I'm not crazy, you have to be seeing someone else. That's the only logical explanation there could be. You're never home anymore — even on weekends. You come home from work after I'm asleep. You pay no attention to me. And I'm supposed to believe that it's all because of work? That you're a seemingly healthy thirty-year-old man with no sex drive? Is that what I'm supposed believe? Please, I'm not stupid, Barry."

That was the worst part of the whole thing. The bald-faced lying. Linda deserved better.

"I'm going to ask you for the last time, Barry. Are you seeing someone else?"

The jig was up. I wanted to stop spinning plates. I wanted

the lying to end. If I was ever going to regain my self-respect, this was the step I'd have to take.

"Yes. There's someone else," I said, looking at the road straight ahead, hoping she wouldn't want more information.

She sat quietly for a moment, looking out the window, processing what I had just said. "Is it Donna?" she asked wearily, making a plausible guess.

"No," I answered emphatically.

"Then who?" she asked, in a more demanding tone.

"What difference does it make, who?" She already knew I was a liar. Did we have to get into the gory details?

"It makes a difference to me. You know, I've asked you this a hundred times over the past few months. I've asked you point blank, 'Are you sleeping with someone?' And you always said no. I could have dealt with the truth. I would have had options with the truth. That's why you didn't tell me. Everything has to be on your schedule. You didn't want to give me the choice of leaving . . . or working to fix any problems. No. You had to lie. Well, now things are on my terms. It's me who's kicking you out. But not before I know who it is." She wasn't falling apart like I had imagined. She was controlled.

"It's Marcia," I said weakly.

"Your secretary? You're fucking your secretary?" She let

out a laugh. "Oh, that's priceless. You're like the king of cliché."

I tried to defend myself. "You don't understand . . . it just happened."

"I understand completely," Linda said with confidence. "This thing with your secretary . . . it's all based on lies. Feelings . . . real feelings between a man and a woman . . . well that's one of the main reasons Vishna had me do the Pistil and Stamen Ritual."

"Please. Not Vishna. How can you take advice from a thirteen-year-old kid?"

"He's only thirteen in *this* life, Barry."

"Oh, right. What was I thinking? And what, may I ask, is the Pistil and Stamen Ritual? I don't know why, but it sounds filthy."

"Because that's where your head is. The Pistil and Stamen Ritual is a beautiful way for men and women to explore their sexuality together," Linda explained, smugly.

"Wait a minute. Did someone put their pistil in your stamen?" I asked, hoping two and two did not make four.

"Yes. That's part of the ritual."

It was all I could do to keep the car on the road. This couldn't be. Not my Linda. I didn't want to hear any more and yet there was a morbid curiosity.

"How many?" I asked.

"Rituals or pistils?" she inquired.

"There was more than one pistil?"

"Not at the same ritual. And actually, you have it backwards—the pistil is the girl and the stamen is the guy," Linda explained, as if this new information would make things better.

"Wait a minute. You're leaving me because I slept with my secretary but you've been with . . . I don't know . . . how many men?"

"Ten . . . no, eleven," she said, remembering one last stamen with a none-too-comforting smile. "But I was only doing it because I didn't understand the trouble you were having in bed. I thought maybe your impotence was my fault. I was looking for answers. I was searching for the truth."

"Oh, I see. It was my fault that you . . . eleven? There were eleven?!" Suddenly I was the lover, scorned.

"That's correct. It *was* your fault."

"Well, excuse me, Linda, but I'm having trouble seeing the difference between what I did and what you did."

As we pulled into the driveway, Linda looked me straight in the eye and explained, "I did the Pistil and Stamen Ritual. You fucked your secretary." With that, she got out of the car and headed for the house. Linda had played her trump card. Of course she was right. In the game of life, "fucked your secretary" beats everything.

TEN

If He's Good Enough for Zsa Zsa

I woke up the next morning with a monster hangover, unable to appreciate the scenic view of the Santa Monica beach from my hotel room. I prayed to God that He would mercifully relieve my pounding headache before the end of the hiatus. Judging by the pain surrounding my temples, I would be lucky if comfort came in this lifetime.

Waiting for two Alka-Seltzer tablets to noisily dissolve, I thought back to the wee hours of the previous night that were spent checking into the Sheraton, unpacking the few things I took from the house, and finding a bar in which to have a drink. Not that I felt like celebrating, exactly. I just wasn't ready to be alone, so I thought that a bit of the bubbly with some other fun-seekers might be a suitable initiation into the single life. Unfortunately, the only

open, late-night bar I could find wasn't the hip, single-scene party
I was hoping for but rather an old, dingy, hard drinking place, full
of alcoholics. They looked like mostly older, working class people,
from the generation before the advent of recreational drugs. They
were content with their mass produced rotgut with just a smidgen
of prescription drug abuse thrown in for good measure.

The Frolic Room on Pico Boulevard near Centinella
Avenue was dark, with a blue haze of cigarette smoke, a TV
showing an old black-and-white movie that nobody watched, and
about ten burned-out bodies nursing drinks along the bar. None of
the people were talking to each other, preferring to linger in their
own private misery. Occasionally, one or another of the rummies
had thoughts that would prompt a heavy sigh, which the other
patrons would courteously ignore. There was not now, nor had
there ever been, any frolicking in the Frolic Room. It wasn't my
kind of place, but I figured I was already there and a drink might
help me get to sleep. Otherwise I'd have to either count sheep or
the ways I had messed up my marriage and life in general. That
could keep me up all night.

The bar was small so I was forced to sit next to one of the
resident winos. I took my chances alongside a guy who appeared
to be about fifty years old. He hadn't shaved in a few days, his
gray stubble matching his dirty, matted hair. He wore a black,

double-breasted suit that hadn't been pressed in years, along with a yellowing, open-collared, white shirt. His bloodshot, light blue eyes were deeply set in his leathery, suntanned face, the probable result of spending his daylight hours wandering the streets in the strong, southern California sun. A lit cigarette trembled slightly between his fingers that surrounded an old-fashioned glass filled with whiskey.

Although disheveled, I could tell that it was an expensive suit. My guess was that this guy had taken a long fall from the top. What had he been to afford that suit? A network exec? A TV producer? Was I about to join him on the bus to Craptown? I decided; one drink and I'm out of here.

It had been years since I had consumed any liquor stronger than wine, but the atmosphere of the Frolic Room called for something with a bit more bite. I ordered a Jack Daniels Black on the rocks, a bourbon call back to my college days in Kentucky. The bartender, paying homage to the maudlin pall that filled the room, gave me my drink and took my money without saying a word.

The strong bouquet of the bourbon took me right back to Kentucky, where the potent liquor was used to keep Linda and me warm at college football games. Thoughts of Linda. Man, I was a screw-up. I let out a loud sigh as I quickly embraced the spirit of the Frolic Room.

I took a sip of whiskey, aware that the adjacent, well-tanned lush was staring at me. Not knowing Frolic Room etiquette, I returned the stare, added a nod, and then headed back to my longings for Linda with no intention of engaging in conversation.

"Hey, how ya doin'?" he asked.

"Not so good, to tell you the truth," I answered, betting he had enough troubles of his own and wouldn't want to hear mine.

"You don't look like a guy who usually drinks in a place like this," he noted, sizing me up. "I bet you your wife kicked you out . . . didn't she?" he said with a great deal of self-satisfaction.

"I'd rather not talk about it," I said, looking up at the TV in an attempt to disengage from the nosey boozehound.

"She did. She kicked you out. I know the look. I'm never wrong." He smiled broadly, my misfortune now his great fun.

"Yes, she kicked me out," I acknowledged reluctantly.

"I knew it, I just knew it!" he cackled. Now he was more than having fun. He was frolicking. "Lou Williams, attorney at law," he slurred, offering me his hand, which was already shaking before I took it.

"Barry Klein. Nice meeting you, Lou." I wanted to down my bourbon and get out before the conversation continued, but I was not in any drinking shape. I couldn't gulp down the fiery liquid. I had to sip it.

"So, what were you doing? Fucking your secretary?" Lou asked quietly, as if it was okay to take him into my confidence.

"To tell you the truth, Lou, I don't think that's any of your business," I said curtly.

"I'll take that as a yes," Lou replied matter-of-factly. "Look, I used to be one of the biggest divorce lawyers in L.A. Maybe I could help you. Why don't you buy me a drink?" Like all lawyers, Lou wanted his retainer up front.

"I'm not going to be here that long," I said, thinking the Frolic Room was not the best place to find competent legal representation.

"You don't believe me, do you?" he surmised, the point so obvious even in his pickled state. "Have you ever heard of the Gabors?" he asked. "I represented them in all their divorces. And they did pretty damn good," he said, proudly.

Zsa Zsa Gabor had been married and divorced at least seven times and made a bundle on each settlement. Her famous sisters did as well. If Lou was on the level, he might be able to offer some sound advice.

"You were really Zsa Zsa Gabor's divorce lawyer?" I asked, hoping for truthful confirmation.

"I've told you all I can. If I told you more, I'd be breaking a confidentimentality," he said, the numbing effect of the booze making all fifty-cent words inaccessible to his brain's speech center.

Finishing my drink, and feeling a little loose myself, I leaned toward Lou, "Forgive me for saying so, but you don't exactly look like one of L.A.'s biggest divorce lawyers."

"Well forgive me for not meeting your standards, but I kind of fell apart when my doctor told me I only had six months to live," Lou explained with a surly attitude and proceeded to finish his drink, bottoms up.

"Gee . . . I'm sorry," I replied with stunned sincerity. I had been so wrapped up in my life that it never occurred to me that Lou was a human being whose problems might be worse than mine. I signaled the bartender to pour another round for Lou and me. As he did, I said to Lou, "I've got to tell you, I don't know how I would handle that kind of news. Six months to live. Wow . . . when did the doctor tell you?"

"Four years ago," Lou said as he gulped down his freshly poured drink.

"Then you're not going to die?" I was confused as much by the bourbon as by the logic.

"Don't sound so disappointed. The doctor says I'm still going to die. He just doesn't know when." Lou ordered us another round.

"So you've been living like this for four years?" I asked, referring to his less-than-productive lifestyle.

"No. For the first six months I did what everybody does. I lived life to the fullest. I lived every day like it was my last. Do you know how tiring that is? Living life to the fullest? That alone can kill you," Lou said, raising his glass to me.

We touched glasses and downed another shot. "Then after the first six months, when I was still alive, I didn't know what to do," he continued. "The doctors were still promising me I would die, so I put everything on hold while I waited. You know a divorce case usually takes more than six months. That's why I didn't take any new cases—I didn't want to leave my clients in the lurch with a dead lawyer. People going through divorce have enough problems. You'll see," Lou said, reminding me of my own mini death sentence.

Lou and I sat quietly for a moment. He, I assumed, was pondering the mysteries of life. Me, I was wondering whether I had to pee badly enough to try and make it to the men's room. Then he asked me, "Do you love her?"

"Who?"

"Your wife. Do you love your wife?"

"Yeah, I love her. That's what I can't figure out about the whole thing. My wife and I had something special. My biggest

confusion tonight when I closed the house door behind me was
how I could have been so wrong about what was meant to be. In
my soul—at the deepest level of my core—I always felt that Linda
and I were meant to be together. We met on a blind date. Fate had
brought us to each other. We were from such different worlds yet
we made sense as a couple."

"Do you love the other one? The secretary?"

It was a question that deserved serious consideration. I
thought for a moment before answering, "No, I don't believe I do."
I knew I could never spend the rest of my life with Marcia.

"That's good. Nothing's worse than being in love with two
women," Lou said in way that indicated he knew from first hand
experience. "You want some free advice from a guy who knows
more about divorce than you'll ever want to know?" he asked, as
he caught himself before falling off his bar stool.

"Sure. Why not?"

"Divorce is like a little death. For the next six months, start
living like you're dying. It's your choice. You can either wallow
in your sorrow, or you can live each day like it's your last. Don't
waste time. If you don't love the secretary, move on. If you want to
try and save your marriage, try. What do you have to lose? You're
dying anyway. The truth is, you probably don't know what you
want. So stay loose. If you live past the six months, then you can

figure out what to do."

***

The Alka-Seltzer went to work and my head began to clear. Lou Williams's advice, although blurred by booze the night before, seemed to make complete sense this morning. I would attack my new life with gusto, spending the morning back at the house, collecting some more things, and facing Linda. Confronting our new reality. Lou Williams had talked about trying to save the marriage. Is that what I wanted to do? I wasn't sure. Stay loose. The afternoon would be spent finding my new bachelor pad. And although I knew I'd have to cope with my feelings of remorse, the prospect of no more lying, no more cheating, and a lot less plate spinning was a huge relief.

Heading out of the hotel, I stopped by the front desk to get some change for a newspaper. I would need the classifieds for my afternoon apartment search. I was helped by one of the assistant managers, Tanya Lake, perhaps the most stunning black women I'd ever seen. Her skin was the color of rich, hot chocolate and she had the most incredible eyes that made direct and very friendly contact with my own. We made small talk and I made her laugh. Then I made her laugh again. After about ten minutes, she asked me out to dinner. I couldn't believe it. She asked me! Did I suddenly smell single? Was it an aura thing? I asked myself, "If this was my last day on earth, would I want to go out with her?" I gave her a definite "Yes." I'd pick her up at seven. My first day away from Linda and I was already cheating on Marcia. Safe to say, Marcia would surely not be the next Mrs. Barry Klein.

When I arrived back at the house in Topanga, I found Linda packing a suitcase. She had decided that she didn't want to stay in Topanga, either. Not wasting time herself, she had already found an apartment at the beach in Venice. If she was going to have to start her life over, she didn't want to do it in a house that was half chosen by me. She was acting cold and distant—it was understandable under the circumstances. Still, on some level, I hoped we'd be able to help each other through this.

We talked about a few more details, like car insurance payments, mail, and how much money she'd need each week for expenses. She made sure I understood that this was only the amount for now. Once her lawyer got into things, the numbers could change.

Linda finished packing and was headed out the door before me. I didn't know what to say. Goodbye? I'm sorry? It's been great? Who knows what to say at a moment like this? Linda knew.

"Barry, don't forget. My lawyer needs the name of your lawyer." She seemed confident and in control of the situation.

I felt overwhelmed by the prospect of interviewing lawyers who would help divvy up my life. I pulled Lou Williams's card from my pocket. He had given it to me the night before just as he shoved me into a cab back to the hotel. The phone number on the card was handwritten. I wasn't sure if it was his or the Frolic Room's. I wrote it down for Linda. So far, his advice seemed sage. For now, my legal life was in the hands of my new lawyer, Lou Williams, Esq.

ELEVEN

You Can Manage with Friends Like Warren Beatty

I had a very successful afternoon of apartment hunting, finding one on the third try. It was a great place, overlooking the big, wide beach at Marina Del Rey. It was vacant, ready, and the quintessential bachelor pad with big, high ceilings and a huge stone fireplace. I figured, hey, if I'm living the cliché, I might as well live the good parts, too. No sense moving into a monastery. After signing the lease, I rushed back to the hotel to get ready for the first date of my new life.

I didn't know what to expect when I picked up Tanya for our date. The truth was, I was racially naive. Oh, I had spouted the liberal line about being color-blind and not caring whether someone was black or green or purple. I was, however, as close to as many green and purple people as I was to any blacks. Tanya lived on Cochran Street. I'd never heard of it. Was it in the ghetto? Would I be in danger? Probably not. Still, there was a sense of relief when Tanya's door opened and I saw her and not some well-armed, exiled, radical member of the Simbianese Liberation Army.

Tanya looked gorgeous. At the hotel, her inviting eyes had been surrounded by a look that was all business. Now she had literally let her hair down and looked downright delicious. She had a much better body than her Sheraton uniform had indicated. Her hot-red leotard and tight jeans revealed possibilities that any new bachelor boy would love to explore. I couldn't take my eyes off her even when she introduced me to her sister who had come over to baby-sit for Tanya's two kids. For a second I wondered what these little seven- and five-year-old people thought about this white guy who had come to pick up their mom, but I was more concerned about the roller skates Tanya had draped around her neck. Weren't we going to dinner? After she kissed the kiddies goodnight and extracted promises of good behavior from them, Tanya told me with great excitement that she had gotten us into celebrity roller skating in Reseda.

I guess married life had kept me insulated from the hip Hollywood social scene because I had no idea what celebrity roller skating in Reseda was. I barely knew how to get to Reseda. I figured if I headed out in that general direction, I might be able to find out what the celebrity skating thing was without letting Tanya know how socially lame I was. When I saw the sign on the Ventura Freeway for Tarzana, I panicked. Reseda was out here somewhere in the San Fernando Valley, but so were Van Nuys and Azuza and a whole lot of other places that might have celebrity roller skating, for all I knew.

As Tanya and I passed the time on our way to wherever the hell we were headed, we told each other our histories. I told her about my coming to Hollywood to seek my fortune and about the recent demise of my marriage. She told me of her rather messy divorce from an ex-professional football player whose playing days ended when he got heavily into cocaine and guns. The Raiders got tired of his irrational, violent outbursts and let him go. Eventually, after many threats to her life, so did Tanya. A restraining order kept him away from her except when he visited the kids. Those visits were much better since he had been through a drug rehab program.

Those intimate details were nothing compared to what I was about to tell her.

"Tanya, I don't really know where celebrity roller skating is. In fact, I don't know what it is," I said, as we whizzed by the Tarzana exit headed toward Oxnard and points north.

"You're kidding, right?" I don't think she meant to, but she asked in a tone that suggested that if I was indeed serious, she might want me to pull over to the side of the freeway and let her out.

"Of course I'm kidding! But what is it?" I made myself as vulnerable as possible as I asked. It worked. She was kind enough not to leap out of the car.

"Once a week, a bunch of celebrities take over the roller rink in Reseda. It's so they can skate without being hassled. It's run by that actor, Ed Begley, Jr. Cher goes. And Nicholson. It's all by invitation only." Her face glowed with enthusiasm as she told me. I didn't want to bring her down with the next question but felt I had to ask.

"So, then, how are we going to get in?"

"Barry, you're the producer of the number one show on television. You count. Besides, my ex-husband is the bouncer at the door. I've been trying to get him to let me in for weeks. He said if you're on the level, we're in. Turn here." She confidently gave me instructions to get us going the right way. It was difficult concentrating because I could only think about my upcoming meeting with the cocaine-snorting, gun-toting, ex-jock, mad at the world, who was going to be checking out the little white Jew who obviously wants to make it with the woman he still loves. Hey,

Barry, still love the night life? Still love to boogie?

Bubby Lake had been a linebacker when he played ball and still had the chiseled physique and madness in the eye that the position requires. Wearing a black T-shirt, which appeared to be painted on his huge frame, he looked more menacing than even my poor pathetic cowardly mind had envisioned. As we approached him, I mentally prepared for trouble. If he even lifted a finger, I would fall to the ground, cover my head with my arms, and scream, "Not in the face! Not in the face!" Tanya seemed quite calm, considering the gun story she had told me only minutes earlier. She reached up and kissed him on the cheek.

"How you doin', Bubby?" she asked sweetly.

"Hey, Baby." He was responding to her but not taking his eyes off me. "I'm sorry, Barry, I'm going to have to bash your head in for messin' with my woman," I thought I heard him say, as he held me with a cold stare.

I stood there waiting for the pain, so overcome with fear that my "not in the face" strategy completely left my mind. After a moment I realized both Bubby and Tanya were waiting for me to do something. Perhaps I had heard him wrong.

"Excuse me. What did you say?"

"I said, I'm sorry, Barry, but I'm going to have to see some I.D."

I tried as hard as I could to keep my hands from trembling as I pulled out my wallet and searched for my license. I dropped it only once.

"You two have a nice time," Bubby said, sincerely enough, as he held the door open for us. We wouldn't be made to stand outside with the assembled crowd of onlookers who hoped for a glimpse of a recognizable celebrity. I could tell the crowd was disappointed that we weren't anybody they knew from *People* magazine or, if they couldn't have that, that we weren't denied entrance. The crowd loved it when Bubby wouldn't let someone in. It meant that the person had to suffer the same humiliation every member of the star-hungry mob had experienced. But that wasn't going to happen to Tanya and me. We were in.

The Reseda Roller Palace was an old dilapidated place that had been built in the late fifties, when the Valley was starting to boom. Wooden bleachers surrounded the skating floor except for the snack area, which consisted of six small tables and a number of vending machines. The only things that had been updated were the sound system and the lights. Huge speakers in each corner, cranked up to keep the base line of every song vibrating throughout your body, made the whole building shake while strobe lights made the skaters appear to jump from one part of the floor to the next.

"We are family, I've got all my sisters with me" were the

words that consumed my entire being as we entered. Tanya and
I wouldn't be talking tonight, we'd be screaming if we had any
hopes of being heard at all.

Tanya was trying to tell me something while my eyes were
adjusting to the pulsating light. I couldn't hear a word she was
saying, so she moved very close to me, putting her mouth next to
my ear. I put my arm around her waist as she spoke. It felt great
pressing her body against mine.

"You need to go to the pro shop and rent your skates," she
told me.

"Why can't we just stand here like this?" I whispered in her
ear as I gave her an extra little squeeze.

She gave me a smile and a wink and pushed me toward the
pro shop. She didn't realize it wasn't just the thought of holding
her that made me want to stay where I was; I hadn't roller skated
since I was seven years old. I had gotten a pair of skates for my
birthday, the kind with metal wheels that clamped onto your shoes.
When you'd skate on cement sidewalks, you'd vibrate so much,
fillings would come loose. Every time you'd hit a crack, you'd
wind up on your butt with a bloody knee or elbow. It wasn't my
idea of a good time so I stopped skating at a fairly early age, seven
years and one day to be exact. I didn't want to tell Tanya how I felt
about skating because, well, I assumed she'd find out what a wuss I

was soon enough.

As I headed for the pro shop, I grabbed a glimpse of the skaters, and judging by the speed the crowd was traveling on the floor, I was going to have a hard time looking cool as I held onto Tanya or the guardrail for dear life. My fearful thoughts were interrupted when I heard, "Hiiiiiiiiiiii, Baaaaaarrrrry." I turned and saw Lorraine LaBarbara waking by with Penny Marshall and Terry Garr. Lorraine waved and continued walking. I was glad she didn't stop to talk about the show but disappointed she didn't stop to introduce me to her celebrity friends.

The walls of the pro shop were covered with eight-by-ten glossies of the top stars in Hollywood. Each picture had a personal note to Jack Clanton, the manager of the pro shop and, at one time, one of the top roller skaters in the country. I figured the notes were fake. The handwriting on all of them was exactly the same, and I just don't think Raymond Massey or Wallace Beery, Jr., did that much skating in their time. Even though roller skating, like bowling, is one of the second-class sports in our country, you still had to admit the pictures of Jack winning the national roll-off in his sparkly suit were pretty slick.

Standing behind the counter, a fifty-year-old version of the Jack in the pictures was giving a pair of skates to Warren Beatty.

Warren Beatty? Barry, you're skating with Warren Beatty!

"Hey, how ya doin'?" I greeted him as I walked up to the counter. I said it so that it was hard to tell if I was talking to Jack or Warren. I wanted to talk to Warren, but who wants to be just another schmuck bothering him? He's one of my mother's favorites. I figured if I told her I met Warren and he sent his regards, she might not be so upset about me losing Linda. I hadn't told my parents yet. I was waiting for either the right time or the courage. I knew they wouldn't be pleased. They loved Linda. No, I'd have to find something better than regards from Warren Beatty before I called them. Besides, Warren didn't wait for me to decide what to say. He had taken his skates and left me alone with Jack.

"That was Warren Beatty," Jack told me excitedly.

"Yeah, I know. Can I have a size nine, please?" I was courteous, but I made it fairly evident that I didn't want to chat.

"I can't believe the people we're getting in here. Warren Beatty . . . man!" After reveling in the memory of Warren, Jack got around to me. "Are you somebody?" he asked tentatively, as he studied my face. He was trying to remember if he had seen me on TV or in the movies.

"Yes, I'm somebody. Everybody is somebody." Shame on Jack for suggesting that celebrity somehow made one person better than the next.

"Who are you?" Jack asked, not bothered in the least by my

attitude.

"Barry Klein, producer of *In the Swim*."

"I'll get your skates."

I was nobody. Jack returned and asked for my shoes.

"You didn't take Warren's shoes," I protested.

"What would Warren Beatty want with an old beat-up pair of skates?" Jack asked rhetorically. He was stating the obvious. I was nobody and probably would steal an old beat-up pair of skates unless threatened with the loss of my shoes.

Skates on, I inched my way out of the pro shop hanging on to the wall like a baby who knows it's being weaned from it's mother's breast. I was not giving up my wall. Judging from the amused looks I was getting from people heading for the pro shop, however, I soon realized that it would be impossible to impress Tanya and remain attached to the wall all night. My first attempt at standing on my own had my arms flailing, first forward then backward in giant windmills fighting to maintain my balance. My second attempt had me simply falling on my ass. If this was happening to me before I got back to Tanya, I could only imagine the damage I would do to myself once I got out on the floor.

As I cautiously stood up, I suddenly remembered something that Lorraine LaBarbara had once told me. I had asked her how she became such a gifted physical comedienne, able to perform whatever extraordinary feats we wrote in the *In The Swim* scripts? She answered with a shrug, "I'm an actress. I act like I can do it." Maybe Lorraine's simple technique would work for me. I would act as if I could skate. I took one step and then another telling myself I was a dandy skater. From what I could tell, I was moving forward. I made it back to Tanya and on to the floor without another major prat fall. For my first attempt after so many years, I did all right. By the end of the night I was even moving to the music. Tanya made it look like we were roller dancing. I managed to stay up while she skated backwards in my arms. We laughed a lot. I felt really free. We skated until one o'clock in the morning when they closed the palace. Outside, the crowd of onlookers was waiting. The paparazzi were there, too, taking pictures of the stars who were waiting for their limos. I found myself once again standing next to Warren Beatty.

"Well, take it easy," I told Warren, as if we had shared a fine evening together.

"Yeah. You, too," he answered with a look that said, "Who is this jerk?" The flashbulbs were popping all around as Tanya and I made it to my car.

I told her what a fun time I had skating. She had, too. We kissed. It turned out to be a longer kiss than I expected. And although I kept one eye open, searching the parking lot for an enraged Bubby Lake, I found this woman very exciting.

I wanted to ask her to come back to the hotel. I wanted to, but the fear of rejection, wouldn't let me. It was a fear I had dealt with all my life. What if she said no? What did I mean, *what if*? Of course she'd say no. Well, she might say yes. So, go ahead and ask her. I couldn't ask her, and I couldn't believe that I'd spend the rest of my life going through these mental machinations. Life is different now, Barry. Here's a chance for a fresh start. Be strong. This fear is irrational. You felt the kiss, Barry. Ask her. There's no way she's going to reject you.

"Would you like to go back to the hotel?"

"No."

Clutching my heart, gasping, I slumped behind the wheel as if I'd been shot. It wasn't a stretch. It's the way I felt. I did it to get a laugh and to avoid the reality of the situation. Fortunately, she did laugh as she grabbed the steering wheel and kept us going straight.

"Barry, I can't go back to the hotel—I work there. It wouldn't be right." She touched my inner thigh and kissed my cheek. "Why don't we just wait until you have your apartment set up, okay?"

I would survive. This was no rejection at all.

The next morning was spent at my new beach pad watching

the movers unload all the furniture I had just rented. The rental agent didn't understand why I wanted everything delivered immediately. She didn't know I needed the place ready for Tanya. At first, Madeline, the rental agent, said it would be impossible. A couple of *In the Swim* T-shirts and the promise that I'd have her in to read for a part once the next season started got the truck right on the road. Madeline, of course, was not just a woman who rented furniture. She was a rental agent/actress complete with a pile of eight-by-tens and resumes in her desk.

While the guys unloaded, I made a couple of phone calls. First I called Tanya, to tell her again what a great time I'd had. Evidently, she really had enjoyed our date, too, because we decided to get together again that night to christen my new apartment. The next call was to Marcia. Now that the show was on hiatus for several months, I wouldn't be seeing her at the office and knew I'd better tell her that Linda and I had split. The difficult part would be explaining why I hadn't called her sooner. I definitely wouldn't want her to know about Tanya.

"Hello, Marcia? Guess what I'm doing?" I asked, imagining she would scream with joy when I told her.

"Are you reading this morning's *L.A. Times?*" This was a pretty lousy guess, considering the amount of excitement in my voice when I asked the question.

"No. I've been busy packing to move to my new apartment. I'm no longer with Linda." I waited for the scream.

"Well, there's a picture of you and Warren Beatty at celebrity roller skating in Reseda in the View section. Who's the black girl?"

"You're kidding? A picture of Warren Beatty and me in the paper?" Doug, the delivery guy, looked up immediately upon hearing the news.

"Really?" he mouthed as not to disturb my call. I nodded. Without hesitation, Doug instructed his assistant to see if there were nicer throw pillows in the truck. Hey, this being pals with Warren was all right.

"Look, Barry, I know you've got some wild oats to sow . . . and I want you to. You need to get it out of your system." Marcia was going to give me enough rope to hang myself. "I just want you to tell me when you do. Okay?"

What fun would it be if I had to tell her? I was conflicted about Marcia. If it felt so good being done with the lying and cheating with Linda, why was I willing to continue it with Marcia? I already knew the relationship wasn't going to survive the long run, so why keep it going at all? Because I was an addict, for God's sake. A victim of the devil's work. If I were able to simply walk away from the pleasures of Marcia's flesh, I might still be with

Linda. No, rather than bravely tell Marcia the truth, I'd have to slowly reduce my dosage of her. The whole thing was pathetic, but it was the best I could do.

"Are we getting together tonight? She hadn't waited for me to answer. "I can't believe you can actually sleep with me after you sleep with me," Marcia giggled at her little joke. She was looking forward to being together.

"Not tonight. I need to get the apartment set up. I'd like it to be perfect for you. How about tomorrow?"

"You don't want any help with the move?" Marcia wanted to be with me. Either because she genuinely wanted to or because she suspected I wouldn't be alone tonight. Why shouldn't she suspect me? She had seen me lie to Linda so many times.

"I'll be fine, thanks. I'll see you tomorrow." I threw her a kiss over the phone. She threw one back, and that was that.

With the furniture in place, I called the set decorator from the show and had him bring over a bunch of plants and bachelor pad knickknacks. In just three hours the apartment looked lived-in. Chilled champagne, candle light, fresh flowers, make-out music. The place looked great. I looked great. I felt beyond great. I had a ball preparing a fabulous dinner of linguini in white clam sauce with Caesar salad, going easy on the garlic in anticipation of the evenings, hoped for, activities. It seemed like a very long time since I'd had this much fun.

Tanya arrived looking beautiful. Her eyes sparkled in the candlelight. She wore a gardenia in her hair, making her look more exotic than ever. The perfume from the flower surrounded her. It didn't take long for us to forget about dinner and pick up where we were the night before.

There's no question that there's something special about being with someone of another race. Something rebellious. Something forbidden. Her brownness was irresistible. We began to touch each other. We couldn't get enough. It was wild, uninhibited sex that started in the living room and moved to the bedroom only after a stop in the dining room for a candle and then the kitchen for some wine. It was fabulous. I felt alive—electric—like I had never . . . hey, wait a minute. This was the way I felt when I was first with Marcia. My mind started to wander and wonder. Was this so terrific just because I was cheating on Marcia? Had it been great with Marcia just because I was cheating on Linda? Thinking about all this made the sex with Tanya better than it might have been had I been paying attention. It certainly made it last longer

When we were finished and nestled in each other's arms, I reflected on my cheating-makes-it-exciting theory. It was an interesting premise. Over the next few months I'd test it rigorously with Tanya and a few other new lady friends. Sure enough, as the months went by, sex with Marcia became less exciting and I couldn't keep my hands or my mind off Tanya.

I didn't spend my hiatus seeing only Marcia and Tanya. Donna Morris was also a regular. She was the only person from work, other than Marcia, I wanted to see. We spent a lot of time together, still the closest of friends. She was still trying to make her affair and marriage work, so it was less complicated when she hung out with me. I needed someone nonjudgmental to confide in about the volatile mixture of seeing both Marcia and Tanya. We spent most days on the beach, trying to forget the past season and occasionally having thoughts of the upcoming one.

I was also seeing Linda, once a week. That was Lou Williams' doing. As the settlement meeting between Linda and me and our attorneys approached, I felt extremely anxious. It dawned on me that hiring Lou Williams, as my lawyer, was perhaps the most colossal blunder in the annals of jurist prudence. Lou and I met three times to prepare for the scheduled rendezvous with Linda's legal team. Each of our meetings was held at the Frolic Room. Each time Williams was three sheets to the wind. I tried to fire him but he wouldn't let me.

"You believe in 'meant to be,' Barry," Lou explained after I had given him his pink slip. "Well, I think *we're* meant to be."

"We're not meant to be, Lou," I assured him.

"Are you kidding me? Look around," he said, pointing out the depressing interior of the Frolic Room. "Do you think you'd come back here time and time again if we weren't meant to be?"

On my way to the settlement meeting, I anticipated Lou Williams arriving late, drunk as a skunk, and singing a dirty verse of "Barnacle Bill the Sailor." I would be paying record amounts of alimony. However, when Linda and her lawyer, Cheryl Kayman, sat down with me and my lawyer, the punctual, clean-shaven, freshly bathed, smartly dressed Lou Williams, we all got along famously. Lou had put forth a Herculean effort to pull himself together. Kayman knew of Lou's pre-bender reputation and treated him with deference and respect. He, in turn, was funny, charming, seemingly sober, and more than competent. Lou suggested that we work out the separation agreement as if the divorce was inevitable. But, he added, we would not be in a hurry to file. Unless Linda or I was madly in love with someone else and wanted to get married, what was the rush? He explained his "six months to live" theory and suggested that Linda and I continue to see each other during the separation. To my surprise, she agreed. It was our attempt at working on the marriage. For my part, there was very little work involved.

Our dates were nice and I always looked forward to them. Sometimes we'd discuss what went wrong with the marriage.

Sometimes we'd simply enjoy each other's company without dredging up the recent past. Sometimes we'd even wind up making love. At first, this seemed very strange. But we were in bed as an act of love. We still cared about each other and, in some way, we were helping each other through a tough time. Right or wrong, it didn't matter. I had only six months to live. For right now, anything that felt good was okay. Being in bed with Linda felt natural. Our once-a-week get-togethers ended, however, after a chance meeting. It wasn't just Linda and I who met. It was Linda, Marcia, and I.

Although not thrilled about it, Linda knew I was still seeing Marcia. After we'd been separated for a few months, she knew I was seeing Tanya as well as other women, too. She had asked me point blank if I was, and I went with the truth. But she had never actually, physically, in person, seen me with anyone. I had always imagined it would be no big deal. In my mind, like most guys involved with two women, I assumed there was no reason why Linda, Marcia, and I couldn't all be friends. I spent time with Linda. I spent time with Marcia. They both liked me. Why couldn't we all spend time together? Not only couldn't we spend time together, we couldn't even face the reality.

Marcia and I were in the grocery store disagreeing about what to buy for dinner. The encounter happened quickly. Like a flash. Almost like it didn't happen at all. Judging by the rate my heart was pounding, it must have. Marcia and I had rounded the corner from the Marshmallow Fluff aisle (her dinner idea), just as Linda had done the same, only in the opposite direction. Linda and I practically bumped into each other. In an instant, we both read the situation and hated what we saw. It was embarrassing and revolting and agonizing all at once. Linda immediately turned and ran. I took Marcia's arm and headed her back toward the Rice-A-Roni. I didn't know what to do. I was flushed. I was confused.

"What's the matter, Sweetie?" Marcia asked. It had happened so quickly she completely missed it.

"Let's get out of here." I said, leading her toward the door.

"What about dinner?"

" I'm taking you out."

"Oh, Baby, I love you," she said as she lovingly took my arm.

I pulled away from her. It was wrong, at this moment, to even have contact with her. I felt terrible for Linda.

When we got back to my apartment I asked Marcia to go home.

"But we were going to spend a couple of days together. You cleaned out a drawer for me," she protested. Earlier in the day, she had won a small victory. A dresser drawer had been designated as Marcia's. She would be allowed to leave a few necessities.

She thought it meant she was moving into my life. I thought it meant that now my socks and my underwear would be temporarily bunched together in an unruly mess.

"Look, Marcia, I just need to be alone. I'm a little nutty right now. That's all." Being nutty had been a successful excuse before. There was no reason not to go back to the tried and true.

"You know, sometimes I wonder if you love me at all," she said unhappily, as she got her overnight bag.

"Would I have given you a dresser drawer if I didn't love you at all?" I asked, as I gently pushed her out the door. I had to talk with Linda. I wanted to make sure she was okay. What happened was awful. I called Linda and told her I wanted to see her. She said no. I begged. She finally agreed to see me—in the car. She didn't want me to come into her apartment. We would meet outside.

When she got in the car, she didn't look at me. She'd been crying, and she still held onto a crumpled piece of tissue. I took her hand, not knowing what to say. We sat there for a few minutes, by the curb, saying nothing, noticing the occasional passerby.

"I'm so sorry. I had no idea you shopped at that store." I finally said, in an attempt to get a conversation started.

"I don't anymore." Linda was furious for having been put through this humiliation. She probably thought she was safe, shopping in her new neighborhood, the place she had come to heal.

"We have to stop seeing each other, Barry," she continued. "I mean completely."

"I thought things have been going pretty well," I said. They had, for me.

"It's too much of an emotional drag on me. I thought I could handle it, you being with other people while we try to figure things out. But I can't. I honestly can't do it. I don't think we should see each other. Or talk to each other. Nothing." She gave my hand a little squeeze as she said it. Then, she quickly got out of the car and headed to her apartment without looking back.

Suddenly, I felt a sickening sense of finality. During the first couple of months of separation, when we occasionally saw each other, it seemed like the "meant to be" part of our relationship was still alive. Linda was still in my life. Now, if she kept her word, it really was over.

I wasn't ready for this. I needed a diversion—something to keep me from dealing with reality. My mind raced wildly. No more Linda. For real. What would make me feel better? Maybe another bout of wrestling a nude woman would help? I looked in my wallet. Sissy-two dollah. More than enough. Possibly enough to wrestle with someone more attractive than Aki. There was no guarantee that would be the case. A mental picture of the old

Chinese woman unzipping her Caesar's Palace outfit flashed across my scattered mind. No relief there. I needed human contact. There was a sudden remembrance of my improv days with Funny Bones. Nothing felt better than being engulfed in a wave of laughter from an appreciative audience. A big laugh meant they loved you. That's what I needed.

It was a weeknight. Funny Bones was not an option. I drove toward Hollywood, heading for "Open Mike Night" at Mitzi Shore's Comedy Store. My thoughts flip-flopped. I wondered what I'd do once I got on stage. I wondered what I'd do without Linda. I had no act—no five minute chunk of material to get the audience love I craved. I had no act to get the Linda love I wanted to keep.

As I stood in the lobby, writing my name on the sign-up sheet, prepared to wait my turn to perform, Mark Baxter, the Comedy Store mc, approached. Like so many comics who hoped to break into acting, Baxter had read for a guest part on *In The Swim* during the previous season. We hadn't hired him, but that didn't mean he wouldn't get another chance in the upcoming season. That possibility sent him right into ass kissing mode.

"Hey, Barry, great to see you. I didn't know you did stand-up," Baxter said as he shook my hand warmly. Before I could respond he added, "You don't have to put your name on the list. I'll get you up next." A wink, a pat on the back, and he was headed for the stage. I followed him into the main room. A black kid who was doing Richard Prior's act, word for word, was just finishing up. A large contingency of his friends gave him a rousing round of applause as he left the stage. Mark Baxter grabbed the mic.

"How many of you watch *In The Swim*?" he asked the audience. They responded with a big cheer. "Well I've got a real treat for you. Here's one of the producers and head writers of the show—a very, very funny guy—let's hear it for Barry Klein!"

Baxter had unwittingly given me the comedy kiss of death. He promised them a very, very funny guy. Their expectations were too high for a guy with no act. Still, I wanted love from this room full of strangers. Somehow, they would make my life right. I walked on stage in a daze. Baxter handed me the microphone and whispered, "Kill 'em, man." Possibly with a gun. Not with the comic thoughts firing in my brain. There were none. I was blank. I stared out into the audience. The bright spotlight prevented me from seeing them but I could feel them waiting for a very, very funny guy. My heart began to pound. What little moisture there was in my cotton mouth made a bee line for my arm pits. I could feel the flop sweat dripping down my shirt. What was I doing up here? Tears began to roll down my cheeks.

"I lost my wife tonight," I said, through the tears. It got a huge laugh. Mark Baxter had promised them a very, very funny guy and now their simple anticipation had them laughing. It didn't feel as good as I had hoped. The crowd quickly settled down as I began to sob. This wasn't so funny. They were ready for jokes. An improv audience is tolerant. They understand the comedy is being made up on the spot. They're amazed at the process. They're pulling for you. A stand-up comedy audience expects jokes. Lots of them. I was just standing there crying. I could feel the discomfort filling the room but there was nothing I could do. I had nothing to say.

"He's stealing Andy Kaufman's act," someone in the back of the room shouted. Andy Kaufman was a successful comic known for making his audiences uncomfortable for long periods of time before getting to anything funny.

A guy in another part of the room, showing off for his friends, began to boo. A smattering of others joined in. I wondered if anyone had ever been heckled before during a nervous breakdown. I'm not sure how long it took, but eventually Mark Baxter came on stage and took the microphone from me.

"Barry Klein, ladies and gentlemen. Barry Klein." As I headed off stage he added, "Don't give up the day job, Barry." He got a big laugh. Bigger than any laugh he ever got from material he wrote. I could hear him introducing the next comic as I snuck out the back door into the alley. Other comics were out there smoking their cigarettes and shmoozing with each other. Still crying uncontrollably, I obviously wasn't in a shmoozing mood. I moved to the back of the alley, next to the dumpster. I sank to the ground and curled into the fetal position. This was alone.

After a few moments another comic came over to throw a candy wrapper into the dumpster. Here's what's great about really funny people. Nothing is sacred. It's all fair game. He deposited his trash, saw me bawling on the ground, gave a look of mock concern and asked, "Bad set?"

I had to smile, then added, "No, man, I killed. I just can't get a really good spot from Mitzi." He laughed. I might survive.

TWELVE

Hello Mudda, Hello Fadda

What little equilibrium my life had regained while Linda
and I were seeing each other during the separation left along with
her. There was no relief from feeling lost. Even the days on the
beach with Donna lost their luster as I became argumentative and
irritable. One day she asked me to give her a lift to the Harley
Davidson dealer. Donna had bought a hog. This was before owning
a Harley was chic. More over, even biker chicks didn't drive
Harleys. They rode on the back looking tough and slutty. Not a
bad look, mind you. But not a look that suited Donna. She loved
the idea of being a big girl on a big bike. Instead of reveling in her
bravura and unique sense of style, I went on and on about how
dangerous and impractical a motorcycle would be. I told her that
buying the Harley was stupid and made no sense. She calmly got

up and left the beach. She would find another ride. In my funk I forgot that Donna and my relationship wasn't about making sense. It was about fun. I wasn't holding up my end of the bargain.

I couldn't wait for the hiatus to end, hoping the regiment of working on the new season would return some normalcy to my life. I also, secretly, couldn't wait to see the look on Scotty O'Rourke's face when Donna rolled up to the Paragon gate on her Big Mama Electra-Glide.

The first day of the season was always fun when you worked for Bobby Mitchell. He made it feel like the first day of camp. He'd have the writers from all of his shows meet in the studio commissary for lunch. Each show would have its own table with the producers sitting at the head, very much like camp counselors. This being the first full season at the helm of *In the Swim*, Tommy and I would be given the head-of-the-table honor. I looked forward to seeing all the other counselors and campers as I pulled up to the Paragon Studios gate.

Much to my surprise, there was no line at the gate. On normal days, Scotty O'Rourke would have as many as five cars backed up waiting to get in. No matter how big the name, Scotty would put everyone through their paces before letting them through his hallowed archway. Now it was a young Latino with a nametag that read "Torres" who stuck his head out of the guardhouse, said "Morning, Mr. Klein," and waved me through. Scotty was gone. A show business tradition had ended.

As I drove onto the lot, I was surprised that I was able to muster up a few fond feelings for the old fart. Sure, he was crotchety to everyone, but Scotty took his job seriously. How many people do that today? I flashed on him sitting in his tiny Hollywood apartment, looking gaunt, not bothering to put in his teeth, our beloved Scotty withering away to nothing, forgotten by the world he had served so faithfully. Good . . . if anyone deserved to rot away in lonely isolation, it was Scotty. As a final act of defiance, I parked in Tommy's spot instead of mine. Tommy wouldn't care, but Scotty, wherever he was, would sense something was wrong. I win, old man. Let anarchy reign!

As soon as I arrived at Camp Bobby Mitchell, I heard, "Hiiiiiii, Baaaaarrrry." I recognized the voice but not the face. It sounded a lot like Rhonda Silverman, but the woman standing in front of me looked much too pretty.

"Rhonda? What have you done? You look great!" There was probably too much surprise in my voice, like there was no way on earth she could possibly look this good. She could have been offended but was just so happy that someone noticed.

"I'm getting laid regularly," she said proudly.

"That's it? You didn't have another nose job or something?"

"No," she said as if she couldn't believe that's all it took, either. "I was sitting home one day, depressed, and I actually had thoughts about suicide. I mean, I've spent a lot of money, Barry, on trying to look good, and it wasn't getting me any results. I was so lonely. Well, I didn't want to kill myself because there was a sale starting the next day at Jona, you know, that clothing store on Ventura Boulevard? So I called 911. They sent over the biggest, blondest, dumbest hunk of a man I've ever seen and he fucked me like I've never been fucked before."

"That's really nice, Rhonda." I wanted to get away before she became any more graphic in her storytelling. I didn't make it.

"The next day, I was depressed because I realized I'd never see this guy again. So I figured, what the hell, and called 911. They sent Butch over again. His name is Butch. Do you believe that? Butch. A guy with a nickname. I'm so happy."

"That really is nice, Rhonda. So, you guys are like an item?"

"No, we're not an item. He's just a big dumb cock. I've been calling 911 three times a week. They keep sending Butch. It's what they're there for, you know—emergencies."

There was no doubt about it, this was taxpayer dollars well spent. Rhonda looked better than ever. I only hoped she would still be funny now that she was sexually satisfied. You never know with comedy. You can never be sure what fuels somebody's joker. If Rhonda's particularly funny outlook on life was rooted in the fact that she had no sex life, well, in that case, she'd be in for a long season. Sure, she might be happier now than she'd ever been, but what about me? I needed good scripts from her . . . and from me. I prayed that the emotional tilt-a-whirl I'd been riding hadn't done any permanent damage to my comic view of things.

I gave Rhonda a friendly kiss on the cheek, told her she looked fabulous, and moved on as soon as I saw Donna Morris arrive. I immediately gave her a big hug and a bigger apology for having been such a stick in the mud our last few times together. She returned the hug and said, "Honey, who's better than you? . . . Nobody." It was a ritualistic reassurance that we gave each other whenever our behavior made us wonder if we deserved to remain on the planet. It was always said with a thick Jersey, wise-guy accent that always made us both laugh. One more hug and she excused herself to go find Brian Fox. Donna thought Brian's wife had been phoning her house and hanging up when Donna answered.

As Donna went on her way, I noticed Howie Clark, surrounded by a group of secretaries. For some reason, Howie had a parrot on his shoulder. One by one, the secretaries would try to pet the bird, which in turn, would try to rip their fingers off.

"Hey, Barry, I want you to meet Paco," Howie said, as I passed by.

"I don't really like birds, Howie. What are you doing with it?" I didn't intend to whistle or cackle or talk to Howie's new feathered friend.

"The doctor says I can't fall down the steps anymore, so I figured I needed a new shtick."

"You look like a gay pirate covered with bird shit. You can't keep him here."

"What am I going to do with him?" Howie replied, heartbroken.

"I don't know, but we can't have that thing squawking in the rewrite room."

As I walked away, Howie was trying to figure out if I was serious about getting rid of Paco. His concern made him oblivious to Paco, who, now sitting on Howie's head, was depositing yet another fresh bird turd.

When I saw the confident smile on Aki Nakamura's face, I was reminded of what a good job with lots of money can do for self-esteem. In the three months since I had last seen her, Aki must have lost a hundred pounds.

"A hundred and ten," she proudly reported. "What do you think?" Aki spun around, showing off her new look, waiting for my response. She was getting dizzy as I searched for the right thing to say. Yes, she had lost an amazing amount of weight, but that got her down to around two hundred and forty pounds. Hardly a girlish figure. Still, you want to encourage this kind of effort.

"You're getting there, Aki." Gee, Barry, would it kill you to give the woman a compliment? "How did you lose so much weight?"

"I found the most wonderful diet doctor," she said, grabbing a chair while waiting for her world to re-stabilize. "He gives me these vitamin shots from France. I hardly eat at all. But I have so much energy."

Ah, yes. Vitamin shots from France. Southern California's obsession with bodily perfection has turned out an endless stream of Dr. Feelgoods willing to shoot up their patients with who knows what in an effort to obtain rapid weight loss. Judging by the way Aki was grinding her teeth, there was a little too much speed mixed with her vitamins.

I headed toward the *In the Swim* table when I saw Tommy walking toward me. Tommy was one of the few people who genuinely hated Camp Bobby Mitchell. He found it sophomoric, self-serving, and an imposition on his morning getting-high time. He didn't care to know people on other shows, and he didn't want to hear Bobby's welcoming speech, even if it was incredibly funny.

Bobby worked harder on his welcoming speech than he did on writing anything else all year. It was as if impressing this room full of comedy writers was much more important than entertaining the rest of the country. Tommy knew how funny Bobby was and didn't need to spend three hours of a morning pretending he cared. In past years, Tommy made sure he was stoned enough that none of the morning's festivities would register on his mental Richter scale.

As he came closer, Tommy looked very different than usual. First, and most obvious, his face seemed symmetrical. There was no cocaine-induced collapse of the left side. Besides both sides matching, his skin had a healthy tone. There was no alcohol bloat. His eyes were clear. I assumed he had spent his hiatus at yet another facility to exorcise the chemical demons from his body. He approached me with a big smile and then, in the shocker of shockers, he hugged me.

"Barry Klein, isn't it?" he asked in mock confusion.

"Yeah, that's right. But who the hell are you?" I couldn't believe how good he looked. He had lost about fifteen pounds in the three months since I'd seen him doing his hatchet job on Ben Fisher at the wrap party. He had also been lifting weights or something. He looked very fit.

"I'm just a guy who's found Jesus," he answered, still smiling.

I smiled back in anticipation of the punch line. Tommy was the king of bad taste. He would make the most graphic jokes about bodily functions and fluids. Part of my job was to make those jokes usable on television. It was worth the effort. The jokes were too funny to dismiss just because they were truly disgusting. With a target like Jesus, I assumed the punch line would be pushing the bounds of good taste. I waited for a payoff that wasn't coming. All I heard was, "Boy, it's great to see you," followed by another hug.

Suddenly, I was no longer so happy about his newfound sobriety. "Is this for real?" I asked, not worrying whether he'd find my lack of belief in his sudden conversion offensive. I needed to know. It's not that I have any bones to pick with Jesus. If believing in him makes someone happy, then I say, "Hey, bless you my son." And even though I tend to tease, I appreciate people seeking a vehicle to take them to higher consciousness. With Linda, I didn't think Vishna was much of a vehicle, but I understood her wanting to go for the ride. Even my introduction by Linda to crystals and meditation served me well until my present state, where all the magic of Houdini himself probably wouldn't help. In the case of Jesus Christ, however, I had seen this Son of God ruin a few fine comedy writers. It was as if the King of Kings had performed some type of comedy lobotomy on these previously funny, albeit hedonistic, souls. Suddenly, there were topics they wouldn't tackle.

They didn't really want to make sex jokes or drug jokes or jokes that were at another human being's expense. What did that leave? What would happen now that Tommy had been welcomed into the kingdom of God?

"Yes, it's for real." His smile dominated his radiant face. You wouldn't believe what's happened to me. All I want to do is testify to the glory of God."

"Oh, shit." It wasn't the proper response but, really, what was I supposed to say?

Tommy didn't let my lack of enthusiasm stop him from telling me the story of his miracle.

"It happened the night of the wrap party. I was driving home and somehow I hit a tree up on Mulholland."

"Somehow? You were bombed out of your mind," I reminded him, knowing you can only enable an abuser up to a certain point. After that, it's no fun for either of you.

"That's true. Anyway, I must have been going about sixty miles an hour when I hit this thing. But the Volvo kept me alive. Just like I knew it would."

Tommy had taken a lot of crap from everybody when he bought his Volvo. After all, how many rich, single guys in L.A. buy Volvos? Only the ones who never want to get laid. How do you pick up a woman in a Volvo? Can't be done. You stop at a red light, look over to see a babe in a Jaguar, and you're sitting in your Volvo. What can you say? "Hey, how'd you like to fill this thing up with kids?" Cool, man.

Tommy was funny enough that he didn't need the car to attract women. He needed the Volvo for a much bigger job. He knew that eventually the car would have to save his life. That one night he'd be a boozed up, stoned-out crash dummy and only the energy-absorbing steel from Stockholm would be able to keep him alive.

Tommy continued. "I was lying there in the car, all mangled and bloody, and I looked over at the passenger seat, and there was Jesus. He saved my life, Barry. Hallelujah."

"Yeah, hallelujah . . . Maybe it was just the drugs, man. You were pretty whacked out." I started trying to find holes in the "Jesus saved my life" theory — I had to if I was going to sit in a room with this man for an entire season and attempt to be funny. Once someone starts using the word hallelujah, and they mean it, well, comedically it's pretty much over.

"That's what I thought," he explained. "But then Jesus showed up again at the hospital. When I was on the operating table. He said that if I surrendered to Him, He would save my life."

"Come on, Tommy, you were under the gas. That doesn't count as a vision. It was a drug induced hallucination."

"It was real, Barry." He wouldn't be moved.

"Well, did Jesus say you were still going to be funny?" I asked. I didn't want to beat around the bush. If he wasn't going to be funny, I didn't want to spend the next nine months hearing about Tommy's personal savior or how I could join up and be saved, too.

"Yes, He did. On His third visit."

"You had a third visit?"

"Two days after my operation. I was lying in bed wondering if the first two visions were for real. I had the exact same doubts you have. I was worried that if I did take Jesus into my life, I wouldn't be funny anymore. And if I wasn't funny, then who was I? It was noon, and I was sober as a judge. And there He was, standing in my room, wearing a pair of Groucho glasses. You know the ones with the fake nose and moustache?"

"Jesus was wearing Groucho glasses?" Normally I wouldn't ask the question. I would assume Tommy was kidding. But he looked completely serious as he described his Lord and Master wearing this cheap plastic novelty.

"He was as real as you are now," he said as he looked skyward.

"So then what did he do? Sit on a whoopee cushion?" I was getting worked up. "Did he give you a piece of hot pepper gum?

Don't you think it's odd that you've never seen Him in Groucho glasses in any religious paintings? I mean, He's been worshiped for two thousand years and nobody's ever seen Him with the Groucho glasses before. How come? We've got some important theological questions to answer here before we can really accept this saved-my-life-thing, don't we?" I asked in what would be my final attempt to deprogram Tommy. He just smiled that God-awful, I-found-Jesus smile of his. I stood there looking at him, saddened by the loss of my comedy buddy, when Bobby Mitchell went by.

"How are you guys doing?" he asked.

"Tommy's found Jesus," I said.

Bobby just kept walking. He either knew he had lost a great comedy writer and didn't want to talk about it or he was too focused on the speech he was about to give.

Bobby would officially start the festivities by giving a speech welcoming everybody back to work. He'd then have a comedian friend do five minutes of special material written especially for the occasion. It was a nice touch that really did promote a sense of belonging to something bigger than just each writer's show. We were all part of the Bobby Mitchell family. Bobby reminded us that although we had a lot of work to do, he didn't want us neglecting our families at home.

"Life is more important than show business," he told us. It

was a lovely thought, but we all knew what was expected. If you had a flu ridden wife at home, feeling like she was knocking on death's door, with all manner of bodily fluid being expelled from every possible human orifice, and you also had a joke that didn't work in a script, you took care of the joke first. If you chose to head home, you might find more than your beloved's head in the commode. You might also find your career in the toilet.

Just as Bobby was finishing his remarks, we heard a loud siren. Suddenly, the doors to the commissary burst open and twelve knock-out gorgeous girls in sexy police outfits came running in. Bobby always had a bit of a production number at Camp Bobby Mitchell. The girls formed an aisle on either side of the door as the siren continued to scream. Then, striding down the isle came Scotty O'Rourke, wearing his uniform, a riding crop tucked under his arm. He was the general inspecting his troops and doing a pretty funny job of it. Even I had to laugh at this little glimpse of Scotty, which hinted at the possibility of a personality. I stopped laughing as he continued to stride directly toward me. Scotty grabbed me by the arm.

"All right you, you're coming with me. You've parked in the wrong spot for the last time." Scotty was really into playing this pain-in-the-ass cop. It wasn't a stretch. He had the room howling. There was nothing for me to do but go along with the bit.

I pretended to struggle as he pulled me out of my chair and out the door. The place went wild. It was a great end to Camp Bobby Mitchell. Everybody was in a good mood as they headed back to their offices. For Tommy and me, after I begrudgingly moved my car, it was time to meet with Lorraine and Mimi.

In addition to my problems on the home front, I was also already worried about work. After all, it was the first day back. If Lorraine and Mimi remained true to form, Tommy and I would probably be fired before the end of the season. I wanted to find a way to head them off at the pass. Because most of the producers who had been fired from *In the Swim* left after having disagreements with The Ladies over the stories being told, I decided to involve Lorraine and Mimi in the process. Why not learn what they wanted to do? Most of their ideas weren't bad. They were just different from what the previous producers had planned. When I first told Tommy about the idea of meeting with The Ladies, he was too loaded to care. Now, as we headed over to Lorraine's dressing room, he was blessing me for having foresight.

"No more blessing," I pleaded, after he had just pointed out how blessed we were to have such a beautiful day. "We're in southern California. Every day is like this. You want to talk about the weather? Fine. But let's not pretend that God has made a special effort to make it sunny and seventy in L.A. If it's sunny and seventy, it means God had other things to do." If he didn't stop with all the blessings, which had also included blessing the beautiful landscaping on the studio grounds and blessing Bobby Mitchell for giving us the job, and blessing an obviously faked sneeze to see if it, too, would be blessed, I'd go insane.

"Sorry, Barry. I'm just so full of joy. And you have to admit, that's a blessing." Tommy put his hands together in a praying position when he said this. It's the same move the pope makes when he's happy about just about anything, including how good the spaghetti sauce is in Rome.

"Are you sure you wouldn't like a drink or maybe a pound of cocaine?" I asked more seriously than not. I knew I had to get Tommy back on the bottle. Jesus was going to make my life miserable.

We arrived at Lorraine's dressing room and knocked on the door.

"Who is it?" she shouted, in her crabby witch's tone.

"Tommy and Barry," I answered.

There was a long pause. Surely by now, Lorraine and Mimi knew who we were. After some mumbling behind the closed door, the "Come in" scream was issued.

Both Lorraine and Mimi were holding copies of *Variety*, the daily newspaper of show business. They had both been reading in an effort to avoid conversation. We were starting the third year of the show and they still had nothing to say to each other. I asked them how their hiatus had been and they both gave me an uninterested "Fine."

The moment of silence that followed made it clear they weren't the slightest bit interested in how our hiatus had been. That didn't stop the new Tommy from announcing, "I found Jesus over the hiatus."

Without missing a beat, Lorraine responded with a cold, "Look, I've got to be out of here in fifteen minutes."

It was a bad start to a meeting I knew was crucial to the success of the season. Lorraine had no intention of putting much effort into the process.

"So, do you ladies have any story ideas?" I asked in an attempt to get things moving.

"I think we should be hypnotized and act like chickens," Mimi blurted out.

"On the show or in life?" I joked. It made Lorraine and Tommy laugh. Mimi wasn't smiling.

"I think it would be funny, Barry," she said, as she went back to perusing her *Variety*. She didn't like having fun made at her expense. When people become stars, they are above all that. Mimi's feelings had been bruised.

"I'm just kidding, Mimi. It's a great idea," I said, as I wrote it down on a legal pad. It was funny. It was the kind of thing only a silly show like *In the Swim* could pull off.

"I also think we'd be funny in a Murphy bed and we should go skiing," Mimi added. She had obviously done her homework. Although she wasn't giving actual story ideas, she was giving funny scenes. It would be our job to build stories around those scenes. That was fine by me. If I had suggested something as silly as The Ladies being hypnotized and acting like chickens, they might have said the idea was, well, silly. But having them sign on this early in the process would make things much easier.

"How about you, Lorraine?" I asked, knowing that if we didn't use an equal number of Lorraine's ideas, we'd be in trouble.

"What if we went somewhere and we were really bored?" she said, followed by a giggle. The giggle was an effort to sell an idea that hadn't been given much forethought.

Tommy and I looked at each other. We both knew a basic rule of comedy: boring is boring. If characters play bored, chances are the audience will be bored as well. I had to decide how to respond. Should I cave in and write down her terrible idea? Or should I be honest with her risking the same fate experienced by most of my predecessors?

Tommy jumped in before I could choose. "I've sworn not

to lie to people anymore, Lorraine. I can't, now that Jesus is in my life. And, well, if you two played bored, it won't be funny."

She looked at him coldly and then said, "You're probably right."

"Thank you, Jesus," I proclaimed, in my best southern preacher imitation. It broke the tension and we all, including Tommy, laughed.

"Well, what if we were buried in sand on the beach? We'd be pretty funny in sand." There was a little nervousness in Lorraine's voice. She didn't want to get shot down twice. Not after Mimi started out so strongly.

"That's great," I said, as I wrote down her idea. It wasn't great. But it was doable.

We were rolling. The four of us batted ideas around for about an hour. Apparently, Lorraine's meeting was put on hold or it wasn't for real. She was making a credible effort with us. It was evident they both wanted the show to be good. When Tommy and I left the dressing room, it felt like we had broken new ground. Short of that, for the time being, we'd be able to hold The Ladies at bay.

The next few weeks would be spent breaking stories, that is, taking notions like getting hypnotized and acting like chickens and developing them into full-blown ideas that could be turned into scripts. The more details we could provide for the writers, the easier their writing would be. It is the most tedious part of the job, but we got into it. We even found a funny scene where The Ladies were bored. Bored people aren't funny. Bored chickens are. The plan was to start the season with the hypnotized chicken episode to show The Ladies we were serious about implementing their ideas.

The days of breaking stories and writing scripts were separated by nights of skating at Flipper's, a private, members-only, roller disco in West Hollywood on the corner of La Cienega and Santa Monica Boulevards. Flipper's had been created to take advantage of the skating craze sweeping Los Angeles. It was a bowling alley, recently converted to a much swankier version of the Reseda roller rink. Skating alone for hours and hours was somehow therapeutic—the pulsating lights and music drowning out thoughts of life personal and professional. Occasionally, on the ride home after skating, I'd stop at the Frolic Room for a night cap with Lou Williams. I'd buy us a round and tell him that I was often tempted to call Linda. He would remind me that her decision not to see me was the way she wanted to spend her six months to live, and that I should respect that. There's nothing worse than a drunk who makes sense.

There also seemed to be plenty of time for fighting with Marcia, who was becoming increasingly demanding. Besides wanting me to stop seeing Tanya every Monday, when I would

skate in Reseda, and some Saturdays, when Tanya and I would go
on a real date because, well . . . because I liked being with Tanya—
there was no pressure with her—Marcia wanted me to stop seeing
other women. And that was something that was happening more
and more as I searched to find out who I was and what I wanted.
Marcia hated all the changes. The final straw came when I fell in
love again—not with a woman, but with a Ferrari.

I desperately wanted to find some *thing* that would
magically turn my life around. Not just my personal life. The show
was also sucking the life out of me. Slowly. Not painfully. But
I was aware of the toll the hours were taking. I needed a boost.
When you're floundering in the turbulent waters of a chaotic life,
it's amazing how much an Italian sports car can look like a life
preserver. Conveniently forgetting the "dangerous and impractical"
speech I had given Donna over her Harley, I was convinced that a
Ferrari would easily make me the happiest man on earth. A Ferrari
is, without a doubt, the most breathtakingly beautiful thing on four
wheels. It's also about the most irresponsible thing you can buy.
Ferraris are notoriously bad cars. They constantly break down.
When you start looking at Ferraris, the salesman actually tells you
not to sell your other car. You'll need it when your Ferrari is in the
shop. All the warnings in the world can't stop you though, once
you've been bitten by the bug. And I had been bitten badly.

Near the end of the previous season, on a day when we were caught up on our writing and I had a couple of hours to kill until the run-through, I stopped off at my local Ferrari dealer to look at a 308 GTS. I made sure my salesman, Ron, knew I produced *In the Swim* and probably made enough money to buy what he was selling.

"I love that show," was followed by a test drive and by Ron writing up an order. The forty-three-thousand-dollar price tag, however, prevented me from actually placing the order.

When I got back to the office, I slipped the papers into my desk drawer. I looked them over every day, wondering if the car would make me happy—suspecting that buying it would be crazy. But I couldn't get it out of my mind. I kept the papers deep in the drawer like a dirty magazine. Then, one day, Marcia walked into my office, unannounced, and caught me with the papers. I quickly slid them back into the drawer. Evidently, not quickly enough.

"What was that?" she asked, as she walked over to the desk.

"Just some papers. What do you need?" I wanted to change the subject. The Ferrari was just another part of my fantasy life I wasn't planning to share with Marcia.

"Come on, Barry, what was it? You've got a look on your face like I just caught you with what's her name . . . you know, the black one."

I just shook my head in disgust, pulled the papers from the drawer and threw them on the desk. The smirk on her face said she knew she had gotten to me with the remark about Tanya. She looked them over, this girl who had promised me nothing but fun only nine months earlier. Then, in the blink of an eye, she became the wicked witch of NoFunsVille.

"I forbid you to do this, Barry," she said, as she held the papers behind her back.

"You forbid me? Why would you forbid me?" I was almost laughing as I asked. The idea that she had that much power over me was a joke. Perhaps at one time, she could have gotten me to forget a Ferrari. Not anymore.

"Well, for one thing, I know you only want this thing to pick up women," she said, stating the obvious.

"May I remind you that you, yourself, said I could sow some wild oats? So just think of the Ferrari as a tractor . . . a really fast tractor."

She completely ignored my logic and continued. "The other reason you're not getting it is that this money would make a nice down payment on a house for us."

A house instead of a Ferrari? Is this what happens when "the other woman" thinks she's become *the* woman? Just a few months earlier, Marcia wouldn't have thought about denying me a

Ferrari. If she did, she would have at least put her foot on my desk, hiked up her dress, and shown me her shapely thighs. She would have whispered how if I ever wanted my head between those legs again I better forget the car. And I would have. I would have taken her right there in the office, forgotten the car, and been forty three thousand dollars richer. That was months ago. Now there was no leg on the desk. No promise of fun. The only thing I could look forward to was coming home each night to Marcia. And I wouldn't be coming home in my Ferrari. It was a terrifying thought.

I picked up the phone and dialed 465-FAST having memorized the number for Hollywood Sports Cars during my daily reading of the Ferrari papers. Two days earlier I had received a twenty-five-thousand-dollar tax return from Uncle Sam. I now had the money and the motive.

"Hi, may I please speak with Ron? Barry Klein calling."

There was one last warning from Marcia as I waited for Ron to pick up. "Barry, if you love me, you won't do this." She was shooting blanks.

"Ron? Barry Klein. I was wondering if you had a ruby red 308 in stock? Sure, I'll hold." I wanted Marcia to leave the room while there was still time to hang up. If Ron called back, I'd tell him he had received a phony phone call from the writers on the show. Marcia stayed, drilling me with her snake eyes.

"Barry, I don't have the car in stock but I've located one. I can have it ready for you tomorrow. I'll pop over to your office right now to complete the paperwork, okay?" Ron wasn't messing around. He was closing in.

"Sounds great, Ron. I'll see you in a couple of minutes." I hung up the phone and smugly looked up at Marcia. "Would you please leave a drive-on pass for Ron from Hollywood Sports Cars?"

Marcia slapped me across the face and stormed out of my office. I hadn't even taken delivery of my Ferrari yet and already it was giving me trouble.

Donna picked me up the next morning on her Harley and drove me to Hollywood Sports Cars. I hung on for dear life hoping I wouldn't die before I got a chance to kill myself in my Ferrari. There, waiting right in front of the showroom was my Ruby Begonia. It was exquisite. Ron had me fill out a few more papers and write the check for forty-three thou. I sat in the car as Ron went over a few last-minute details.

"What are these lights on either side of the steering wheel?" I asked. The light on the left had "1–4" imprinted on it. The light on the right read "5–8."

"Those tell you, when you foul a spark plug, whether it's in valves one through four, or five through eight," Ron said, quickly changing the subject to where the spare tire was kept. I shouldn't have let him move on so quickly. Here's a tip: never buy a car that has lights to tell you which spark plug has been fouled. If they've bothered to put in the lights, the car is a dog. I wouldn't come to know this until many months and many fouled plugs later. Those lights are kept busy on a Ferrari. But when you've been blinded by the beauty of a 308, they could have a loud speaker blaring, "This car is an Italian piece of crapola!" and it wouldn't matter.

I told Donna only beautiful women would be allowed in the car and proceeded to give her the first ride. As we drove, strangers smiled and gave us the thumbs-up sign. We laughed joyously. After an all too quick spin, it was back to the studio.

"Enzo Ferrari to see Barry Klein," I said, as I watched Scotty check his list to see if Mr. Ferrari had been cleared.

"I've got a Mr. Foster to see Mr. Cohen," Scotty reported, without looking up.

"That's me." I didn't wait for Scotty to signal me by. I put Cara Mia in first and rolled onto the lot.

We didn't get much writing done that day. Most of our time was spent walking to the parking lot to see my new toy. I gave everyone a ride. Even Marcia had to admit the car was beautiful.

"Are we going to go for a ride tonight to break it in?" she asked, her ranting from the day before long forgotten.

"Actually, I'd like to have a little time to drive it by myself first. How about tomorrow?" As soon as I said I wanted to be by myself, Marcia turned and headed for the office. She couldn't even let me enjoy my first day with my Ferrari. Her moodiness was getting old. As I watched her walk back to the office, I decided, privately in my mind, to give her two weeks to straighten up. If she didn't, she was gone. Two weeks seemed fair, and it would take me that long to find the courage to tell her.

I hung around the office until about seven o'clock before heading home. I wanted to take the Ferrari down Sunset at night with the top off, brand spanking new, to let the world know I had arrived. Feeling totally in control, I slipped the top off the Ferrari, popped in a Boz Scaggs tape, and proceeded to Sunset and Vine. My plan was to drive down Sunset as far as Doheny. I figured by then the Ferrari would have performed its magic and I would have some fabulous babe next to me.

The trip started out pretty much as I planned. People couldn't stop complimenting me on the car. At Sunset and Highland, a red light put me next to a fabulous redhead in a Porsche.

"Great car," she said, with a big smile.

"Thanks," I smiled back. That's all I could manage. Come on, Barry, ask her if she'd like to go for a ride. Tell her you like her car. Say anything. The light turned green, she gave me one last look, and then, urged on by the jerk honking his horn behind her, she drove off. What a let down. I was sure the Ferrari would be able to get women into the car all by itself. If I was going to have to talk to strange women, well, if I was able to do that consistently, I wouldn't need a forty-three-thousand-dollar sports car, would I? I was determined to have more success with my next eye-contact encounter.

I was all the way to Fairfax before I hooked up with a brunette in a Mustang. Traffic was moving so we were sort of sneaking glances at each other. Finally, she couldn't help herself.

"It's beautiful," she yelled, after rolling down her window.

"Thanks. I just got it." Okay, Barry. A little better than last time. Why not ask her if she'd like to go for a drink? Once again we smiled at each other. We were both smiling and driving and waiting for Barry to talk. Having worked up the courage to pop the drink question, I began to speak. "What's your name?"

"Marcia." Well, I wouldn't have any trouble remembering that, I thought. However, while deciding whether the fact that this girl's name was Marcia was a blessing or a curse, I realized that she had fallen back. I was now smiling at an old man in a '72 Buick. He, on the other hand, was not smiling but was pointing frantically at something in front of me.

I quickly turned and saw the words "Ford" and "Pinto" getting bigger and bigger as they rushed toward me or I rushed toward them. The Pinto had stopped. The Ferrari hadn't. Although I managed to slow to a mere five miles an hour, that's not a speed a Ferrari will tolerate if it makes contact with another vehicle. The sound of crashing glass filled my head as Ruby Begonia came to a jarring halt. I couldn't believe it. This wasn't happening. Not on the first night I had my Ferrari. As Marcia in the Mustang drove by, she mouthed "Sorry," then threw me a kiss. Well, that was certainly worth forty-three thou, eh Bar?

Now all the people who I had passed, people who had smiled and given me words of admiration and encouragement, went by me shaking their heads. I knew what they were thinking: What kind of idiot cracks up his Ferrari the first night he has it? And of all things to hit—a Pinto?

I reluctantly got out of the car to assess the damage. The Pinto was fine although the decrepit woman in the housecoat who got out of it was rubbing her neck in that "Oh boy, I've been hit by a Ferrari" kind of way. My car had a crumpled front end, and the headlights, which used to pop up from the sloping nose, were now pushed back and not working at all. I convinced the woman we should pull off to a side street and exchange insurance information. There was no need to cause a traffic jam on Sunset. Fortunately, she agreed. I gave her the name of my State Farm agent who I knew would love the call. The last thing he said to me, earlier that very same day, was, "Please, please, please, be careful. We don't usually insure these things." I swore there would be no problem. Looking at the Ferrari's smashed bumper, I knew having my renter's policy as well as my car insurance was going to be little consolation for him when he told his boss what happened.

Lulu in the Pinto smelled a little too much like Scotch to want to stay around for the cops any more than I did. We took each other's info and split. I headed back to the Marina with my parking lights on, the only illumination still working on the Ferrari. Well, that and the 1–4 light, which promptly came on, indicating I had fouled my first spark plug. It shouldn't have been a surprise. I had already driven 12.4 miles.

The next morning, I had the car towed back to Hollywood Sports Cars where Aldo, the head of the body shop, gave me the good and bad news. He could have the car fixed in a week. Everything, that is, except the headlights. It would be at least three months before he could get the parts to fix that. For three months I'd be able to drive my beloved Ferrari. Just not at night. It's not that easy impressing women with a car that has to be home by sundown. Even Cinderella had until midnight. I would have to deal with people as myself. There would be no magic bullet, no lucky rabbit's foot, no potion nor talisman to pull me from my funk. I was just another producer of the number one show on television. With my self-esteem at a new low, that was hardly enough ammunition.

* * *

The six weeks of pre-production didn't fly by. I wasn't sure whether time seemed to be dragging because of the drudgery of the show or because each morning I'd see my gorgeous Ferrari, sitting in the garage, and know there was nothing I could do to get those damned Italians to put my headlight parts on a plane any sooner. Whatever the reason, it was a relief to finally get into production. It was time to shoot our first show of the season.

The week leading up to the filming went smoothly. The Ladies were reasonably content and only bothered Tommy and me with an occasional "A hypnotized chicken wouldn't do that." Then we'd go around and around, explaining that there were no hypnotized chickens. The characters, Patti and Connie, were hypnotized. Since Mimi and Lorraine had never been hypnotized, how would they know whether they would act a certain way? On Wednesday, Mimi suggested we bring in a hypnotist to put both Lorraine and her under. That way, we could find out how they would really act if they were hypnotized and were chickens. Lorraine would have no part of it.

"What if we get hypnotized to act like chickens and we get stuck that way?" she asked Mimi. "Then every week on the show, we'd have to act like chickens. Wait a minute. It wouldn't be just on the show. We'd be chickens."

Mimi laughed. Then, after giving it some thought, she wasn't sure whether Lorraine had a point or not. No, it would be better if they weren't hypnotized in real life and just guessed what it would be like. Hopefully, their performances wouldn't suffer too much.

Before filming, I stopped by Lorraine's dressing room to give her the normal "Have a good show" speech.

"So, are you happy with the show so far?" I was fishing for compliments and we hadn't even shot the first show yet.

"I hate the show," she said, looking me right in the eye. She wasn't kidding.

"I don't hate what you're doing with it, Baaaarrrrry. I just hate doing it. I hate Mimi. I hate Willy. I hate Billy. I really hate Ben Fisher. I know I'm making a fortune, but I don't need it anymore. I've got a fortune. I dread coming to work every day." Her eyes teared up as she rattled off everything about the show she despised. She was really miserable. She had achieved what every actor wants and found it to be an empty experience.

"What do you want to do?" I asked, trying to find a solution to her problem. An unhappy Lorraine would be a festering sore.

"I want to direct feature films," she said, totally unaware of the competition she'd be facing from all the Marcia Heilger types in the studio secretarial pool.

"Why don't you? If you don't need the money and you're miserable . . . what is it that Bobby always says? Life is more important than show business. You should do what you want."

"Maybe I will. I just found a great script by this guy, Dave Larson."

I didn't want to ruin Dave's career, but I had heard that he was no longer just selling pot. He was also dealing cocaine. Lorraine needed to be warned before she bought a script from a coke dealer.

"How well do you know Dave?"

"He's my coke dealer," she said without a trace of hesitation. "He's got this wonderful script about a writer who has to become a drug dealer when this guy who's his best friend starts working on a hit television show won't give him any work."

"Sounds pretty far-fetched. I don't think that could happen," I said innocently.

"You should read it. It seems so real."

"Not to me. Have a good show," I said, as I slinked away.

Drum roll. Well, close to a drum roll. Howie Clark had

been unable to find a suitable adoptive home for Paco, the parrot. As a result, Howie was having more trouble than usual making the drum come to life for his Bobby Mitchell introduction with Paco walking up and down his arm. The bird wanted to perch on the drumstick. Howie did the best he could.

"Ladies and Gentlemen, the number one . . stop it, Paco . . . producer in television today . . . Bobby Mitchell!"

Crisscrossing spotlights. Standing ovations. The audience went wild. The show was a bigger hit than ever. Bobby was about as happy as he could be as he welcomed everyone back for the fourth season. Why shouldn't he be happy? All we had to do was make it through this season and he'd have his one hundred episodes of *In the Swim*. Because the show was a hit, after the first season's order of twenty-two episodes, the network began ordering twenty-six episodes a season. At the end of this season we'd be in the promised land — fat city — TV syndication.

Lorraine and Mimi were brilliant as chickens. They even improvised a chicken fight when Mimi got in one of Lorraine's close-ups. Lorraine wasn't about to share the camera with Mimi so she began to peck her. Mimi pecked back. It went on for about three minutes. The audience thought it was great. Watching from behind the cameras, Tommy and I knew The Ladies were really going after each other. The real question was whether the fight would continue after the show. It did. Lorraine and Mimi took their bows together after the last scene. They held hands and kissed each other on the cheek just as they did after every show. Then they got backstage and the fireworks began.

"I'm not putting up with this for another season, you bitch. When the camera's on me, stay out of my goddamn shot!" Lorraine was much bigger than Mimi and she backed her up toward the wall as she yelled.

"I don't know what you're talking about," Mimi answered, in a way that said she knew perfectly well what she had done and that it was just too bad.

"I think what Lorraine is saying . . ." For some reason, Howie decided to step in and be the peacekeeper. It was a dumb thing to do. The Ladies had many battles over the previous three seasons. None of them had gotten physical. This season would be different. Just as Howie stepped between them to allow cooler heads to prevail, Lorraine took a swing at Mimi. She missed, hitting Paco who was still perched on Howie's shoulder. The bird went flying. Not your natural bird flying, mind you, but caught in the side of the head by a wicked left hook kind of flying. Paco lay on the floor, a pile of beautiful green, red, and blue feathers. Everyone stood still waiting for the bird to shake it off and return to Howie's shoulder. He didn't move. Mimi was the first to rush to Paco. She cradled him in her hands and held him by her ear, hoping to hear him breath. Howie watched in total shock.

"Paco? Come on, Paco." Mimi was one of the few people on the show who liked Howie's parrot. "Can you fly, baby?" As Mimi asked, she launched the bird into the air. I guess she figured that if there was any life left in Paco, he'd start flapping his wings rather than crash and burn. He came down with as much of a thud as a bird can make. Mimi, again, held the lifeless body.

"Is he dead?" a shaken Howie asked.

Lorraine, who was not a big fan of the bird, put her arm around Howie. It appeared compassionate. But she couldn't hide her true feelings. "Maybe not, Howie. Maybe he's just stunned. Why don't we have Mimi throw him up in the air again? It may not help but it was fun to watch."

"You are the coldest cunt . . ." Mimi didn't swear that often but she obviously knew how.

"I don't have to take this," Lorraine said, as she stomped off to her dressing room. Mimi again dropped Paco and ran after Lorraine.

"Don't you walk away from this, Lorraine. This was your fault!" Mimi was a yappy dog at Lorraine's heels.

The crowd that gathered for the fight watched our two gracious stars scream at each other as they headed for their dressing rooms. Our attention was finally diverted by Howie, who was now crying over his deceased parrot.

"Why? Why? Why did this have to happen?" Howie was sobbing and looking for answers. Specifically from me.

"I don't know what to say, Howie." I looked to Tommy. "Reverend?"

"Howie, who knows why the Lord chose to take Paco at this time? But He must have some plan for Paco."

My guess was that the Lord's plan for Paco was that he be put in a shoe box and buried in the back yard. It's a bird, for crying out loud. I must be a bit less sensitive than others about these things because quite a few people, including Marcia, decided to go home with Howie to make sure he was okay. Marcia's trip to Howie's was fine by me as I wasn't looking forward to going to her place after the show. It wasn't just being with Marcia that I was dreading. I didn't feel like socializing at all.

On the way home, I realized what the problem was. This was the first show of the season. Linda always came to the first show of the season. Even if she missed every other show, she came to the first. I missed her. It was another reminder of how I had blown things. How many chances are we given in a lifetime for a special relationship? Hopefully, more than one. There was an emptiness in my life. No one was supplying that special connection. The step beyond the fun. All I wanted to do was talk to Linda, and that was against the rules.

Pulling into the garage, seeing the crippled Ruby Begonia, it was crystal clear that my Ferrari wasn't the only thing missing an important part.

THIRTEEN

You Don't Have to Hit Me
over the Head with a Turkey Leg

Monday morning I arrived at the office in time to find Marcia on the phone with, I assumed, a man. I came to this conclusion based on the fact that as she kept the phone cradled between her ear and shoulder, she was creaming her legs. Normally that wouldn't have aroused any suspicion. This time, Marcia was creaming them all the way up to the top. The tippee top. That is, until I walked in and said, "Good morning." Then, the legs came instantly down as Marcia told the person on the phone she'd call them back.

"Who was that?" I asked, as I casually looked through a small pile of phone messages.

"Just a friend," she answered, her face slightly flushed. She was hiding something. "John Bracca wants you in his office right away," she added, almost as an afterthought.

"John Bracca? What does he want? Did he say anything?" My reaction was rapid fire. In all my time at Paragon Studios, John Bracca had never called me into his office. Except for the annual note, thanking me for a great season, obviously written by a secretary on his stationery, we had almost no contact. I had nothing to say to the Executive Vice President of television and took comfort in the fact that he had nothing to say to me. We had an understanding of sorts, about having nothing to say to each other. When we'd pass each other on the lot, I'd give him a very curt "John" and he'd give me an extremely curt "Barry." Then we'd both have to smile at how curt we were. It had become our little joke and often, after passing him on the lot, I'd find myself smiling for quite some distance at our ability to have such a good time while saying almost nothing. At some point, I sensed he even liked me.

I rushed out of my office, heading to Bracca's, stopping only to give Marcia a hard time as I left.

"That was a guy, wasn't it?"

"Who was a guy?" she asked innocently.

"On the phone. You were talking to a guy and practically playing with yourself, for Christ's sake."

"Barry!" She was flustered. It was a guy.

If Marcia had a new boyfriend, breaking up would be much easier than I anticipated. That pleasant thought got me all the way to the administration building and up to John Bracca's office. As head of Paragon's very successful television division, he had a huge office that featured an impressive art collection. The waiting area alone had original works by Willem de Kooning and David Hockney. They were both gifts from the studio. John Bracca had taken Paragon Television from a low point, seven years earlier, when the studio only produced *Big Freddie,* a horrible show about an inept Mafioso, to where the studio stood today, Hollywood's most prolific and successful maker of TV product. It was Bracca who convinced the likes of Bobby Mitchell to create their shows at Paragon Studios. Bracca nurtured the relationships with the networks to get his shows on the air. It was Bracca who convinced the stars to come to work at Paragon.

Although only thirty-seven years old, John Bracca was one of the most powerful men in Hollywood. As his secretary told me to go right in, I looked forward to giving him his "John" and getting back my "Barry." The anticipation of the exchange put a smile on my face as I entered the office.

"Why the fuck did you tell Lorraine LaBarbara to quit the show?" Bracca bellowed as I entered. I was dumbfounded. His greeting left no room for my "John." I looked around the office and saw we weren't alone. Bobby Mitchell was on the couch along with Mason Green and Stu Phillips. Phillips, the head of current programming at the network, was Green's boss.

"Quit the show? Why would I tell her to quit the show?" I asked, my heart pounding in my ears.

Bobby Mitchell picked up the interrogation.

"I got a call from Lorraine's agent this morning. She's left the show."

"She wants to direct some fucking movie." Bracca couldn't keep quiet. He was livid. He paced, his face as tight as a drum. "She says you told her to do whatever she wants. Well, she wants to direct a fucking movie. I want her in my fucking TV show, and you've got her directing a fucking movie!" He was spitting each time he said "fucking."

I wanted to say "Say it, don't spray it," to take some of the tension out of the room, but I didn't dare.

"Why would you say something like that to her?" Bobby asked, trying to calm things.

"We were just making conversation. She said she was miserable. You're the one who says life is more important than show business." I wanted Bobby to share the blame.

"Life *is* more important than show business. But not for

actors. They have to act. They have no choice. You never tell an actor that life is more important than show business. Never." They all shook their heads as Bobby said "never."

"I was just trying to be honest with her," I said, in my defense.

"Not with an actor," Bobby added. I waited to hear the rationale behind this blanket disregard for all actors, but there was none coming.

"Well, what are you going to do?" Mason Green asked Bracca and Mitchell with authority. He loved putting people like John Bracca and Bobby Mitchell on the spot. Green had no real power over them. He wasn't about to miss taking advantage of a situation like this.

"Maybe I can talk to Lorraine and change her mind," I offered.

"We told her we'd double her salary and that didn't work. What are you going to say that can top that?" Bracca continued to pace.

A hundred and fifty grand per episode and she wasn't coming back? What was wrong with this girl?

"What are we going to do to protect the franchise?" Stu Phillips interrupted. It was a fair question. It's not easy getting the number one show on television. A network doesn't want to give it up when it gets one.

"I think we should shut down for a week and threaten to sue her ass if she doesn't honor her contract." Green was enjoying this tough guy act. Everybody in the room knew that he would pee in his pants if Lorraine so much as looked at him the wrong way.

"We can't shut down because of Mimi's deal," Bracca explained.

"Mimi? I thought the problem was with Lorraine?" Phillips was confused.

"Lorraine quit. Mimi's got to be done by the end of January, because she's making a fucking movie." This time Bracca caught me with a rather large gob of spit seen by everybody in the room. Something had to be said besides Bracca's "Sorry, Barry."

I gave him his usual, "John." It made him smile. It was safe to breathe again. Bracca shook his head. We had a problem on our hands.

Since it appeared the whole thing was my fault, I was glad I came up with an idea that the others seemed to accept.

"Why don't we just do a few episodes without Connie? That'll give us time to continue talking with Lorraine. If she changes her mind, it's no big deal. If she doesn't, we'll have time to come up with a story that'll make her leaving an event. You know, she could run off to get married. Or get killed. Something we could promote."

Stu Phillips cautiously warmed to the idea. "I suppose killing her could be promotable. Could we kill her during the November sweeps? Can you make it funny?"

"I'm sure Barry and his gang can make Connie's death very funny," Bobby assured the executives.

By the end of the meeting, they were in love with the prospect of Connie dying. They had convinced themselves that the show would actually be better with her dead. I knew otherwise. Walking back to my office, I went over all the stories we had lined up for the season. Each one depended on Connie and Patti being alive. Not just Patti. We had lost all our preproduction work. We were, in essence, beginning a new season in four days without so much as a notion of what the new show would be. We were only in round two of the twenty-six-round fight, and it looked like we had been hit by a knock-out punch.

The writing staff gathered and spent about ten minutes chastising me for ever talking to Lorraine and about twenty minutes hilariously roasting me about it. Then we began to pitch ideas of what Mimi could do alone. For the first two hours, it seemed the answer was nothing. Then Mimi stopped by. She wanted to give the writing staff a pep talk.

"I came down here as soon as they told me what was going

on. I want you to know that I appreciate how hard this is going to be on you. If there's anything I can do to help . . ." She stopped because we were all laughing. It was the voice.

"I'm sorry, Mimi, we're not laughing at you. We're just a little punchy. We've been looking for ideas for the past couple of hours and we haven't come up with anything great." I decided, contrary to Bobby Mitchell's advice, I better be honest with her.

"Well, I certainly hope you weren't laughing at me. Because, as of now, I'm an executive producer on the show. I'm going to be very involved in the whole process. All stories have to be approved by me. I want to see every draft of every script. Nothing is to be done without my O.K." The voice didn't sound so funny anymore.

It had only taken two hours for Paragon Studios to give Mimi the key to the store. Her agents had demanded, and gotten, Mimi the title of executive producer with all the power that the title brought. They said Mimi would only do the show by herself if she got both her and Lorraine's salary—one hundred and fifty thousand dollars per episode. Larry Brogan her, philandering, alcoholic, oh-so-very-talented husband, was to be a consultant on the show, making sure that no one was doing or saying anything that wasn't in Mimi's or his best interest. My job, which was hard enough under ideal conditions, would now be hell.

"Well, any ideas for the next show?" I asked, thinking we might as well get Mimi right into the mix. In the past, her ideas were pretty good.

"I think I'd be funny wearing big hats. You know, really big. That's what I want for the first show. Let me know when you've got something." With that, Mimi left the room. Normally, that would have been a relief. With her gone, we'd be free to bitch and moan. Instead, when she left, Larry came in. He sat down, obviously planning to stay. It was very awkward. We couldn't carry on about what a lousy idea Mimi had just given us. "Big hats?" "How do you do a show about someone wearing big hats?" We couldn't call her lewd names or rant or rave or do all the things writers do before they settle down to work. We all just sat there looking at each other. Finally, Tommy Cross, the old Tommy Cross, took over.

"Get out of here, Larry, we've got work to do," he said, giving Larry a cold stare.

"No, you don't understand." Larry was going to challenge him. "See, Mimi wants—"

"I don't care what Mimi wants. Either you're out of here or we're out of here. Are you and Mimi going to write the show yourselves?" It wasn't exactly the old Tommy. He wasn't screaming, swearing, or physically threatening Larry. Still, he had all the power of the old Tommy.

"Let's see what the studio says about this." Larry wasn't about to leave quietly.

"Fine," Tommy said as he picked up the phone and dialed John Bracca's extension. "John Bracca, please. Tommy Cross calling and it's urgent." Normally, John Bracca would not be bothered by a show's producer over day-to-day operations. This day, however, was different than most. It only took a second for Bracca to get on the line with Tommy.

"John, I just wanted you to know that if Larry Brogan is in our writers' meetings, I quit. So does Barry. And, I assume, so does the rest of the writing staff." There were nods of agreement all around the table as Tommy took a stand for all of us. Donna Morris blew Tommy a kiss.

Larry Brogan was not shaken by our show of solidarity. "You're all going to be sorry for this. We'll just get new writers."

"Yeah," Tommy reported into the receiver. He's here—just a minute." Tommy offered the receiver to Larry. "It's for you."

"John, Larry Brogan." Brogan listened for a moment as Bracca was trying to keep the peace and a great writing staff in tact. "I don't think Mimi's going to be very happy about this. And, to tell you the truth, neither am I."

If Larry could get John Bracca to back down, the game was over. Mimi would be able to get whatever she wanted, whenever she wanted it. The shark smelled blood.

John Bracca did not get to where he was by backing down from the likes of Larry Brogan. Suddenly, Larry's face turned ashen as he pulled the receiver away from his ear. Bracca's screaming could be heard across the room. The tirade went on for about two minutes. "Fucking" this and "fucking" that. Bracca's phone must have been dripping wet. Then, Bracca's end of the phone was silent.

Larry Brogan stood up, stiffly, glaring at us. "You people are going to rue the day you crossed Larry Brogan," he said through clenched teeth.

I couldn't let well enough alone. "Rue the day? Who are you, Snidely Whiplash?" I asked, comparing Larry to Dudley Dooright's arch enemy. The other writers cracked up as Larry, the defeated bully, turned quickly and left the room without saying another word.

For the next five minutes we celebrated our victory and profusely thanked Tommy for his courage, which he, of course, credited to the power of his Lord, Jesus Christ. That was the only disappointment. I thought the old Tommy was back. He wasn't. The party finally ended when Rhonda Silverman brought us back to reality.

"What if Patti somehow got into a fashion show and she had to wear a big hat? Maybe it could be something about foreign countries. You know, a big Eiffel Tower hat for France and a big gondola hat for Italy." God bless Rhonda Silverman. The now regular emergency visits from Butch hadn't affected her writing ability. We wouldn't be knocked out in this round. We would do our show about big hats. It didn't matter that the story made little sense and the show turned out terrible. What mattered was we didn't shut down.

Instead of celebrating the shooting of the big hats show, on the way home I stopped at the Frolic Room to console myself. No matter how bad things got for me, I could always hold my life up against Lou Williams's and ask, "How about now?" I found Lou on his usual bar stool. He was more depressed than I'd ever seen.

"What's wrong?" I asked after signaling the barkeep to give me the usual and pour another for Lou.

The bartender delivered my bourbon just as Lou delivered the news. "I went to the doctor today," he said sadly, tears welling up in his eyes.

"Is it bad?" I asked with real concern. I had grown to genuinely like Lou.

"It's worse than bad. I'm not going to die. Either the

alcohol killed whatever was killing me or they were full of shit or something. I'm going to live." He was choking back the emotion.

"That's great!" I raised my glass in a toast.

"Is it?" he asked, looking down at his glass. "I can't be a drunk anymore." He sat silently for a moment then growled, "Fuck!" With that he downed his shot of whiskey, threw a twenty-dollar bill on the bar and walked out. There was nothing I could do for him. He would have to fight the good fight himself. I knew from Tommy's occasional, pre-Jesus, attempts at sobriety, Lou's journey would not be easy. It put my problems in perspective.

After the terrible show about big hats, we did two more stinkers: one about Patti helping some seniors avoid eviction from their apartment building and another about Patti saving some dogs from the pound. Mimi's input was simple. She wanted Patti to do good things. Her thinking was, America would love her.

America wanted to laugh at her. They wouldn't care if she killed babies as long as it was funny. Patti being good wasn't funny, and America stopped watching. Not all at once, but slowly. It was after the third show aired without Lorraine that we slipped from our number one spot. We were number five that week.

At first the network and studio did their best to rationalize the ratings slippage. CBS ran *The Wizard of Oz* against us. That always did well. The following week the excuse was that ABC had

a very special *Three's Company* where Jack dressed up as a girl.
Special? Denial was the soup de jour. They didn't want to face the
fact that, without Lorraine, the show wasn't working.

For a couple of weeks, Bobby Mitchell got involved in
trying to find a solution to our problems. Each week he brought
in a new guest star to play opposite Mimi. Some were better than
others. But even JoAnn Worely, the best of the lot, didn't have
Lorraine's chemistry with Mimi. The magic was gone, yet we
plowed on. We were still a top fifteen show, and a network doesn't
get rid of a top fifteen show.

* * *

The Santa Ana winds had been battering L.A. for three
straight days. They blew in hard from the desert, making the city
unbearably hot and a sizable portion of the population certifiably
mental. There was something about the scorching winds that put
the City of Angels on edge. The maddening breezes along with the
mounting problems on the show made it impossible for me to go
to work. I needed to go. I just couldn't motivate myself. Eleven
o'clock in the morning and I was walking the beach. Small waves
were breaking close to shore, sending water up around my ankles.

Death in the family. I tested excuses for my absence as I
walked. If I didn't go to work, I'd have to have an explanation for
Bobby Mitchell. I dismissed death in the family. If you use that

one, it could happen. I've got enough guilt in my life, thank you.

Sitting at the water's edge, I thought about telling Bobby I was sick. It wasn't a total lie. I was definitely feeling ill. Mentally ill. I was seriously depressed by my life, both in and out of the office. The questions about life, my life, were relentless. How could I have betrayed Linda? How would I break up with Marcia? How could I make the show better? What did I want from life? I had no answers.

"Playing hooky?"

Looking up, over my shoulder, into the morning sun, I couldn't clearly make out who was talking to me. He had gray hair. Not a full head. Just around the sides. A slight paunch peeked out from his baggy bathing suit. Sunglasses hid his eyes. A good tan along with bare feet and chest made him look like a middle-aged beach bum.

"Do I have that 'playing hooky' look?" I asked, as I looked back to the ocean. I wasn't sure I wanted to chat with a stranger in the little time I had left before I absolutely had to head for the studio.

"You look like you have a lot on your mind. Want to walk?"

Okay, normally a strange guy on the beach asks you to go for a walk, you say, "No way." By 1980, enough chopped-up bodies had been found in the high desert for you to know that even adults shouldn't take candy from strangers. But somehow this was different. One of the things about Linda I missed the most was her New age Lessons in life, like the importance of listening to your inner voice. If she said banging a gong would open a certain chakra that, in turn, would unblock my funny bone, then the gong banging would begin. I just never had the discipline to stick with any of it when left to my own devices. Now an inner voice was telling me to go with this man. It was screaming.

"Sure, what the hell?" I said to the stranger as I stood. I was tired of listening to myself whine. Why not let the kind stranger listen to my tale of woe? We walked toward the Venice Pier, starting with introductions but quickly moving on to what was going on in my life. After he told me his name was Marty Wachs, I didn't give him much chance to jump into the conversation. But he didn't seem to mind. He was obviously a good listener as I rambled and gave him the whole story: Linda, Marcia, Tanya, the job, the fouled spark plugs; life was supposed to be great, and it was all turning sour. By the time we got back to my spot on the beach, I had talked so much, I was beginning to lose my voice.

"What do you do, Marty?" I asked. I figured I'd let him gab for a while so I could take a break. I was drained.

"I'm a psychologist," he said, picking up a few small shells from the beach. He threw them in the water one by one.

"A shrink? What do you do, just troll the beach looking for psychopaths?"

"You just looked like you needed to talk. And judging from the amount you did, I'd say I was right." His smile was warm, his tone supportive.

"A shrink? Geez, you should warn people. So what happens now? Just because I've told you my life story, I'm supposed to come lie on your couch once a week?" I don't know why I was challenging him. I had spilled my guts to him and was already feeling better.

"If I were you, I'd come twice a week. At least in the beginning. With someone as bright as you, it shouldn't take that long to figure things out." He gave me a pat on the back, another flash of the warm smile, then started walking away. "My office is in Santa Monica. I'm in the book." That was it. He was gone.

I looked at my watch. It was twelve-thirty. I had to get to the office. Running across the hot sand, back to the apartment, I again thought about Linda and how she used to say the universe always sends what you need. How about this quick service? I had just started thinking that I was cracking up and a shrink appears.

Staring at my open closet, trying to find something to wear to work, I leafed through the trousers. I didn't want to get dressed. What would happen if I showed up at work in my bathing suit? What would happen if I didn't show up at all? What should I do? Should I go? Should I light a joint? No, it was too hot to be stoned. It was too hot for anything. Sitting on the floor by the bed just looking at the wall, sweat dripping off my face, I had to find a way to make things better. There had to be answers to at least some of the questions. My relationship with Linda had failed. My relationship with Marcia had failed. Even when I saw a woman casually, something that shouldn't create emotional baggage, there seemed to be drama involved if we didn't see each other again. Where were the shallow women only interested in meaningless sex? Why couldn't I find them? Why couldn't they find me? What was wrong with me? What would make me happy? Spending eighty-five dollars an hour to discover whether this was all my parents' fault wouldn't be my idea of fun. But I had to do something. In the technical terminology of Dr. Freud, I was going coo coo.

"In Santa Monica, I'd like the number for a Marty Wachs. He's a psychologist." I closed my eyes and waited for the operator to find the number. A cooling breeze came through the window signaling some welcomed relief.

For the next six weeks, every Tuesday and Thursday morning, I'd spend an hour with Marty. He didn't mess around.

He got right to things. Marty didn't believe in years of analysis. Identify the problem and figure out how to deal with it. I liked that.

We started right in with Mom and Dad because that's where I thought therapy was supposed to start.

"It's as good a place to start as any," Marty assured me. "We usually learn how to act in an intimate relationship from what we saw growing up." It didn't take long to realize that Muriel and Irv did the best they could. Yes, they made some mistakes, but all in all, they did a pretty good job. Muriel treated me like a prince, and the only thing Irv did that I could consider damaging and, therefore, the cause of my deviant behavior, was being so damned faithful to Muriel. He didn't tell me that when you got to be a man, you thought about sex constantly. Monogamy? He made it all look so easy. Too easy.

I had my first revelation. I could take the next five sessions wondering why Irv held back on the secrets of life or simply forgive him. A little quick mental math made me realize I'd save four hundred and twenty-five dollars by forgiving. Mom, Dad, I love you. Moving on.

As badly as I felt about losing Linda, I didn't think I felt badly enough. My adjustment to single life seemed much too easy.

"How long do you want to punish yourself?" Marty asked.

"How long am I supposed to punish myself?" I was new to

all of this.

"As long as you want to," Marty informed me. "But I've got to tell you, Barry, I don't think your adjustment has been as easy as you think. The guy I met on the beach was in a lot of pain."

"Losing a woman like Linda, I should be crushed. Nonfunctional. Life should not be worth living," I explained, not wanting to get better any quicker than I should.

"Barry, your suffering is real. Honor it. If you need more time that's fine. But I think you seem okay with this."

I figured Marty should know. He was the doctor.

The next issue was a bit more difficult. Why couldn't I make an emotional commitment to any of the women I was sleeping with? I mean, I was starting to wonder if I'd ever be in a successful relationship again. Surely, a question as complex as this would take longer to solve than my first two problems. It did take longer, but not much. Instead of leaving me to flounder around, trying to find an answer on my own, Marty did me a great favor and passed on some advice from his older, more experienced self. Marty was in his early sixties, from a different generation. Yet he seemed like a contemporary. He was in good shape for his age. He still had the confidence and the air of the fighter pilot who flew bombing missions over Germany nearly forty years earlier. He was a man. A he-man. He knew women. He lived life.

"Barry, guys are just different. Those women don't want you to be a man. They want you to be a woman. Then you would understand what they want. The truth is, you do understand what they want. You just don't want to give it to them."

"You're right. If I really felt something for them, there wouldn't be a problem. For my first eight years of marriage, before Marcia's lovely legs were dangled in front of my face day after day, I was totally committed to Linda. It wasn't that hard to do." I was beginning to see the light. "But what about all the nagging?" I was hoping Marty would keep the wisdom coming.

"They're probably not nagging, Barry. But that's the way you feel. You have to decide when the price is too high. When they're asking more than you're able to give, you've got decisions to make. Do you stay or go? And the sooner you make those decisions, the less complicated they are."

There was the catch. I would have to make decisions. If you decide not to start spinning a plate, you don't have to keep spinning it.

"But what if the answer is always that I'm not happy? That's the way it seems, lately."

"Then you'll be alone. You might even find that it's actually okay," Marty said with a reassuring smile.

Alone? There was a scary thought. When Linda and I split

up, I thought I'd be alone a lot. It had now been many months
and I hadn't been alone much at all. Well, this didn't answer my
question. If anything, it brought up more to think about when I was
alone.

There really wasn't that much alone time available, the
main reason being that the show was taking up more and more
of my life. From the day Lorraine left, we were playing catch-up.
There was no time to do second or third drafts of scripts. We'd
think up stories, write them, shoot them, and ship them. It was no
wonder the quality was suffering.

We were nine shows into the season when the second big
bomb hit. Willy announced that he, too, was leaving. He didn't
care that we had a contract and might tie him up in litigation for
the rest of his career. He didn't care that we, once again, would
have to throw out any stories we had that contained both Willy and
Billy. Once Lorraine, was gone, we depended even more heavily
on the boys to carry the show. Willy especially didn't care that
Billy, his partner for the last three years of the show and the seven
years before that when they worked as a comedy act, would be
totally lost without him. Willy had been offered an opportunity he
couldn't turn down. When Lorraine LaBarbara cast him as the coke
dealer in her movie, he jumped ship.

The news of Willy's departure was much less dramatic than

when Lorraine left—a simple phone call from Bobby Mitchell saying that Willy was gone. That was it. No "Sorry for the inconvenience," no "I don't know how you guys are going to keep this thing going." He just gave me the news and hung up. It was Wednesday when he told me. That gave us three days to come up with a new script for the following week.

"How about a show where Billy wears big hats?" Donna Morris said as we began our search for new levels of mediocrity.

"What if Billy and Patti go into business? Then we wouldn't have to kill ourselves to get them together. It would also be easier to bring in outside characters." Aki Nakamura was rapidly becoming an important part of the staff. She was coming up with more and more usable ideas. We bounced it around and decided that Patti could get wrapped up in the roller skating craze and want to open a skate rental shop at the beach. Short of money to open the store, she'd turn to Billy, who, in his grief over Willy's sudden marriage to a mud wrestler, would lend her the cash as long as he got to be an equal partner.

It wasn't great but it was good enough. That's all we were looking for. Aki would write the script in two days. She was the logical choice. Since she began taking vitamin shots, she needed less sleep than the rest of us. She'd hand it in Friday morning, we'd give it the once over, and be ready for Monday. Things would be jumping. While Aki was writing, the rest of the staff would be coming up with new Patti and Billy stories to get us through the season. I only wished we had more time.

Be careful what you wish for. Before I knew it, the show had slowed to a crawl. After only three episodes featuring the new team of Patti and Billy, Mimi began to break out in hives, on Monday mornings, when she didn't like a script. The studio brought in a parade of doctors in an attempt to alleviate the unsightly skin blotches to no avail. It got to the point where if Mimi didn't like what she read on the first five pages of script, she'd be scratching and breaking out before the end of act one. The next three episodes took nine weeks to complete. We'd begin work, Mimi would break out, we'd close down. The writers would attempt to rework the script to Mimi's liking and we'd try again.

When Mimi's skin problems first started, everyone was very sympathetic. The studio and network encouraged her to take it easy. Their main concern was Mimi's health. Then it started to cost them money. "To hell with Mimi, we've got a show to do." They began to wonder if we could work the skin disorder into the show. If Mimi had rashes, why couldn't Patti?

The network would have liked to cancel *In the Swim* and replace it with another series. But we had stopped our ratings slide and settled in as the number twenty-five show on television. Hardly a hit. Still, you don't cancel the number twenty-five show without having something better with which to replace it.

The slow pace of the show gave me plenty of time to skate at Flipper's. Each night, I'd circle the floor trying to come up with a way to finally and completely break up with Marcia. Her fling with her guy on the phone was all too brief, leaving her with plenty of time to figure out ways for us to be together. The time had come to move along. One night, it hit me. Literally. I was rolling along when a novice skater, having great trouble keeping his balance, bumped into me, then grabbed me and pulled me to the floor. To make matters worse, he couldn't get himself up. I had to help him. We struggled to the side of the rink and I deposited him on the rail.

"Thanks for the help, man. Sorry about that," he yelled, to be heard over the blaring music.

"Don't worry about it," I replied. I could be generous. Everyone had seen me help him off the floor. It was quite evident that he, not my skating ability, had caused the fall.

Before I skated away from him, he gingerly removed one hand from the rail and extended it for a handshake. "Harold Kimmel."

"Barry Klein. You take it easy out there."

"Are you the Barry Klein who produces *In the Swim*? he asked, quickly returning his hand to the railing to keep his balance.

"Yes, I am," I answered proudly. Even though the show was no longer a hit, producing it was still a power position.

"I worked with your former secretary, Beth. She was my assistant."

Kimmel! I could kill him and not spend a day in jail. Justifiable homicide. I wanted to kick his skates out from under him, but he fell again without my help.

From the floor, he said, "You know, Beth left me about a month ago. I still haven't been able to find anyone to replace her. She was one of a kind, wasn't she?" Kimmel wanted to be buddies as I once again helped him to his feet.

"Actually, Beth wasn't nearly as good as the secretary I have now, Marcia Heilger. She makes Beth look incompetent," I told him. "I'll never let her get away the way I did with Beth. Are you going to be okay?" I didn't care about his well-being. I wanted the Marcia remark to be heard loud and clear.

"Yeah. I'll be fine. Nice meeting you." Kimmel inched along the rail, hand over hand, until he made it off the slippery wood surface and onto the carpet where he could walk.

The nice thing about Hollywood scum is there's a level of consistency. If a person is willing to steal your secretary once, they'll do it twice.

"My new title will be assistant to Mr. Kimmel." Three days

after my chance meeting with Kimmel at Flipper's, Marcia was telling me about her new job. She was waiting for me to get upset, waiting for me stand up and say I wouldn't let her go.

"That's great, Darlin'. You know, because of the secretaries' union, I could never make you my assistant. I'm not going to stand in the way of a great career move like this," I said, forcing myself not to jump up and click my heels.

"I feel like I'm abandoning ship, leaving in the middle of the season. Are you going to be okay? We'll still see each other outside of work." Marcia was fishing for reassurance more than checking up on me.

"I'll be fine." Yes, I would be fine. Marcia was on her way out of my life. In one week she'd be making Kimmel coffee. In three he'd fall for the creamy legs and they'd be sleeping together.

It only took two weeks before Marcia told me about their relationship, I acted as hurt as I could. I'm not much of an actor, though. It's why I became a writer. I said I would have trouble getting over her. The huge smile on my face said otherwise. The one nice thing Marcia did do for me was she gave me the bad news in bed. One last fling with my pal Red, the news about Kimmel, a sweet kiss, and good-bye. That left Tanya as the last plate on a stick.

Tanya and I had Thanksgiving dinner at my place. It was more than just Tanya and I. Bubby Lake and the kids joined us.

When Tanya and Bubby had split up, Tanya promised that Bubby would always be able to join her on Thanksgiving. It was his favorite holiday and the thought of having to eat turkey dinner by himself at Denny's made him a touch suicidal. We had a great time. We had all gotten used to the idea of me being with Tanya during our many trips to Reseda. Bubby had his substance abuse under control and I'd come to like him a lot. I could see how Tanya fell in love with this friendly, bright, funny, giant. Bubby had a great sense of humor. I was almost tempted to have him write a spec script. Remembering Tanya's stories about his rages of temper, however, made me think better of it.

I cooked a turkey with all the trimmings. I'm a good cook. Bubby can attest to that. The man ate an enormous amount of food. The kids cleaned their plates, too. When dinner was over, as I cleared the dishes from the table, I saw Bubby take Tanya's hand. After I brought in the apple pie, they asked me to sit down so that we could talk. We didn't have to. I knew from the look Tanya had given Bubby when he took her hand what was going on. She was once again in love with Bubby. They were going to try and make their marriage work again.

Sitting there, the five of us, was an amazing experience. There was no anger or jealousy because I had slept with this man's wife. I knew I would miss Tanya, yet I couldn't help being happy for them. I liked him. I loved her. Not enough to fight for her. Not enough to be there for her. But I loved her. We swore we'd get together all the time. That the kids would call me Uncle Barry. It was a Thanksgiving fable. When they left, after a bear hug from Bubby and a loving hug and a much too short kiss from Tanya, I was alone. For about a second. I picked up the phone to call someone. Anyone. Then, with a new determination, I hung up. There would be no calls to Marcia or Linda or anyone else. Breathe, Barry. It's okay. I sat down with another piece of apple pie and a fresh cup of coffee. Alone.

I thought back to my childhood when, if I misbehaved, my parents would send me to my room as punishment. Once I got there, I was with my little yellow stuffed dog, Ted, and my imagination. It was an escape to a wonderful world of adventure. They thought they were punishing me. I loved it in my room. Now I was back. Being alone was all right. There were no plates spinning this evening. I would make it though the night with just Barry Klein. No Ted, but that was okay, too. In reality, for a stuffed animal, Ted was too damned needy.

FOURTEEN

Hurry Up, There's Another Crazy Guy Waiting

The next two months crawled by. The show had become a chore. The once-hilarious network flagship was now a run-of-the-mill sitcom populated with forced jokes and canned laughter. We knew we were riding a dead horse. Some of us just rode longer than others.

The first to dismount the decaying steed was Rhonda Silverman and, surprisingly, Donna Morris. I thought Donna and I would work together forever. Why would she leave me? The chance to make more money than God by creating her own show. Rhonda and Donna had pitched a pilot to NBC and they bought it. Their show, *Little Doggies,* was about two girls who leave their home in Seattle to become rodeo stars in New Mexico. According to the NBC executives, it was a breakthrough concept, this two-girl thing. Because Donna and Rhonda were doing the show at Paragon Studios, they were able to convince John Bracca to let them off *In the Swim.* There was no telling when we'd finish production and they needed time to write their pilot script. Donna gave me the news while we were having dinner together. Her new office would be in "J" building right next door. We'd still be able to sneak over to each other's office to provide moral support or just hang out when we needed a mid-day break. Once she swore to me that this dinner together would not be our last, I gave her my blessings. The next day, Donna and Rhonda left.

I was down to one session per week with Marty Wacks. Other than wondering if I would ever again have a long-term relationship, I felt relatively sane. I had begun to recognize the early warning signs of trouble when dating new women, and rather than indulging in unnecessary plate spinning, I would exit stage left, quickly and with as little emotional damage as possible. It was honest and much less painful for everyone involved. I came to terms with the fact that the show would never again achieve greatness. I was now a professional comedy writer providing a service — doing the best I could with what I had. It still beat the hell out of selling underwear.

I missed Linda. Our six-months-to-live period had come to an end with no miracle cure from the doctors. No call from the governor. And no call from Linda. We still had no contact. We were finished. I coped with that reality, taking solace from the adage that time heals all wounds—even those that are self-inflicted. No amount of perceived mental health, however, could prepare me for my next bout of separation anxiety.

"Barry, I think we're finished seeing each other," Marty Wachs, my lifeline, reported on that fateful Tuesday.

"Why? What did I do?" I assumed I must have done something to make Marty not want to see me any more.

"You got better," he said with a smile.

"How can I be better? We've only been doing this for three months." I wasn't that opposed to being cured, but I didn't want to stop seeing Marty. I liked our sessions, even if they did sometimes leave me feeling emotionally exhausted. They provided clarity.

"I think you have the skills to cope with what's going on in your life. We're done for now."

I was afraid. "Just because I can cope, you're dumping me? Who's going to give me good advice? Who's going to be there if I need someone to talk to?" I was rambling. "I don't understand. Woody Allen's been in therapy for, like, fifteen years. How can I be done in three months?"

"I think that's something that Woody Allen should ask his therapist," Marty said as he moved from his usual therapist's chair and sat next to me on the couch. He put his arm around my shoulder and explained, "Look, if the people who get better don't leave therapy, then I can't help new people. That's what I do. That's my job."

"What? Have you been walking on the beach again?" I asked. "You found some new nut to take my place?"

He chuckled. "If something specific comes up and you can't handle it, call. We'll deal with it. You'll come in for a tune-up." Marty stood with open arms, inviting me to join him in a hug—a long-lasting bear hug. Then, holding me at arms length, he said, "You've done the work, Barry. You did good. Go live life."

* * *

It was a beautiful Saturday morning when I woke up feeling physically and emotionally fit. I decided to put on my outdoor wheels and skate to Santa Monica and back. It's a fun trip that takes you through the bizarre parade of people along the Venice Oceanfront Walk—the jugglers, the psychics, the Muscle Beach crowd all make for an interesting skate. I normally don't stop to watch any of the side-show acts, but this time a small, old, dark-skinned man, dressed in saffron-colored robes caught my attention. He smiled and waved me over to the card table where he was sitting. His smile was incredibly inviting, considering how many teeth he was missing. I couldn't ignore him. I skated over

and read the sign that was taped to his table: BABA NAM, PAST
LIFE READINGS.

"Excuse me," he said in a thick East Indian accent. "But are
you a writer?"

"Maybe," I answered suspiciously, assuming that after his
lucky guess he was going to try and separate me from my money
in some kind of psychic game of three-card monte.

"You must be a very important one. You have powerful
spirit guides all around you," he said, nodding with great
assurance.

"Yeah. And you wouldn't believe how much they eat. It
would be nice if they'd pick up a check once in a while," I replied.

He laughed, then added, "You're lucky. They very much
like you sense of humor."

"You see spirit guides? I thought your thing was past life
readings?" I figured, as long as they like my sense of humor,
there'd be no harm in asking.

"I do many things. Past life readings is just how I make a
buck," he whispered, as if letting me in on his little secret. "Would
you like a past life reading?"

"Well, I don't really believe in them," I whispered back,
letting him in on my take on things.

"There is much you can learn from your past, you know.

Your distant past," he said, sounding like some gypsy fortune teller. "I can tell you this, these spirit guides around you have things they very much want you to know."

"Really?" I asked, letting down my guard for just a second. I wasn't ready to skate away. What if old Baba Nam had some secret-of-life message for me? After all, the idea of a past life reading wasn't new to me. Linda had exposed me to it, among many other alternative concepts as she traveled the road to enlightenment. The road that led her to becoming some kind of Aquarian hooker. Eleven! That's a lot of guys. You fucked your secretary, Barry, remember? Oh, right.

"Okay, here's my problem with it," I said, deciding to give it to Baba Nam straight. "Every time I talk to someone who's had a past life reading, they tell me their lives were fabulous. They were always some wealthy prince or beautiful princess. Nobody ever shoveled shit during the Inquisition."

"Oh, there were shit shovelers. This time around they are working for the I.R.S.," Baba Nam said with a laugh. Then he quickly turned serious. "You have a crystal, don't you?"

"Yeah, I do." I noticed, as I answered, my heart was beating faster. In the guess-about-Barry department, Baba Nam was now two for two.

"El Morya, one of your spirit guides, wants you to know

that it needs sunlight. Where do you keep it?"

"In my desk drawer." I had put my crystal there so that it would be nearby yet out of sight. I'd take it out when I was writing alone or sometimes I would just hold it for a few minutes. But it always went back in the drawer. I still wasn't ready to answer all the questions it would bring up from the other writers.

"Sunshine. It needs sunshine," he said firmly. His eyes rolled back into his head, slightly, as he continued. "I see El Morya, a member of the Brotherhood of Light, Djwakul, and . . . Homer. In ancient times you used to write with Homer."

"Homer? The *Iliad* and the *Odyssey*, Homer?" I asked, incredulously.

"Yes. You were partners but you broke up before he wrote those. But they were your ideas."

"Oh, come on. I thought up both the *Iliad* and the *Odyssey*? Even my ego isn't that big."

"They were supposed to be part of a trilogy," he continued in his trance. "The third book was to be about two girls who left Athens to live on Mount Olympus."

"I guess it could have been me." The idea of being in the same league as a great writer like Homer was intoxicating. Still, a healthy dose of skepticism kept me from buying into what Baba Nam was saying.

He must have sensed my reluctance because he took my hands in his and said, "I can say no more. They want to talk to you themselves. Please.

Inner voice, intuition, whatever you call it, suddenly, as Baba Nam held my hands, there was a strong, firm voice in my head. I tried to ignore it, but it wouldn't go away: "Stop wasting your time and your talent. There is something important that we must write. Together. It will be a great work. A masterpiece that will affect all of mankind. You must be alone so that you can hear us. It must be soon. Accept your destiny." With that, the voice was gone.

"Are you going to do it?" Baba Nam quietly asked.

"You know what I heard in my head?"

He simply nodded.

"I can't just leave the show to go write because voices told me to."

"It will be a masterpiece. How can you not?"

"Maybe when the season is over," I said, in an attempt to stay rational.

"That may not be the right time. I have a retreat in Ojai. You could come stay there. You'd have the quiet you need."

"And how much will that cost me?" I asked, figuring we'd finally gotten down to the bottom line.

"The truth is always free," he said in a slightly insulted tone.

This was insane. Even if the show was in trouble, I had a job that most writers would kill for. To leave it because of my experience with Baba Nam was more psychotic than any behavior I had revealed to my psychologist, Marty Wachs. Still, if the possibility existed, no matter how slight, to write something special…something to alleviate every writer's worst fear – the fear of being a hack…

I needed a sounding board. Someone who would not arbitrarily discount the Homer scenario, but would help me weigh the pros and cons of this major decision. The last person on earth for me to turn to would be my father. There was no way he would understand the Baba Nam connection. Past lives? Voices from another plane? Please. His idea of divine intervention is when the girl at the ice cream shop puts sprinkles on his cone without him even asking. But I was at my wits end. So during our weekly phone conversation, I broached the subject.

"I'm thinking about leaving the show," I reported in response to the "so what's new, Buddy Boy?" that started every phone call, ever, with my father.

"You got a better offer?" he asked. He was already amazed at the obscene amount of money I was being paid. A better offer would be past obscene. It would be something he could be really proud of.

"No. It's not a better offer. I don't know if there's any money in it at all. I want to go off by myself and figure out what I want to write. Crazy, huh?" I couldn't tell him about the voices. There was no way he'd get it.

"Barry, do you know how Windows By Klein got started?" he asked. The way he asked I knew there was a story coming. I prayed that it was relevant. It was a prayer I had uttered many times while growing up – a prayer rarely answered. He pressed on.

"Your mother and I had been married for about three years. I was selling piece goods in the garment district. I hated it. I didn't have two pennies to rub together. One day, I'm eating a hot dog on the street and this...I don't know...this voice...this idea... something...it pops in my head, Windows By Klein."

My God, I'm not just crazy. It's worse. It's genetic. I'm carrying some recessive gene that makes my family hear voices. I'm one chromosome away from being the Son of Sam. Before refocusing on my father's story, I made a mental note that I must never have children.

My father continued, "Windows By Klein? What the hell does that mean? Then this other thing pops in my head, 'Slats, any color you want.' Once that happened, bingo, I had no choice. Do you know what I'm saying, Barry?"

"I don't have a clue," I answered, hoping he'd get to the

point.

"What do I always tell you?" he asked. "The Klein Clan is special. And you always think that's bullshit, right?"

"Sort of." I was unaware that he was so aware.

"Well it's not bullshit. We're special because we're not afraid to listen to that *mishigoss* that goes on in our heads. Let me tell you something, Barry. Everybody has bumps in their road. How you go over those bumps determines how you live your life. I've always believed that if you put the bumps in your own road, then there won't be room for the bumps that life wants to throw at you. You may not know how big the bump is going to turn out to be, or how gracefully you're going to get over it. But you're going to have bumps anyway. Make your own bumps, Buddy Boy."

The big question, as I entered the studio on Monday morning, was how to tell Bobby Mitchell I was leaving the show. Would I tell him the truth—that I heard voices? In spite of my father's pep talk, a lot of people don't like working with someone who displays one of the major symptoms of schizophrenia. I could say I was leaving to grow as an artist. Surely that would fall into the "Life is more important than show business" category. If Bobby truly believed in this philosophy, except for actors, of course, then maybe he wouldn't go berserk when I told him my plans. I'd tell Bobby right after the Monday morning script reading. If the reading went well, maybe it would seem the show could survive my absence.

One thing you learn in comedy is that timing is everything. Bobby, Tommy, and I were talking together before the script reading. Actually, Tommy and Bobby were talking. I was mentally replaying over and over how I'd tell Bobby the news of my departure. They seemed to be discussing Bobby's idea to bring in Vicki Lawrence as a new regular on the show, when Tommy announced, "Bobby, this is my last week on *In the Swim*.

Bobby remained calm. News of someone leaving the show was now becoming commonplace. I, on the other hand, was panicked. If Tommy was leaving, surely I couldn't. And if Tommy was leaving, I would have to run it alone. That didn't sound very appealing.

"Where are you going?" Bobby asked, still managing to keep his cool. He assumed Tommy had gotten a better offer.

"There's a new Christian cable network. They want to do programming to attract a mainstream audience. They've given me an on-the-air commitment for twenty-two episodes of a sitcom I came up with for them. It's called *Hey, Jesus*. It's about Jesus and his disciples before the crucifixion. John's the really smart one. Paul's the worrier. Matthew's the hypochondriac. Judas the wacky neighbor. It's a gang comedy. I feel really blessed."

Tommy had a holier-than-thou grin on his face as he told Bobby of his good fortune.

"Well, you're not blessed, you're fucked. Because I'm not letting you go." Bobby's calm suddenly had an edge of anger as he told Tommy what's what.

"Come on, Bobby, it's an order for twenty-two. I don't have to do a pilot." Tommy was appealing to Bobby's business sense, knowing Bobby wouldn't be moved by the real reason for *Hey, Jesus*, which was the chance to spread the word of God.

Bobby got right in Tommy's face. "Nobody's leaving this show anymore. Not you. Nobody. If you try to, you'll find out that 'you'll never work in this town again' isn't just some tired cliché. It'll be the story of your life." With that, Bobby walked away and announced that it was time to start the script reading.

Perhaps this wasn't the day to tell Bobby about my plans.

The reading went badly. We had come up with a story entitled "Billy's Revenge" where, because business was bad at the bait shop, Uncle Sal had to come work for Patti and Billy at the skate rental place. Billy constantly put Uncle Sal down and treated him like dirt. The story went nowhere. It was the same joke over and over. By the end of the reading I was cringing each time Billy took a shot at Uncle Sal. I knew we'd be in for an all-night rewrite. I was about to tell the cast the rewrite plan when

Ben Fisher stood up.

"I'd like to say a few words about this script and about the show in general." As Ben spoke, everyone around the table looked down. We knew we were in for one of Ben's diatribes and we were embarrassed for him. "I'm not doing this crap anymore, and I'm going to see to it that none of you do it, either." With that, Ben pulled a large gun out of his briefcase. I have no idea what kind of gun it was—I'm not the kind of guy who knows guns. I do know that it made an unbelievably loud noise when he shot it at Michael Zylik. The bullet just grazed Zylik's arm, yet it was enough of a hit to knock him out of his seat and spray blood all over Mimi, who was sitting next to Zylik. The women in the room began screaming hysterically. The men began diving under the table. I wasn't sure of my sexual orientation as I was both screaming and diving.

"Stop making fun of me, Billy," Ben half yelled, half belched, as he fired another shot. Luckily, Ben hadn't spent much time at the firing range before embarking on his rampage. He missed Billy by a mile, knocking out one of the tall work lights that stood nearby.

Thankfully, Zylik was not badly hurt. He sat crouching behind a chair, holding his arm while he tried to calm Mimi who cowered on the floor next to him. "It's all right, Love. I'm quite fine," he repeated in his soothing English accent. She was still terrified but managed to do it quietly.

Real fear is much different than what most of us think of as fear. I had been afraid to tell Bobby I was going off to Ojai. But that wasn't genuine fear. As I lay on the floor, my script covering my head, as if forty-three pages of paper might somehow slow a bullet aimed my way, I knew I had never really been afraid before. I could only repeat the words, "Oh, fuck" over and over again, a mantra that proved to be anything but calming.

Ben fired two more rounds into the ceiling while still screaming at Billy. I was sure we were all going to die. Where the hell was Scotty O'Rourke? Wasn't this the kind of moment he lived for? Tommy was under the table on his knees having assumed the prayer position. I hoped he was asking Jesus to put down the Groucho glasses and pick up a big stick or something with which to bash Ben over the head.

There was a short cease-fire as Ben looked at his gun, much the same way King Kong looked at Fay Rey the first time he picked her up. It's that big, dumb monkey-taking-a-break-from-his-ransacking-the-city look. He seemed to be thinking, "Hmmm, how'd I this get into my hand? Well, as long as it's here . . ." Ben spotted Mimi and pointed the gun directly at her. He was about to pull the trigger when Bobby Mitchell got up from under the table.

"Ben, stop it!" You had to be impressed with Bobby's

courageous move to challenge Ben Fisher. Not only was he telling Ben to stop, he was using a stern, parental tone of voice. A tone of voice that, when used by most parents, makes their children want to shoot them.

"I'm not taking it anymore, Bobby. You don't know what it's like to be the brunt of every joke. It was one thing when the show was a hit. But now? I can't even get laid. Hookers are turning me down."

As I watched from under the table, I wanted to suggest that perhaps Ben's cigar breath was the problem and not the quality of the show. Instead I stayed down, only peeking to see how Bobby was doing.

"Let's talk about it, Benny. We can change things." Bobby edged toward Ben as he tried to calm him.

"You're jerking me off. You're not going to change anything, you lying sack of shit." Ben raised the gun and pointed it right at Bobby. Mimi screamed. Bobby just kept walking toward Ben.

"You can call me that after all we've been through together? When have I ever lied to you?" Bobby's offensive caught Ben off guard. As Ben thought about the question, Bobby walked up to Ben and, without hesitation, hit him with a roundhouse left. I was surprised to see how much power a small man like Bobby possessed. Ben went down in a heap. Bobby grabbed the gun.

"That was nnnnniiiiiiiiice," I said as I got up, in an effort to ease the tension. No one laughed, but there were smiles all around.

"Okay, that's it. Show's over," Bobby announced to the room.

"That's right." Mason Green, the network representative, thought he was helping get things back to normal. "Let's let the writers get to work on the script. There's a lot to be done." There was no way anyone was going to write any comedy after what we'd been through. I was about to say as much when Bobby jumped in.

"No. You don't understand. The show is over. I'm closing it down. I've had it."

"Hold it. I know we're all upset, but let me call Stu and John Bracca." Green didn't want this happening on his shift. He was supposed to take care of any problems. He wasn't prepared for anything like this.

"You can call anybody you like. I've hated this show for years. I hate that my name is on it. This isn't a Bobby Mitchell show. Bobby Mitchell shows are fun. This isn't. Nobody wants to do it, and nobody should have to. I'm pulling the plug." With that, he headed for the door. He was still carrying Ben's gun. We were all dazed, not sure what to do with Ben or the wounded Michael

Zylik. Harvey Lipshitz finally went to the phone to call for help.
Ben sat slumped in his chair. Alice Martin and Aki comforted
Michael Zylik. It was Billy who immediately got down to business.

"Well, I've got a contract. I'm getting paid for all the
episodes." He said it out loud, but the thought had already gone
through everyone else's mind. Those of us with contracts for the
twenty-six episodes would still be paid by the studio. It was the
best of all worlds. No more *In the Swim* and a big check.

After the police arrived to take Ben away and Zylik
was safely on his way to hospital for bandaging, Tommy and I
walked to our office. He was going on about how God worked
in mysterious ways. It was God's will that he go do *Hey Jesus*. It
was the only rational explanation of the morning's events. Ben's
outburst must have been part of God's plan. I wasn't so sure God
had planted the gun in Ben Fisher's briefcase. The only thing I was
sure of was that the team of Homer and Klein had some writing to
do . . . or should it be Klein and Homer?

FIFTEEN

We Love to Go a Wandering

Baba Nam's retreat was nicer than I expected. He had a small, well-kept house and a guest cottage situated on three acres a few miles outside of Ojai. Things must have been good in the past-life reading biz. The house was light and airy. It wasn't musky like the home of John Reilly, the crystal man. In fact, it was lemony fresh. I would stay and write in the cottage and share my meals in the house with Baba Nam, who turned out to be an excellent vegetarian cook. The rest of the time, I was free to walk the hills of Ojai. Arid, full of scrub, hot days, cool nights, the setting was perfect for a peaceful time of introspection. Yet there was no peace. I was constantly waiting for Homer to keep his end of the bargain. Where was he? It was voices, damn it, that had sent me to Ojai. There had to be a huge revelation coming. Why else was it taking so long? The anticipation was driving me crazy. Especially at night. That's when I expected the supernatural to happen, in the dark of night. Sitting outside the cottage, once darkness had fallen, every noise, every twinkle of every star made me wonder if it were a sign.

Days weren't much better. Since Homer was obviously busy with another project, I spent a lot of time thinking about how life can turn things upside down. Ben Fisher had gone from being a TV star to a resident patient in a mental hospital in little more than an instant. I was no longer the producer of the number one show on television. In fact, if Homer didn't deliver the goods, I was unemployed. Would I ever work again? Was the downfall of *In The Swim* my fault? Most of my contemplation, however, was spent on my marriage to Linda. My conclusion: being in love and faithful isn't easy. It never has been. But it's a choice. Over the previous year, I had experienced the luxury of greener grass on the fooling-around side of the fence. It was fun for a while, but eventually, it got old. And confusing. Not that monogamy is any easier. Being faithfully in love can be a struggle. In a 1976 *Playboy* interview, then candidate Jimmy Carter admitted to lusting in his heart for other women. If a God-fearing, bible toting, man like Jimmy Carter is lusting, what's supposed to happen to a guy like me? How am I supposed to stay on the path of righteousness? A day at a time?

A minute at a time? Is being faithfully married like being in some kind of lifelong twelve-step program? Yes, it is. "Hi, my name is Barry and it's been fourteen seconds since I've thought about a naked woman." Applause from the supportive brotherhood.

Perhaps there is price to pay for not separating fantasy from reality. So you better know what you want your reality to be. And what do you really want, Barry? Do you want a lasting relationship? Or do you want the parade of neurotics who have kept you warm over the past year? Tough questions. What could be more comforting and supportive than a lasting relationship? Who doesn't love a good parade?

I looked for the answer during the days. At night, I waited, terrified, for the burning bush or some sign from Homer that it was time to get started on our masterpiece. It had been more than a month since I had left L.A. What was taking so long? Baba Nam continually told me to have patience. His hospitality and friendship were barely enough to keep me on course. I was rapidly tiring of his advice and his cooking. His clear corn soup, which only weeks before had seemed so perfect, now looked to me like no more than nibblets in dishwater.

Two o'clock in the morning and the air still hadn't cooled off. I lay in bed sweating, unable to sleep while large mosquitoes took turns sucking the life out of me. Thirty-three days away from home and I was more miserable than ever. I began to give God ultimatums. "If I don't hear a voice or see a vision pretty darn soon, you can find yourself another writer. I'm out of here." Just what God needs, more whining from a wayward pilgrim. What does He care if I go home? He'll find someone else who's willing to wait for a miracle.

A flash of light streaked across the cabin window. I immediately began to hyperventilate. This was it. I'd pushed God too far and now he was sending a messenger. The loud knock on the door rattled the whole cabin. It wasn't a peaceful Baba Nam kind of knock. It was an Angel of Death kind of knock. It was too deliberate to be knocked by anything alive.

When I got to the door, I yelled, "Who is it?" in as deep and gruff a voice as I could muster. That should make the Angel of Death think twice before dragging away this tough guy.

"It's Baba Nam. There's an emergency telephone call for you from your agent in L.A. You better come down to the house."

I had left Baba Nam's phone number with Jeff Walters, my agent, with instructions to call only in an emergency. Now, as I ran clumsily in the dark to the house, a list of possible victims of fire, flood, or death filled my head.

"Jeff, Barry. What's wrong?" I asked, trying to catch my breath from the run.

"Hey, Bar, guess who I just spent the last three hours with at a party at Kip Adotta's house?"

"It better have been with someone who's now dead or dying. It's two o'clock in the morning."

"It's better than that. I've been drinking White Russians with Bobby Mitchell. And guess what, I got you a job. Bobby wants you in his office Monday morning." There was joy in Jeff's voice. It's not that often an agent gets a client a job. That's what they're supposed to do. It just doesn't happen very often.

"I can't, Jeff. Not yet." I didn't want to leave without my masterpiece. I couldn't, however, explain that to Jeff. He was a good agent and I didn't want to scare him off by being the guy with the voices.

"You've got to. Bobby just sold a new show and he wants you to run it." Jeff had no idea that what he was saying carried little weight when compared to a once-in-a-lifetime supernatural experience, so he continued on. "Barry, the new show is on cable. They want to be in business with Bobby. You'll be exposed to a whole new group of people. This is important." Jeff was making sense, business-wise.

"What's the show?" I had to show some interest, even if I had no intentions of doing it. Jeff had worked hard for this.

"It's really innovative. It's called *Cherché la Beach*. It's about two girls from Missouri who move to the south of France to become lifeguards. Great, huh?" Jeff thought he had me.

"Innovative? Come on, Jeff."

"The south of France on cable. You can say 'tits.' Bobby thinks you can probably show them. You'll be making television history. Barry, I want you to do this." Jeff's tone was serious. This was a good job. There was no reason not to take it. I was still hesitant. Jeff played his trump card.

"Bobby says you and Tommy Cross are going to run the whole thing. He'll let you do whatever you want."

"Tommy's going to do this show? What happened to *Hey Jesus*?" It didn't make sense that Tommy would give up his personal savior to peddle flesh.

"Tommy wrote the first three scripts. Best stuff I've ever read. Brilliant. But the Christians wouldn't shoot it. They wanted everybody to be nice. They wanted him to take all the comedy out. Tommy went on a bender. He was drunk for a week. Isn't that great?"

What to do? On one hand, I had the opportunity to write something that would have a lasting effect on all humankind and assure my place in history. Assuming, that is, that the voice-of-Homer thing was for real and not some acid flashback shared by a slightly psychic Gunga Din. On the other hand, I had wondered if I would ever again have the opportunity for a long-term relationship, and here it was staring me right in the face. It dawned on me that I had been with Tommy for almost four years. We spent more time together than any married couple. Being with him was more fun and more laughs than with anyone I knew. And other than his brief affair with Jesus, we had been comedically faithful to each other. What more could I want?

"They want me back in L.A. to do a show," I said to Baba Nam, hoping for some advice.

"This is your fork in the road. Your destiny. You must choose."

I really had no choice. The prospect of working with a substance dependent Tommy Cross was too much to resist. And maybe, with Lou Williams' help, I could get Tommy to give the AA path to sobriety one more try. And maybe Tommy was Homer in a previous life. That made as much sense as me writing with Homer in this or any other life.

"I'll be there Monday morning," I said.

Saying goodbye to Baba Nam, I thanked him for his hospitality and asked him if he would be offended if I gave him a thousand dollars to cover my room and board for the month.

"Even three thousand will not be offensive," he said with as smile. As I wrote the check, he gave me one last pearl of wisdom.

"You will know if you did the right thing. When you are on the right road, life is easy. There will be no obstacles in your path."

Those were the words I repeated over and over that Monday morning as Scotty O'Rourke, staring at the admissions list through his coke bottle thick glasses, going over it for the tenth time, said, "I've got a Barney Kane to see Bobby Martin."

SIXTEEN

Cherché la Mediocrité

Thank goodness for breasts. Everybody loves them. Especially everybody who watched *Cherché la Beach*. Renee Dawson and Jill Jarmon, the show's stars, could hardly act. They did, however, have great bodies and weren't opposed to taking their tops off at least once an episode. That was all the executives at Prime Choice, the cable network, cared about.

"Make it risqué, not dirty, Barry," Peter Wootin, the latest version of a network wunderkind assigned to me, instructed. "We're not pornographers. We're doing something revolutionary."

"Revolutionary? The word "naked" is in the second chapter of Genesis. Tits are the oldest trick in the book," I reminded him.

Wootin didn't care about my attitude. All he cared about was that we were a hit. The first bona fide cable hit. People were talking about the show and signing up for Prime Choice in droves.

At first Tommy and I were concerned that nobody seemed to care if the show was funny or not. The third episode was a stinker. There wasn't even one really funny joke. Yet there were no complaints. Not from Bobby Mitchell. Not from the studio. Not from the network. When the episode was reviewed in the *L.A. Times,* they called us "revolutionary." Either we were better than we thought, or Peter Wootin had an unlimited expense account, convincing critics of our merit over fabulous dinners at Spago.

Soon, Tommy and I had replaced our normal "Find a better joke" instructions to the writing staff with "Have them change their shirts again."

The only real challenge was making *Cherché la Beach* not look exactly like *In the Swim.* Both shows were about two girls who become lifeguards. How many compelling lifeguard stories are there? Compelling? How many dull lifeguard stories are there? The truth is, there are only seven stories that are ever told in situation comedy.

Every episode you've ever seen is really just a version of one of the seven. Shows try to disguise the fact that they're doing one of the seven, but there's no getting around them. Every episode is a retelling of: 1. The Rent Is Due; 2. The Boss Is Coming to Dinner and Lucy's Painted Her Hair Purple; 3. Fish Out of Water;

4. The Cabin Show; 5. Wrong X-ray; 6. The High School Nemesis Comes to Visit; and 7. Can't Kill the Turkey on Thanksgiving.

Any time a character needs to come up with money for any reason on an episode of a sitcom, it's The Rent Is Due. Rich person thrown in with poor people or poor person made to live with the rich like in *The Beverly Hillbillies,* it's Fish Out of Water. Like the *Hillbillies*, many shows are the retelling of one of the stories over and over again. *Bewitched* and *I Dream of Jeanie* were both The Boss Is Coming to Dinner and Lucy's Painted Her Hair Purple told a hundred times. The Cabin Show is any episode where the characters become isolated and have to deal with each other in a new dynamic. They usually go camping at someone's cabin, but they could be stuck in an elevator and it's still the cabin show. *Gilligan's Island* was week after week of The Cabin Show.

On *In the Swim*, Tommy and I had done our best to disguise the recycling of the sacred seven. On *Cherché la Beach,* we went a different way. We didn't disguise them at all. In The Rent Is Due, the rent was due. In the next episode, Karen, Jill Jarmon's character, did indeed paint her hair purple just before the head of all French lifeguards came to dinner. It wasn't funny. No one cared. When Monsieur Maurice showed up at the door, Karen, still wrapped in only a towel because she had just painted her hair purple, unintentionally exposes her breasts. Tommy and I felt that

we were pandering to the lowest common denominator. We got
nominated for a Cable Ace Award.

It seemed we could do no wrong. So when I laced up my
skates for what had become a weekly Saturday morning skate to
Santa Monica, I hadn't a care in the world other than to figure out
how the girls would find a live turkey in France for the Can't Kill
the Turkey on Thanksgiving episode.

Turning onto the bike path leading to Santa Monica I
reached workout speed. I flew through the Venice boardwalk area
and waved to Baba Nam who, with his eyes rolled back, was
giving a past life reading to a young woman. He waved back at
me, evidently able to keep an eye on two realities at once. Leaning
forward, with arms swinging side to side, I joyously skated until I
saw an obstacle up ahead. An incredible blonde, at least from the
rear view, was skating about a hundred yards in front of me. Catch
up and talk to her, Barry. That is, if you have the balls?

I couldn't believe I was ruining my workout by nagging
myself about the last vestiges of my mental illness. Although I
had more than my fair share of dates, asking for each one was
a gut-wrenching ordeal. I'd eventually ask but not until putting
myself through the mental ringer. My fear of rejection was too
deep-seeded to be cured by simple self–brow beating, or by
Marty Wachs, or by electroshock therapy, for that matter. It was

part of me. I would just have to accept that. It was a sad thought. There were so many great things in my life. Why would I let a simple "No thanks, not interested" from a stranger, no matter how beautiful she was, make me feel inadequate?

Closing the gap to twenty-five yards only made the view better. The body looked perfect, dressed in electric blue, spandex workout tights and a white tube top. Typical L.A. People don't put on grungy sweat clothes to work out. They have to look fabulous. Blondie had succeeded. What about the face? Haven't we skated by our share of less-than-attractive ladies who, before passing them, held out the promise of great beauty? And what if she's a stunner? Are you going to speak to her? Is today the day you throw away your crutches and walk? Are you healed, Barry? What's the deal, shithead? It's always good to call yourself shithead or some other confidence builder before you try the most difficult things in your life. It didn't matter. I was going to talk to this one. The look was too spectacular to let her get away.

Getting closer to the target, I had to adjust my speed. Too fast meant whizzing by. Too slow wouldn't look cool. I wanted a speed that would permit conversation yet create an illusion of exertion. Not really exertion. The perfect physical output from a guy in great shape. What I wanted was . . . shut up, Barry. You're stalling.

The moment arrived. I was only two strides from coming up next to her. What to say? Don't figure it out. Just get up there and see what happens. Heart pounding. Dry mouth. There was still time to bail out. Not this time, Barry. Don't you dare.

When I saw her face, there was no disappointment. This was no seventy-year-old grandma some Beverly Hills plastic surgeon had liposuctioned into a pair of skin tight jeans. That's a freak show you see quite often in L.A. No, this girl was a genuine knockout. Tanned, fresh, incredible eyes. For a second she looked like Linda. Then for two seconds she looked like Linda. Jesus Christ, it was Linda. Talk about your bumps in the road. I was going to have to make nice to my Ex.

"Good morning." I was starting off right down the middle of the fairway. Nothing clever. Certainly nothing to offend.

"Hi," she said, without looking to see who had addressed her. Looking as good as she did, a lot of men must have talked to her when she skated. Keeping her eyes straight ahead, she wanted to be alone. Fortunately, a crack in the cement made her lose her balance, momentarily. Her arms flailed. I steadied her. She had to look over.

"Oh, hi there." Thankfully, her voice brightened with her recognition. She seemed happy to see me.

"Want to skate?" Pretty lame, Barry. If she didn't want to

skate, she wouldn't be out here.

"Sure." Anything short of "Get your butt off my planet" would have been a relief. This was heaven.

We skated. We talked. Not excessively. It was nice just to skate. We caught each other up on our lives, carefully avoiding information about relationships. I told her what was going on with the show. She told me about returning to school. When we first married, we always thought Linda would go back to college to get her degree. Instead, she took jobs to help us stay financially afloat. She had decided to do something special for herself. She was going to get her degree in art history.

We skated to the Santa Monica Pier and back to Venice in what seemed to be record time.

"This is where I get off," Linda said. It was an awkward moment. Was I just going to skate off and hope for another chance meeting in the future? It had been wonderful talking with her. Once we got passed the initial discomfort, it was almost like old times. There was also no denying that she looked simply ravishing. I wanted to ask her out. I had to see her again. Now my fear of rejection had a new twist. I had betrayed this woman. Why on earth would she go out with me again? It didn't matter. I had to know.

"You don't think you'd want to have dinner tonight, would

you?" Can't get any more positive than that.

"I already have plans for tonight," she said, looking down as she said it. Plans. Of course she had plans. You don't look that good without plans.

I had managed to make it through our separation without thinking about Linda's personal plans. I knew she wasn't sitting around pining for me.

"How about tomorrow?" I wanted the words back. What if she had plans for the whole weekend? What if she was in a relationship? As she looked up, all I knew was that I wanted to see her again. Naked. I wanted to see her naked. I was attracted to her in every way.

"Yeah, that could work," she finally replied. I have to study, but around seven would be good."

"Great." I didn't hide my excitement.

"I'll see you then." She was leaving.

I didn't want her to go. I called to her, "This was terrific."

"Yeah, it was." She stopped and smiled. I skated over to her.

"I'll see you tomorrow." I lightly kissed her lips. My heart was pounding. I was completely alive.

She said nothing and skated away.

Dinner was more cautious than the previous day's skating.

The day-and-a-half wait had given us both time to think about the advisability of seeing each other again. I spent Sunday wondering whether I should call Marty Wachs. Was seeing Linda crazy? Was I going out with her only to avoid being alone? No. I wanted to be with her.

We finished dinner. It was wonderful being on a date where I didn't have to hear some stranger's life story. Or tell mine, for that matter. The conversation was lively even though we both were tiptoeing around any references to what our personal lives were like.

"Do you want to go skating at Flipper's?" It seemed like a no-big-deal question, yet it was a very big deal. I was including Linda in my fun.

"That sounds great." I was a little surprised by her answer, expecting something more sensible like, "Sorry, I've got school tomorrow." Or, "We've just eaten a big meal— we shouldn't exercise right away." Why did I expect that kind of answer? Was Linda that dull? Had she ever been? Or had I simply decided that's who Linda was in my life?

Flipper's was fun. Except for the number of guys who hit on Linda. It seemed like every time I went to the bathroom or to get us drinks, there was someone else trying to get her phone number. Look at her, Barry. Why wouldn't every guy in the place want to be with her?

The ride home took forever. There was just too much sexual tension. We had kissed a number of times while skating. The kisses had become progressively more passionate. Linda put her hand on top of mine, which was resting on the gearshift. She gave a little squeeze and then gently played with my fingers. I drove the rest of the way home in second gear. I didn't want to shift. I was afraid if I moved my hand, Linda would move hers.

Parked in front of her apartment building, the kissing, which had begun at Flipper's, continued. It was different than our kissing before the separation. It was exciting. There was a passion. We were both restricted by the confines of the Ferrari. The damn Italians had finally fixed the headlights. Now I wanted to be in my parent's '68 Pontiac with the big bench seats so we could do some old fashioned making out in the car. I wanted to touch her. To feel her pressed against me. I was afraid if I stopped kissing long enough to suggest such a thing, she might come to her senses. She might realize who she was kissing.

It was Linda who finally came up for air. We were both breathing heavily.

"Do you want to come in for a cup of . . . I don't know . . . pussy?" She actually said that! Then she grabbed me and we started kissing again. It was difficult keeping the kiss going. We both started laughing. It was such an un-Linda thing to say. At the same time, it was a real turn-on. Not because Linda was talking dirty, although I saw that as a bonus. But because she made me laugh. I was used to laughing with Donna Morris. I was not used to laughing with Linda. Not at something she said.

In my best Southern gentleman accent, I said, "Why Miss Harrington, I don't know what to say. I'd love of cup of . . . as you so beautifully put it . . . I can't say it, Ma'am."

Another quick kiss and she was out of the car running to her apartment. "Come on," she called.

The next hour was magical as we took our time with each other. It was wonderful being with Linda again. There was a comfort being with someone I knew so well. At the same time, there was an exciting newness as we had both picked up our share of little tricks over the long separation and we were eager to please.

Lying in each other's arms, I tried to remember the last time I made love to a woman. Not screwed or fucked. Made love. It was with Linda, of course. It had been too long. I closed my eyes and enjoyed her touch as she stroked my hair.

Linda's bedroom was full of plants and crystals. The whole room felt alive and enchanted. There was an actual buzz to it. It was the same buzz I had felt when I first held a crystal. Linda had the place tuned up so that the subtle vibration was everywhere.

"Do you want to go to Aspen with me next weekend?"
Linda asked as we lay quietly in each other's arms. I could hear the
caution in her voice. This was dangerous ground we were treading.

"Aspen?"

"I've got to do some art stuff. I'm leaving on Friday. I don't
know . . . something tells me we should go together."

Something? Something was telling her? I had recently
spent an unfulfilled month in Ojai because something told me to
follow Baba Nam. How many times was I going to put my trust
in this something? However, I could not remember when I felt as
good as I did at that moment.

I told Tommy on Monday that I was going to Aspen.

"What about the Can't Kill the Turkey on Thanksgiving
show?" he asked, as he gulped down his tenth Coca-Cola of
the morning. Tommy was attending AA meetings regularly and
had replaced his alcohol cravings with a fixation for sweets and
nicotine. He was constantly consuming massive amounts of sugar
or had a cigarette in his mouth. If his mouth was full, there would
be no room for the booze.

"How about this?" I said. Then proceeded to make up
the following; "The president of the United States gives the
president of France a live turkey as a Thanksgiving gift. The bird
escapes, and all of France is looking for it. It, of course, makes

its way to the girls' lifeguard stand. They've been down in the dumps, wondering how they were going to celebrate their first Thanksgiving away from home with pâté. Now they have a turkey. All they have to do is kill the poor thing."

"Have a good trip," Tommy mumbled, wishing me bon voyage as he stuffed yet another piece of Juicy Fruit in his mouth.

Aspen in 1980 was still a simple place. It hadn't yet become the mecca for high-profile Hollywood and Euro-trash enjoying the social equivalent of skiing in Beverly Hills. Although it was still early September, fall was already in the air. Leaves were beginning to change, even though the mountain wildflowers continued their spectacular bloom. Our Saturday morning hike to the Maroon Bells Wilderness Area provided a totally peaceful contrast to the tensions of L.A. Total peace except for the confines of Barry Klein's mind. I was completely screwy. Scared silly. Linda and I had seen each other twice more during the week leading up to the trip. Each time was more wonderful than the last. Now, walking hand in hand, I couldn't help but wonder where it was all leading. I thought we were over. What do you want, Barry? Where do you want it to lead?

Saturday afternoon was no better. I tried watching football on TV while Linda went off on her own. What did Linda want? Did I dare ask?

We were both quiet at dinner. Linda looked beautiful, the mountain air giving her rosy cheeks. Looking at her, I couldn't help thinking, "It should be the law: everybody gets a little time off for bad behavior in the middle of a long-term relationship." It would be great, wouldn't it? A little time to get crazy. No divorce. No custody battles. You get some time away from the grind and then, all of a sudden, all better. It *would* be great. Unless instead of letting you get crazy, it made you crazy. You know, crazier than you already were. It wouldn't do that, would it? Of course, it wouldn't. Look how sane you are now, Barry. Help!

"Linda, will you marry me?" I asked as she devoured her dinner.

"Taste this trout. It's unbelievable," was her reply.

"Is that a yes?"

"You know, technically we are married," she said, looking out at the view. I hoped she was more than sightseeing and was considering my proposal.

"That marriage seems dead," I said. "In the past. We've changed. We've both grown. I feel like, this past week, I've fallen in love with you all over again. That's what I want to celebrate."

"This past week?" she sarcastically asked, as if that wasn't nearly enough time.

"How long did it take for us to fall in love the first time?" I asked.

"It took you about five seconds."

"And you?"

"It took me at least seven seconds."

She smiled, then turned away as she thought over my marriage proposal. I was more than asking her to marry me. I was asking to be pardoned for my crimes. Heinous crimes. A capital offense. Waiting for her answer, I desperately wanted to find a joke to ease the tension in case she turned me down. There was none. I had to be emotionally out there. Maybe if I let some water dribble down my chin? No!

Forgiveness. It's a blessing to get. A mitzvah to give. Not everyone can give it. Not everyone gets it. It can come with a multitude of conditions, or in an instant, plain and simple.

"I think we should buy some new rings, walk up into the mountains and, more than just restate our vows, tell each other how we really feel. That's the kind of ceremony I'd like."

Plain and simple—I believed she had forgiven me for my human frailties. In three years I had gone from underwear salesman to producing the number one show on television. I couldn't handle the change. It was no excuse for not fulfilling my solemn oath to faithfully honor, cherish, and obey. Yet it was the only excuse I had. I was human.

The next morning we found a jewelry store, picked out a pair of matching gold wedding bands, and headed up one of the many paths to the alpine tundra. We walked for about an hour. The warm sun and crisp mountain air were intoxicating. Either that or the lack of oxygen from the altitude was making me dizzy. I thought I would pass out. Linda walked easily like she was some kind of Sherpa.

"What's wrong with right here?" I called to her as she continued walking ahead of me with a purpose. She said she would know when we arrived at the right spot.

Walking and wheezing, I thought about how lucky I was. I had gone through a life crisis and come out more than just alive. I was renewed. I had been given the chance to learn about myself. Who I was as a man. And instead of losing this incredible woman who walked ahead of me like some kind of pack animal, our relationship was stronger. She seemed nearly perfect. The willingness to get reinvolved with someone like me was her only flaw. That and her absentmindedness. Is it so difficult, if someone calls, to jot down a phone message? At least the important ones? Would it kill her? Not now, Barry. Not now. You love her, remember? Don't you? Yes, I do.

Up ahead, Linda stopped by a small, weather-worn barn surrounded by the most incredible wildflowers, a bouquet created during the short but lush mountain summer. When I caught up, I could see why she had stopped. With a view of the village below and the still snowcapped Rockies surrounding us, this was one of the most beautiful spots I had ever seen.

"I think this is it," she whispered, showing the proper reverence for a creation of God more holy than any cathedral.

I simply held her hand as we stood silently while taking in the grandeur. An audience of wild goats, six or seven of them, came over the ridge above us, stopped, and watched curiously. Not many people ventured this high up the mountain.

After a few minutes, when the time seemed right, I took Linda's new wedding ring from my pocket and slipped it on her finger.

"Linda, I know what we've been through was rough. The fact that we're standing here together is amazing. I don't know why I deserve this kind of luck. According to my father you may be under some kind of Klein Clan curse. I don't know. I do know, you won't be sorry. I love you, Linda. I always have. I always will." With that, I kissed her. There was general "baaah-ing" of approval from the goats. It was as if these wild animals had real wisdom.

Linda took my ring from her pocket. She slid it on my finger, took my hand, and said the words that will be etched in my heart forever. "Barry, if you ever pull this shit again, I'll kill you."

"It won't happen," I assured her. "Wait until you see how good things are when we get back."

Linda looked out at the incredible panorama before dropping the bomb. "I'm not going back with you, Barry," she stated.

In an instant, I panicked. "What!? Why!?"

"I'm staying in Aspen," she replied calmly. "I got a job at a gallery. That's why I had to come here."

I tried to take control. "But we have to go back. I can't just leave the show." Although I said it firmly, my argument sounded weak at best. Linda was dealing with matters of far greater importance than *Cherché la Beach*.

"Barry, I need some time to make sure that getting back together is what I want. On the way up here I sensed that staying in Aspen would be best. It was my inner voice, Barry."

I was suddenly contemplating my life without Linda again. I had to try something else.

"Well, my inner voice says we should go back to L.A. Maybe you're inner voice is wrong. Maybe you're picking up somebody else's inner voice. Maybe you're just worried about getting back together? Well, so am I—a little." I didn't want to be thrown to the waiting wolves in L.A. without her.

"Are you saying that your inner voice is real and mine isn't?" she asked with an amused smile.

"Yes. That's exactly what I'm saying. You could be possessed, for all we know."

"If we're supposed to be together, we'll get through this," Linda explained. "This is something I have to do. If I'm going to grow . . . if we're going to grow as a couple and as individuals, we have to give each other the room. This isn't kid stuff. Or one of your stupid television sitcoms. It's adult stuff. That's what I'm saying, Barry. It's time to grow up."

There was more "baaah-ing" of approval as I considered what she had said.

"Come on, husband, let's get you packed," Linda said. Then, after a tender kiss, she headed down the mountain.

I stood there, wondering about the time I would have to spend without Linda. Would it be so different than when we were separated? Of course it would. Now, I desperately wanted to be with her. Picking up a small stone, I rolled it around in my hand as I wondered if I could give her what she needed. Would I have the strength to wait? Only time would tell. I wished for a sign, something to give me courage. I got a rousing "baaah" that seemed to say, "You'll be just fine." Then, as I headed down the mountain, wondering what besides the show could keep my attention while I waited to be reunited with Linda, I got another sign. It was a voice — clear as a bell — "So it is, Barry, that this son of Greece, by his oath, calls upon you."

"Homer, is that you?" I asked, alive with anticipation.

"Truly, it is. Got any ideas?"

Made in the USA
Charleston, SC
03 September 2011